CARNAGE ON THE COMMITTEE

Whe_ _the chairperson of_ the _____ pper-
Warburton Literary F_____ cious
circumstances, Robert _____ sane
member of the judging _____ e in
summoning Baroness 'Ja_____ to step into
the breach.

Speculation that a killer may be targeting the judges worries the baroness not in the slightest— it's the prospect of immersing herself in modern literature that fills her with dread. But noblesse must oblige, even when it means joining the ranks of the superciliati sitting in judgement of the literati.

With the baroness at the helm, the judges resume the task of whittling away at the short-list. But the killer, too, has resumed and is whittling away at the judges one by one . . .

CARNAGE ON THE COMMITTEE

Ruth Dudley Edwards

WINDSOR
PARAGON

First published 2004
by
HarperCollins Publishers
This Large Print edition published 2004
by
BBC Audiobooks Ltd
by arrangement with
HarperCollins Publishers Ltd

ISBN 0 7540 9540 1   (Windsor Hardcover)
ISBN 0 7540 9426 X   (Paragon Softcover)

British Library Cataloguing in Publication Data available

Printed and bound in Great Britain by
Antony Rowe Ltd., Chippenham, Wiltshire

To Kathryn and John, both of whom frequently persuade me that the seemingly impossible is easily achieved.

Among those to whom I am grateful for inspiration and/or help are Presiley Baxendale (who got her way), Nina Clarke, Jodi and Bobbie Cudlipp, my brother Owen, Mariella Frostrup, Eamonn Hughes, James McGuire, Robert Salisbury, and the great Frederick Crews, whose *Postmodern Pooh* should be force-fed to all aspiring literary critics. Iarlaith and Máirín Carter deserve special honours for their stunning inventiveness on the imaginary-fiction front. My thanks too to Julia Wisdom, who held her nerve, to Charlotte Webb, a first-rate copy editor, and to Georgina Burns, Debbie Collings, and Anne O'Brien for many kindnesses.

PROLOGUE

'She's dead. Dead. *Dead*. It's a dis*a*ster! What are we going to *do*, Robert? What the fuck are we going to *do*?'

'Who's dead?'

'*La grande fromage*, that's who.'

'Hermione? Are you serious?'

'Deadly.'

'But she looked fine the other day. What did she die of?'

'How do *I* know? Something *ser*ious, obviously. Anyway I don't care. She's *dead*. Oh, God! How *could* she die?' Prothero emitted a great sob.

'I'm sorry to be pedantic, Georgie, but it was only yesterday that you said you wished she'd never been born.'

'That was just because she was being her usual toffee-nosed pain-in-the-arse. Saying you wished she'd never been born's not the same as wishing she was *dead*. How can we get another chairperson at *this* notice? What are we going to *do*?' Prothero's voice rose to a shriek. 'There's a meeting of the committee next *Thur*sday. Have you for*got*ten? The *cru*cial meeting. The *long*-list meeting. What *will* we do without Herm*i*one?'

'Calm down, Georgie. Calm down.'

'How *can* I calm down? Stop being so macho about this. It's my crisis and I'll thweam if I want to. Aaaaaaaaaaaaaaaghhhhhhh!!!!!!!!!!!!!!!'

Amiss held the receiver away from him until the sounds diminished. He put it cautiously to his ear again and seized his moment as Prothero paused

1

for breath. 'Georgie, if you go on like that I'll put the phone down. Let's begin at the beginning. Is it definite that Hermione's dead?'

'Yep. Stark, staring dead.'

'What did she die of?'

'They don't seem to know.'

'She seemed fine on Tuesday.'

'It was Tuesday afternoon she sickened, according to hubby. He very thoughtfully rang me this evening after he heard the news. Have you met him? Lovely, lovely man, William. Wasted on her. Those eyes . . . that . . .'

'Georgie!'

'Sorry.'

'So you need a new chair.'

'Immediately.'

'So whom have you in mind?'

'That's what I'm thweaming about. You *know* who'll insist on being it.'

'Geraint Griffiths. And probably Den Smith.'

'And you *know* what'll happen if the Gee Gee becomes chairperson.'

'Den will walk out.'

'And you *know* what'll happen if the Gee Gee's told he can't be chairperson.'

'He'll walk out. That is, he'll threaten to walk out. I wouldn't be certain he would.'

'He'll certainly make a *huge* fuss. Especially if Dirty Den gets the job. And whichever of them walks or fusses, it'll be *all* over the press in five minutes, the committee *and* the prize will be a *laugh*ing stock, the Big Knapparoonie will fire me and I'll *nev*er work in this town again.'

'I'm sure you're exaggerating, Georgie. You'll work something out, I'm sure.' Amiss's eyes strayed back to his computer screen. No, he thought. A blunt instrument. There wouldn't have been a sharp enough knife in such a seedy flat . . .

'Robert, for God's sake, help me.'

Amiss wrenched his mind away from his putative, to Prothero's real, corpse. 'Oh, sorry, Georgie, I got distracted.'

Prothero was aggrieved. 'How *can* you, Robert? I'm relying on you. I got you on this committee in the first place to hold my *hand*. *And* because I knew you were diplomatic. And if ever the Warburton needed a diplomat, it's *now*.'

'Don't try to make it sound as if you did me a favour,' said Amiss crossly. 'I wish I'd never agreed. Two months reading crap and then all those ghastly rows I don't want you to pretend for even one minute you haven't been titivating the press with. Hermione's well out of it.'

There was a muffled sob. 'Don't be so *cru*el. I *did* think I was doing you a favour. I thought you'd meet some interesting people who loved books. So *help* me, I thought literary prizes were about book-lovers rewarding book-lovers. How *could* I know what the liter*a*ti were like?' His voice began to rise again. 'How *could* I? I'm just a poor bastard who sucks up to people for a living. *Rob*ert, how *can* I stop the Gee Gee and Dirty Den in their tracks?'

'I don't suppose you should just let the best man win?'

As the scream began, Amiss interrupted. 'OK, OK, I have it. Gender. That's how you stop them. Tell Knapper that it's got to be a woman or the sisterhood will go mad.'

'But then Rosa Krap will think she's entitled to it. And you *know* what'll happen then.'

3

'Geraint and Den will both walk out.'

'Exactly.'

'So you can't have Rosa Karp.'

'And how am I supposed to get out of *that*?'

Amiss brooded. 'Find a chairwoman fast and then tell Rosa you had to get a new broom as it was impossible to choose between her and Wysteria.'

'*Hysteria*!!!!!!!!? You couldn't have Lady Bloody Hysteria Fucking *Wil*cox as the chair of a choirboys' *knit*ting competition. I've already had her on the phone in tears four times this week complaining about the Gee Gee's abusive phone calls.'

'Not the point, Georgie. You can mutter about having had to act in haste so *fait accompli* and all that. But it does require you to get someone fast.'

'It requires *you* to get someone fast. I wouldn't know where to *start*. I'm only a poor bloody PR man. *I* don't know which trees grow the kind of bird who can deal with the Gee Gee and Dirty Den. *And* the rest. *And* read hundreds of books in ten minutes.'

An image floated into Amiss's mind. He blenched, but stifled his doubts. 'I don't want to get your hopes up too much, Georgie, but I do know a possible.'

'Oh, you are *won*derful, Robert darling. Who *is* this superwoman?'

'Does the name Jack Troutbeck mean anything to you?'

'Troutbeck? Troutbeck? Troutbeck? Don't think so. Is he a woman? Are we trans*gen*dering here? Rosa Krap *will* be pleased.'

'Baroness Troutbeck. More composite than trans.'

'Would that be that beefy broad who duffed up

4

the art establishment on TV last week? I read something about how someone or other said he'd never *ever* been so insulted.'

'Sounds like her.'

'What are her credentials?'

'Mistress of St Martha's, Cambridge.'

'Loved by the lite*r*ati, is she?'

'I expect any that know her hate her. But she'd know how to deal with Geraint. And Den. And Rosa. And I can't think of anyone else who fits that bill.'

'Is she interested in modern literature?'

Amiss had a sudden memory of the baroness over dinner denouncing as rubbish every novel written since Graham Greene was in his prime. 'Yes. Very. English is her subject.'

'Will she *like* the idea?'

'I don't know, Georgie. Probably not. But if you want her, I'll try to persuade her. In the meantime, you'd better break the news to Knapper and sell him the idea.'

'It'll be OK, I expect,' said Prothero, suddenly sounding more cheerful. 'Her being a baroness will probably be good enough for him. He can't get too *man*y of them. And Cambridge will help. He loves hobnobbing with people from what he calls "the ancient universities". Will you need to know he's keen before you sound her out? I mean you wouldn't want to get her on board and then hurt her *fee*lings if he vetoes her.'

'Jack's feelings don't get hurt, Georgie. That's why the Warburton needs her.'

CHAPTER ONE

Before leaving home to meet the baroness, Amiss switched on the television news. It being August, journalists were starved for stories, so Hermione made the second item. Lady Babcock, it was reported with great gravity, who was better known as the literary luminary and high-profile New Labour peer, Hermione Babcock, had died after a short illness. Her photograph flooded the screen, her handsome features dominated by the prominent nose and supercilious upper lip so many members of the House of Lords had come to hate. 'Lady Babcock, who was sixty, was, perhaps, the most famous face of English literature of her generation. Here is Susie Briggs, our Arts Correspondent.'

Susie Briggs seemed grief-stricken at the loss of someone whom she deemed the *grande dame* of English letters and canonised as a warrior for peace and a towering cosmopolitan spirit, who was, *inter alia*, a fervent enthusiast for European political, economic and cultural unity. An acclaimed authority on the Bloomsbury set, her admirers and friends were legion, invitations to her salon were much sought-after and she was also this year the chairperson of the prestigious Knapper-Warburton Literary Prize, which she herself had won the previous year with *Virginia Falling*, the beautifully observed, tender yet haunting and ground-breaking novel about Virginia Woolf's last day.

A small forty-something in a tight denim shirt

appeared on camera. Amiss groaned.

'Professor Ferriter, what is your reaction to the loss to letters of Hermione Babcock?'

'I'm, like, gutted. Just gutted.' With his familiar feeling of distaste, Amiss observed the flash of the diamond tongue-stud. 'Hermione was like the first truly post-modern Bloomsburyite. Bloomsbury was, like, cool till it became history, but Hermione, she made it relevant again by embracing its provisionality, its fragmentation, its ambiguity, its simultaneity.' As he warmed to his theme, Ferriter's little forehead wrinkled and he waved his fists around like a didactic baby. 'And then, like, she moved on. I mean what she said to me only the other day about how Queer Studies has screwed the deconstructionist prism and reversed the whole Bloomsbury experiment, it was sooooooooooo . . .'

Susie had moved from sadness to desperation. 'But her work, Professor Ferriter. What about her work as a novelist?'

'Pretty dated term, that, Suz, if you don't mind me saying so. These days we don't . . .'

'She won the Warburton for a novel, Professor,' cried Susie, who by now sounded cross. 'Can you tell us about it?'

'Wow! It was like . . . wow! That moment when as she dies Virginia has this anti-marginalising vision of a Palestinian woman who is setting off a bomb in Jerusalem to blow up the forces of fascist colonialism while herself seeing Virginia the oppressed feminist throwing herself into the water . . . is . . . is . . . is . . .' He seemed overcome.

'Yes, very moving. Thank you, Professor Ferriter.' With evident relief, Susie turned back to face the camera. 'But what will this mean for the

8

controversial Knapper-Warburton Prize, the focus for anger and rumour in the arts world and just reaching a crucial stage in the judges' deliberations? And in such a crucial year too, with the winner being eligible for the million-euro Barbarossa Prize?' Georgie Prothero's face and Prada ensemble loomed into view, the horn-rimmed glasses and the sombreness of his expression adding gravity to his very youthful features. 'Who can possibly take over at this short notice, Mr Prothero? Especially when the committee is so split.'

Prothero looked affronted. 'I don't know where you got such a false picture of the committee, Miss Briggs. And I'm afraid that—like all those connected with the Knapper-Warburton Prize will be—I'm still too stunned by this tragic news to think of anything else but our profound sense of loss.'

'It's common knowledge that the judges have been at each other's throats, Mr Prothero,' said Susie impatiently. 'But in any case, you'll have to find another chairperson, won't you? The rumour is it'll be Geraint Griffiths. Or perhaps you might be thinking of Professor Felix Ferriter, who I've just talked to?'

Prothero shook a minatory finger. 'Such speculation is most inappropriate, Miss Briggs. This is no time for rumour. The Warburton—now the Knapper-Warburton—is a great institution, and whatever you say, the committee is dedicated and united and we will get on with the job in hand. In the meantime, let us mourn the heart-wrenching loss of a great lady.'

'And that's all from me,' said Susie Briggs.

'Thank you, Susie,' said the newscaster. 'Now, to sport, where England has scored a surprise victory in the one-day . . .'

Amiss pushed his cat off his lap, dodged the indignant swipe of her claw and went to fetch his coat. His phone rang, he looked at the screen, saw Geraint Griffiths's number and, shuddering, headed for the door.

*   *   *

Interrupted only by a frantic phone call from Prothero about Griffiths's success in getting his name trailed in the media, Amiss spent an agreeable half-an-hour in the Dorchester bar slowly sipping a glass of their cheapest red wine and listening to Cole Porter being played on a piano Liberace would have died for. He held in front of him a magazine he had been reading until he discovered he could see, reflected in the mirrored ceiling, the cleavages of two women sitting behind him. Amiss was no more a voyeur than the next man, but the breasts were large, the necklines plunging and the women—one black, one Chinese—were fantasy fodder. Just before eleven o'clock his reverie was broken into by calls of 'Robert! Robert! Where are you?' and he leaped up and waved.

'There you are! Why were you hiding behind a tree?' The baroness advanced in front of him, cried, 'Look at me' and twirled flirtatiously; a swathe of purple velvet swept a silver bowl off the table. She gestured impatiently at Amiss as he began to pick up the nuts. 'They'll do it. What do you think?'

10

Amiss abandoned the task to two waiters and sat down while the baroness plumped herself into the chair beside him and ordered from the dinner-jacketed major-domo a large ('Now mind, I mean large, a large double, and water in a separate jug and no ice, have you got that?') whisky. 'What are you having?' she demanded of Amiss.

'Another glass of red?'

'But what is it?'

'Another of the same,' said Amiss firmly. As she leaned forward he snatched his glass away before she could sniff it disparagingly. 'I don't want one of those wine conversations, Jack. You said you didn't have long. Oh, and you're looking very nice.'

She forgot about the wine. 'Nice? Nice? What do you mean nice?'

'I mean splendid. Magnificent. Superb. You look wonderful. Is that enough flattery?'

'Nearly. But the earrings? What about the earrings?'

'They almost brained me, but now they're static, I can see they're very impressive. If hardly subtle.'

She beamed. 'I don't do subtle. Green topaz and diamonds.'

'Sounds expensive. Myles?'

'No. My grannie. She didn't do subtle either. Right, that's enough preening. Get on with it, whatever it is. You'd better make it snappy. Myles will be along within half-an-hour to pick me up.'

'Where were you, anyway? Your office was extremely coy about your whereabouts.'

'I don't employ blabbermouths. I like secrets.'

'Jack!'

'I was at an old boys' dinner for Myles's army pals. Don't usually have women, but I was the

11

speaker.'

'What does one speak to the SAS about?'

'I did a bit of warmongering. Now we've done for Bin Laden and Saddam Hussein, sort out Kim Jong-il, ayatollahs, imams, Brussels and anyone else who gets in our way. That kind of thing. They seemed to like it. Where's my whisky?'

It arrived as she spoke. She frowned at the waiter. 'Very small double that. What's the point of paying Dorchester prices if you don't get a decent measure?'

The waiter smiled. 'A very beautiful dress, if I may say so, *Signora.*'

She beamed. 'Italians,' she said to Amiss. 'Bloody brilliant. They always get it right. Can't fight, but boy, can they flatter! You could take a leaf out of their book. Always pays off with women. Now what do you want? Why am I here?'

'Because you're a kind, thoughtful woman who responds to SOSs from friends even when with the SAS.' He saw her expression. 'Sorry. Because I have a proposition for you.'

'I'm the one who makes the propositions.'

'Not this time.'

'I like making propositions.'

'Hermione Babcock's dead.'

'Good.'

'That's a rather callous response.'

'Did you ask me here to elicit hypocritical drivel?'

'No. Sorry. Why didn't you like her?'

'Stuck-up, patronising bitch. Every time she spoke in the Lords she looked as if she had a pole up her arse. What a bloody menace! Do you know she wanted us to stop being called "Lord" and

12

"Lady". How would we ever get a table in a decent restaurant?' She took a copious swig of whisky. 'What did she die of anyway? Aridity? Acidity?' She laughed uproariously.

'A mystery ailment,' said Amiss, rather primly. 'Anyway, her death leaves the Warburton judges without a chairman and I wondered if you'd take over.'

The baroness sat upright. 'Meeeeeeeeeeeeeee-eeeee?'

'You gave that nearly as many syllables as Lady Bracknell did the handbag. And more volume. You've got half the Dorchester's clientele transfixed.'

She snorted. 'If they think that's loud . . . Why would I want to be chairman of the Warburton? It's boring, boring, boring, boring, boring. Self-important judges. Staged feuds. Rotten writers. Why would I want to have anything to do with it?'

'It's more to do with why I want you to. I'm on it, we've got troublesome committee members and it needs a firm hand.'

The pianist moved smoothly from 'I Get a Kick Out of You' into 'Anything Goes' and the baroness broke into tuneless, loud song. '. . . was looked on as something shocking . . .'

'Jack. Pay attention.'

'Why are you on it?'

'As ex-editor of *The Wrangler*, but really because a mate wanted an ally.'

She yawned. 'So you become chairman. You can handle it. After all, I've trained you.'

'You haven't trained me well enough. Even if they'd have me, which they won't, because I'm too obscure, I couldn't do it. Without you in control,

13

the whole thing'll collapse in acrimony.'

'Why shouldn't it collapse? Best thing for it.'

'You don't really disapprove of literary prizes, Jack. It's a way of transferring money from business to poor starving writers who can spend it on food and drink. You were very pleased when your Dean of Studies won the Butterfield.'

'Maybe. But that was history. This is fiction. And all modern fiction is a waste of paper.' She signalled vigorously in no particular direction. A waiter materialised.

'I want a decent cigar.'

'Certainly, ma'am.' He reappeared within seconds with a mahogany box which he opened with a flourish. She sighed. 'I'll have a small one. There isn't time to do justice to a decent one before bedtime.'

'Sir?'

'No, thanks.'

'For heaven's sake, Robert, why not?'

'Afraid I'd go back to smoking cigarettes.'

'Have you any pleasures? How's your sex life?'

'Jack, this gentleman is waiting to light your cigar.'

When the business with clipper and lighter and energetic puffing was concluded and her cigar safely lit, she leaned back in her chair and smiled happily. 'You were saying about your sex life.'

'Non-existent at present.'

'Good God, I don't know what's wrong with you young people. When I was your age I'd have had three on the go.' She swallowed some whisky noisily. 'Or maybe four. Depending on how busy I was at the time.'

Amiss changed tack. 'Den Smith's on the

14

committee. And there are some people you'd hate just as much as him. You'd have endless scope for making their lives a misery.'

'Den Smith? We should be dealing with him too. Second only to Saddam as a public nuisance. Nobody could be as bad as Smith.'

'Rosa Karp?'

'Well, maybe Rosa Karp.' She drew on her cigar meditatively. 'Tempting. Mind you, I'm not having an attack of false modesty, but even if I agreed, which I won't, I don't see how you'd swing it. I daresay they hate me even more than I despise them.'

'Things are desperate. They'd almost certainly have to agree.'

'Who's they?'

'The key man in all this is Ron Knapper. You'll have heard of him, won't you?'

She wasn't listening. Her attention had wandered to a small, fat, swarthy, elderly man who was passing by their table along with his companion, a young and striking blonde a head taller than him, who wore skin-tight, low-cut, micro-skirted gold lamé with thigh-high leopardskin boots. Her slender fingers were festooned with rings, both wrists sported sparkling bracelets, a single large bright stone lay between her vast breasts and her ears were completely covered with a jewelled lid.

'My,' said the baroness. 'He's certainly paying for his pleasures.'

'Maybe it's his daughter.'

'The technical term is niece. This place is a fixer's paradise. Good fixers acquire nieces like that. The currency is rocks. Big rocks.'

15

'Ron Knapper, Jack. Canadian wallpaper manufacturer who acquired the Warburton Corporation a couple of years ago. The Warburton prize came with it. Knapper, apparently, is a writer *manqué*. Always going on about how he wishes he'd been a novelist instead of a businessman. Likes to see himself as a patron of the arts.'

'Like that advertising idiot who spends hundreds of thousands of pounds buying up piles of dirty laundry—knickers they've called "Journey's End" or "Finder's Keepers". That kind of thing?'

'That kind of thing.'

The baroness blew a smoke-ring. 'I had a most enjoyable fight about him last week on a TV programme. With Den Smith, as it happens. Den, of course, so much believes that ugliness is truth, that he'd rather art galleries showed pickled hedgehogs than Michelangelo's "David". He called me a dinosaur.' She smiled and picked up her whisky glass.

'So you called him?'

'A dung beetle. He seemed quite vexed.'

'Augers well. Anyway, Knapper leaped upon the Warburton with cries of glee, renamed it Knapper-Warburton and, because he's the mega-ambitious sod he is, decided it had to be the biggest and best prize ever. Big-money literary prize, Jack. His equivalent of rocks. Got him to the dinner tables of the literati.'

'Who wants to get to their dinner tables? They don't know anything about food. Look at Iris Murdoch. Ate dog food. And not even decent home-made dog food. Tinned. Probably drank bad wine as well.'

'So,' said Amiss wearily, 'once Hermione won

16

the prize he consulted her on how to make it famous. She took him under her wing, he made her chair . . .'

'What!'

'Sorry, chairman, and all our present problems stem from that. Do you want to know the state of play?'

'No.'

A familiar small figure darted into the room, strode down to their table and clapped Amiss on the back. 'Good to see you, Robert. Can't stop. Ida's got to take off for Cambridge at six tomorrow so I'd better get her home to bed. Have you finished?'

'No, I haven't, Myles. I've been trying to persuade her to do something but she won't listen properly and I need an answer tonight.'

Myles Cavendish gazed sternly at the baroness. 'If Robert wants you to do it, Ida, you must do it.'

'Why?'

'Because he's your friend and he always does the things you want him to do. It's a matter of honour.'

She drained her glass. 'In that case, of course I'll do it. Now why didn't you say that, Robert? I thought you were supposed to be good at handling me.'

'I was about to try the throwing-myself-on-your-mercy gambit.'

She yawned noisily. 'Honour's quicker. I'll pick you up at six-thirty tomorrow and you can tell me all about it on the way down to Cambridge.'

As she began shouting for the bill, Cavendish looked at Amiss and winked.

CHAPTER TWO

'Are you ready?'

'Up, dressed and waiting, Jack. Where are you?'

'Hammersmith Bridge. With you in five minutes. Find your umbrella and wait outside.' The phone went dead and, fretfully, Amiss dialled her back. 'I won't wait outside. You'll want to see Plutarch. And what's more you claimed recently that you wished to see where I'm living now.'

'Did I? To check you've improved on the hostel you used to call home? Not the *House Beautiful* tour, though. I've no time to waste. Be ready.'

He was checking his e-mails when the bell rang. As he hastily scanned a message from Geraint Griffiths, the ringing went on and on until, cursing, he leaped from his chair, ran to the buzzer, pressed it and dashed out into the hall.

'Is Plutarch on parade?' she shouted, as she banged the front door behind her.

'Sssshhhhh!' said Amiss, wondering why he was bothering.

'What are you sssshhhhhing for?'

He ran back into his flat, waited until she was in and shut the door gently. 'I was sssshhhhhing in the vain hope that you would remember that not everyone in the vicinity wants to be woken up at six-thirty. But of course I'd forgotten what you've told me often enough.'

She nodded approvingly. 'When I'm up, everyone should be up. Now where is she?'

Plutarch arrived in a whirl of ginger and launched herself at the baroness, who staggered, nearly fell, but recovered herself gamely and scooped the cat into her arms. 'What have you got I can give her? I forgot to bring anything.'

'You should seek to have a relationship free of bribes.'

'Bollocks. Plutarch's a cat. Cats have no sentiment. She's glad to see me because she associates me with pleasure. Get me something. Cats shouldn't be let down.'

'I haven't anything suitable.'

She strode into the kitchen and yanked open the door of his refrigerator. 'Bugger all here. No wonder you're so thin. You need a woman to put meat on your bones. Get Rachel back.'

Plutarch lunged at the top shelf. 'Ah, yes. Clever girl. Sausages.' She handed the packet to Amiss. 'No time to cook it. Get the meat out of two of these and mould them into bite-size pieces.'

As he was wrestling with his task she looked disapprovingly at the label. 'These are unfit for feline consumption. You should never have sausages made from anything except Tamworths. No other pig is worth eating.'

Amiss handed her a few balls of sausage meat. Plutarch, who up to now had been behaving exceptionally politely, snatched one rudely from the baroness's grasp, leaped to the floor and tucked in.

The baroness looked at Amiss disapprovingly. 'I'm surprised she's survived this long if you're feeding her such inferior food.'

'That's what *I* eat.'

'Quite.'

Plutarch finished her first course and was given three more in quick succession. Then the baroness pulled a vast handkerchief out of her Gladstone bag, wiped her hands energetically and turned back to Amiss. 'Are you ready?'

'The flat. You wanted to see it.'

She threw a glance around the living room. 'Is there a decent garden for Plutarch?'

'Yes. Small but secluded. I regret to say she plays merry hell with our feathered friends. I do not enjoy dealing with the corpses.'

'Tough. Nature's nature. Plutarch has to have her fun. Now come on, come on, we haven't got all day.'

Amiss picked up his coat. 'Christ, Jack, I'm not exactly house-proud, but you made such a song and dance about my buying somewhere decent that I'd have thought you'd have a passing interest in what I bought.'

She shrugged. 'It's all right. Indeed a signal improvement on that hideous place you were renting. But you need more bookshelves. It's a tip.'

'Those piles are Warburton contestants. I'll be getting rid of most of them at the first opportunity.'

'And do something about pictures. And get some decent rugs. Then it'll do as a transient stop before you make millions from your novel and move into a Georgian crescent. Have you finished it yet?'

'I only started it last month.'

'What's holding you up?'

'The bloody Warburton for starters.'

Plutarch, who had been yowling lustfully, leaped back into the baroness's arms in search of more sausage. The baroness dropped her unceremoniously. 'That's it, Plutarch. Can't stop any longer. See you shortly. Someone I must introduce you to. I'd take you with me now if I had

20

a Mickey Finn to keep you quiet on the journey.'

Amiss looked at the baroness suspiciously as he closed the door. 'Whom do you want to introduce her to?'

'That would be telling. You'll meet him. At St Martha's.'

'A dog, presumably. Or an ailurophobe.'

'Better than that.' She skipped out of the front door grinning, dashed down the steps through the rain, pointed her key at the car, clicked the remote control and dived into the driver's seat. 'Are you impressed?' she demanded, as Amiss climbed in 'I'm becoming technological.'

'What brought that on?'

'Myles convinced me that it was in my interests.'

'You two seem very Darby-and-Joanish at the moment,' said Amiss, as he buckled his seat belt. 'Are you settling down?'

'I'm too young to settle down.' She revved up the engine. 'Told Myles I might marry him when I'm eighty and have sown enough wild oats. Vrooom, vrooom,' she carolled, as the car took off. 'Now, to business. Is it settled? I presume you'd have got round to telling me if they didn't want me.'

'How am I supposed to settle something like that between midnight and six a.m.?'

'I thought this was urgent.'

'Well, actually, I have. Georgie Prothero . . .'

'Who?'

'The PR guy who's in charge of the Warburton.'

'What an extraordinary name. Sounds like a lovelorn 1930s provincial draper.'

'Well, he's certainly keen on clothes.'

'Woofdah?'

'Very much so, though restrained when on duty.'

21

'The supply of heterosexuals seems to be completely drying up. No wonder I stick with Myles.'

'Except when you're being a lesbian.'

'Except when I'm being a lesbian. But I'd be much less a lesbian if there were more available men. Doesn't mean I approve of woofdahs. They spoil things for us by turning real men into pansies.' The brakes screamed as the lights ahead turned red, and the car juddered to a halt. Amiss squeezed his hands together tightly and mentally rehearsed his painfully acquired techniques for getting through a journey with Jack Troutbeck. There was no point in cajoling, begging or warning.

Rule One: pretend not to notice she's driving fast or recklessly or you'll encourage her.

'Anyway, Georgie was on after we parted last night and reported that Ron Knapper was thrilled to bits that you've agreed.'

'You mean he'd heard of me?'

'He recognised your name, but fortunately didn't know what he knew about you, if you follow me. If he did, he probably wouldn't have wanted you; I can't imagine you are the toast of the literary dinner parties he so enjoys. But he's delighted to have a peeress . . .' There was a deafening blast of her horn and the car in front took off at high speed.

'Imbecile,' she shouted at its rear. 'Were you asleep?'

Rule Two: never remonstrate about bad behaviour; she won't know what you're talking about.

'He's delighted to have a peeress and college mistress all in one and what's more . . .' As the lights ahead turned orange to red, she accelerated and raced through.

22

Rules Three, Four and Five: keep repeating Rule One.

'What's more, he's in no position to be choosy, since Georgie also reported that it's beginning to look as if Hermione may have been murdered.'

'Really? You've taken rather a long time to impart that not uninteresting titbit.'

'I was seeking the right moment. Didn't want to upset you.'

The baroness snorted. 'I'm not upset. There were times when I'd have murdered the bloody woman myself if I weren't too busy.'

'Just because she wanted to get rid of titles?'

'Just because of her disdainful upper lip. When she spoke in the Lords she had a way of looking at us as if we were something Plutarch had dragged in through the cat-flap that riled me not a little. I don't mind people being superior if they've got something to be superior about, but Hermione was rich because of her husband, titled because she sucked up to New Labour and gave them some of William's money, and distinguished because her literary cronies puffed her.'

'She did win the Warburton.'

'Bet you anything you like the judges included some ex-lovers, social climbers and the superciliati.'

'Superciliati is right,' cried Amiss, in sudden anger. 'The way she banned genre novels was a disgrace.'

'What novels?'

'Crime, science fiction, fantasy, romance, comedy—anything that you find in publishers' lists separated from pure literary fiction.'

'But that would have excluded Wilkie Collins or Conan Doyle.'

23

'Or Jonathan Swift or Tolkien or probably Jane Austen.'

'Or Wodehouse. Didn't you make that point?'

'As forcefully as I could, but she had most of the others completely onside. Wysteria looked dubious for a moment, but . . .'

'Who?'

'Wysteria Wilcox. Come on, Jack. You've heard of her. Lady Wysteria Wilcox, author of those short, plaintive novels about angst-ridden, wounded lady toffs nurturing hopeless passions for unsuitable, uncaring brutes well below their station. And a poisonous bitch on the side.'

'That doe-eyed cretin isn't Lady Wysteria Wilcox. For one thing, her first name is Trixie. And for another, she's Lady Wilcox, not Lady Wysteria, or even Lady Trixie, as she wasn't an earl's daughter. Just married one.' As the rain became heavier, she increased the speed of the windscreen wipers but did not decrease that of the car.

'I didn't realise you were such a stickler for etiquette. You'll be complaining any minute that you've wrongly been preceded into dinner by the second cousin of a marquess.'

'I'm a stickler when it suits me. And it suits me when someone I despise as much as Trixie operates under false pretences. She was a contemporary of mine and she was bad then, but she's got worse. How she got anyone to marry her—let alone an earl—beats me. She had all the sex appeal of a bag of golf clubs.'

'Whatever her other deficiencies, you can't blame the poor bloody woman for changing her name from Trixie. After all, you changed yours from Ida.'

24

'I wouldn't, if she hadn't changed it to Wysteria.'

Amiss grimaced. 'Fair enough. Still, for literary purposes I suppose it's an improvement. Anyway, Trixie, a.k.a. Wysteria, a.k.a. Lady Wilcox, also backed Hermione, on the grounds that we must eschew populism in favour of the spirit. Or some such guff. Geraint Griffiths was so keen to narrow the field in the interests of his candidate that he'd have excluded George Eliot, and nearly all the others went along with it because of intellectual snobbery. When I objected, Hermione looked down her nose at me and said, "I am the chair and I have spoken." There wasn't any point in fighting a battle with only one ally, and that one petrified and inarticulate.'

The baroness had stopped listening, and to Amiss's alarm, had turned round ninety degrees and was waving her left hand around impassionedly. 'What is *Macbeth* but a murder story? *Romeo and Juliet* but a romance? *A Midsummer Night's Dream* but a fantasy? What was the silly bitch on about?'

Rule Six: when her eyes are off the road and she's looking at you, show no fear or she'll dally to find out what's wrong with you.

'Couldn't agree with you more, Jack.' She turned her attention back to driving and Amiss breathed more freely. 'Still, I don't know why you're surprised at all this. It's snobbery, pure and simple. I've learned to my cost that the fashionable literati—at least the fashionable literati I've been exposed to—are like that. Can't bear to say a good word for anything the plebs like, so they sneer at their authors. You should have heard the committee when Harry Potter was mentioned.'

'I like Harry Potter.'

'You would. I do. They didn't. "Elitist", "reactionary" and "derivative" were among the least offensive adjectives used. Oh, yes, and Hermione thought the whole Potter phenomenon vulgar.'

'Getting murdered is pretty vulgar,' said the baroness cheerfully. 'Why was she murdered?'

'*If* she was murdered.'

'You're like a bloody secret agent. Careless talk costs lives and all that sort of thing. If she was murdered, why was she murdered?'

'Maybe because she was chairman of the Warburton. That's what Georgie's afraid of and why Knapper's so delighted to have you signed up.'

Amiss's phone rang. He looked at the screen. 'Seven-fifteen a.m. and Geraint Griffiths is ringing again. He left four messages last night—the last one at one-thirty in the morning, after which he favoured me with no fewer than five e-mails.'

'Who he?'

'Geraint Griffiths. One of your committee.'

'Sounds like a pushy Welsh git.'

'Hard to quibble with that description, though I think his Welshness is a bit exaggerated. I believe he was known as "Gerry" until he began a career as a broadcaster and pundit and decided Geraint carried more weight.'

She rolled her eyes. 'Celtic codology.'

'Geraint uses whatever weapons are available. Rather like you.'

'Why's he pursuing you?'

'To enlist my aid in making him chairman.'

'Why don't you tell him to get lost?'

'No point, Jack. With a bit of luck, your

appointment will have been announced before I have to speak to him.'

The phone rang again. After scrutinising the number, Amiss answered it. 'Morning, Georgie. Everything still OK? . . . Yes, I'm with her now. We're on our way to Cambridge . . . Yes, of course I'm briefing her. Why do you think I'm not at home tucked up in bed? . . . OK, OK . . . That sounds fine. I'll run it past her and call you back. Bye.'

'Run what past me?'

'He read me the press release he's putting out as soon as you've given it the all-clear and the committee have been notified. He's evading Geraint Griffiths until he's got Den and Rosa onside, but it's still too early to ring them.'

'They're not being asked their opinion, I hope?'

'Certainly not. Knapper chose Hermione and now Knapper's chosen you. The press release expresses the grief of the Warburton group and everyone involved with the prize at the loss of Hermione and welcomes to the chair the distinguished Mistress of St Martha's. You are quoted as saying something along the lines of "The circumstances are tragic and we all mourn Hermione Babcock, but in the interests of literature I have agreed to step into the breach and I very much look forward to working with the distinguished committee."'

'Pack of lies and banalities, but *noblesse oblige*, I suppose.'

Amiss rang Prothero. 'Jack's happy with that press release . . . Oh, really? . . . No, I don't know . . . Well, they'll just have to look up cuttings. Or the Net. Or ask her when you talk to her . . . I do understand. But no one can blame you. Just keep

27

saying it was Knapper . . . Yes, I'll tell her . . . Don't know. Maybe . . . Good luck.'

'What was all that about?'

'He couldn't understand why you aren't in *Who's Who.*'

She snorted. 'Used to be, but I'm not any more.'

'Because?'

'Because I don't want every Tom, Dick and Harry knowing things about me.'

'You are, I think, Jack, the only secretive exhibitionist I know.'

'It's more fun just to show what you want to show, as any stripper will tell you. What else was he saying?'

'He wants to talk to you this morning. And wants you to talk to Knapper as well. And, if possible, every member of the committee.'

'I'll talk to Georgie Poofdah. Knapper yes. Judges, certainly not. It would give them ideas above their station. Poofdah's paid to keep them happy.'

'Prothero, Jack. Please register that. Prothero, Prothero, Prothero.'

His phone rang again. He looked at the caller's number, groaned and switched the call alert to vibrate. 'Where were we?'

'Talking about murder, what did she die of, anyway? Nothing painful, I hope. If I'm to be a target I'd like the murderer to be inclined towards well-placed bullets in the back of the head.'

'Nastier than that, I'm afraid. According to what her husband told Knapper, the medics suspect poison. She was in good health and there's no obvious natural explanation.'

'Well this certainly livens things up—in a manner

28

of speaking.'

'You do realise this has to be kept quiet. It's only speculation.'

'Yes, yes, yes, yes, yes, yes, yes! Have you been on to our friends in the fuzz?'

'Couldn't raise Jim. Got Ellis. He's nosing round and will be back to us.'

'Quite like old times.'

'I can see you're enjoying yourself. You haven't shouted at anyone for miles.'

'I like fun and this is sounding promising. Life's been a bit tame recently. Haven't had an adventure since we solved the Irish Question last year.' [*The Anglo-Irish Murders*]

'Unfortunately the Irish don't seem to have noticed. They're still asking the same question.'

'There's the Irish for you. Ungrateful to the last.' The car turned sharply from a roundabout into a slip road. 'Stop babbling for a couple of minutes or so. The rain's eased off, so I'm going to do a bit of driving.' He looked at the speedometer with his usual sinking feeling. As it shot up to eighty, she moved into the fast lane and put her foot fully down. 'I'm in the mood to show my paces. Nothing to clear your head early in the morning like doing a ton down the motorway.'

Amiss sank into his seat in obedience to *Rule Seven: when you're really terrified, just close your eyes and feign sleep.*

CHAPTER THREE

'Wake up, wake up,' she shouted a few minutes later. 'Coffee and obits break. And don't even think about eating. I've rung St Martha's with instructions about breakfast.' As she slammed the door, he scrambled out and followed her into the service station. 'I'll get the papers and a table, Jack. You get me a black filter coffee and do the complaining.'

He was already half-way through *The Times*'s account of Hermione's glittering career when the baroness shoved a cup and saucer in front of him and sat down. Ignoring the expected grumbles, he passed her *The Guardian* to distract her and tried to sip the acrid liquid without making faces. Within a few minutes, she jumped up. 'I can't stand any more.'

'Any more what?'

'Any more of this muck or—what's even more rebarbative—this assessment of Hermione Babcock, great-hearted European and scourge of little Englanders. If they're to be believed, she was leading the Warburton towards a New Jerusalem in the teeth of the forces of reaction.' She gathered up her belongings. 'Forces of reaction, indeed. They ain't seen nuttin' yet.'

As they passed the cash desk, she hurled at the cashier the information that the coffee wasn't fit for cattle.

'The quality of the coffee's got nothing to do with her,' said Amiss wearily.

'Rubbish. She works in the place, doesn't she?

30

She should take an interest in the sufferings of customers. You might as well say the food at St Martha's has nothing to do with me.'

She paid no attention to Amiss's feeble rebuttal. 'Stop being boring. There was some good news: Babcock copped it when she was only half-way through her sensitive, ground-breaking new novel.'

'What ground was she breaking this time?' he asked, as they charged back to the car-park.

'Christ knows. The crassness of consumerism came in to it somewhere, as did the neo-Gothic, Mother Courage, post-capitalist meta-narrative—whatever crap that is—White Goddesses, Hillary Clinton and the *Ode to Joy*. Top of the many things I'll never forgive the bloody European movement for is its kidnapping of Beethoven's Ninth: they should be playing *Wellington's Victory* instead. Now get in. Get in.'

The next few minutes were enlivened by the baroness's inability to find the way out, her insistence on driving contrary to the directional arrows and the altercation with the protesting driver who was going the right way. 'That showed him,' she remarked with satisfaction as they finally reached the motorway.

Amiss emerged from the newspaper in which he had prudently buried himself. 'Do you want to hear some more about Hermione? There's quite an entertaining piece in *The Independent* about how she and Flora Massingham, her sister, were at daggers drawn; it also implies she shagged half of literary London. Which, of course, we all knew anyway.'

'How could anyone possibly have wanted to shag a scarecrow like Hermione? I wouldn't have laid a

31

finger on her even on a desert island.' She paused for reflection. 'Well, not unless we were stuck there for a long time. And she agreed to put a bag over her head.' She accelerated. 'Unlike her sister, whom I would dally with any day of the week. What time is it?'

'Just after eight o'clock.'

'When is Perkins announcing I've taken over?'

'Prothero, Jack. Prothero. Prothero. Prothero. Don't know yet. He'll ring me when he's done it.'

She smirked. 'That should upset a lot of people. I'm warming to the whole idea. Where were we before you passed out? What am I supposed to know?'

'That you're supposed to read two hundred works of fiction by Tuesday.'

She emitted a cheerful bellow. 'Nearly four days. In my spare time.'

'A doddle for a woman of your gifts.'

'Have you read them?'

'More or less. The ones one could actually read, that is. A full complement should be on their way to St Martha's by courier van as we speak.'

'Am I inheriting the chairman's set?'

'No. Georgie had spares. It would have seemed rather brutal to have demanded Hermione's when her body is hardly cold. Besides, if she really was murdered they'll probably become part of the investigation since the word is she collapsed on top of them.'

She chortled. 'What a photograph that would be. I could pose purposefully in front of her body, with my hand on the highest pile, promising that right will prevail. Come to think of it, if I've anything to do with it, the Right will prevail. Now, you know what I'll need.'

'Naturally. I'll go through the books, eliminate most of those you'd hate and select those I think you might like because they're throwbacks to half-a-century ago.'

'A century ago would be better. If not a century-and-a-half ago.'

'But you'll have to read the ones that are seriously in contention as well. Then there's the matter of the long-lists we're supposed to provide by Tuesday—minimum of twenty; maximum of thirty, graded by preference. Then at the meeting next Thursday we're supposed to agree a list of twenty-five. Later today I'll give you a draft long-list for yourself, which will have some in common with mine, will reflect your prejudices . . .'

'Tastes.'

'Prejudices and tastes. And will also include the known favourites of your committee. As part of her insistence on making a meal of everything, Hermione insisted on regular weekly meetings where we discussed—or rather fought over—the books we most liked and hated. I'm all too well aware of what my colleagues value.'

The baroness yawned.

'So you'll know what to read.'

'Skim.'

'Skim.'

His phone vibrated. 'Yes, Georgie . . . That's good . . . Right . . . Well, I suppose it's an accurate description . . . Really? . . . No, no, I won't talk to him till you've reported back. Good luck.'

'Was that Pickering?'

'Prothero, Prothero, Prothero. So far he's only managed to reach the women. He says Wysteria

Wilcox squealed a bit and said, "Oh, but she's dreadfully uncouth".'

'What does she mean?' The baroness sounded indignant.

'Rosa Karp was furious because you're a misogynist . . .'

'How did she work that out?'

'No doubt she'll let you know. But neither of them is fighting your appointment since they're smarming up to Knapper . . .'

'What for?'

'God knows. He's rich and everyone's hoping he'll scatter largesse towards their pet projects on the same scale as he's done with the Warburton.'

'So where does the Warburton fit into the prize world? Which I gather is big business these days.'

'The world's awash with literary prizes. Even just in the UK, there are prizes for every genre you can think of. Not just fiction and poetry and history and biography and politics and, of course, crime and fantasy and science fiction and romance and all the other things Hermione despised, but cookery and gardening and medicine and probably pornography.'

'There's the Bad Sex Award. That'd be a lot more fun to judge than this one.'

'I agree. The Bad Housekeeping Award would probably be more fun than this one. Don't forget I've been suffering for months now.'

'And there's a "Lezzies only need apply", isn't there? Named after a piece of fruit?'

'The Orange Prize for Fiction. Confined to women. Not to lesbians.'

'Same thing.'

'How can you say that, Jack? You're the Mistress

of a Women's College. Not a Lesbians' College.'

'That's different. Laid down by statute. Founder's wishes. Which I'm trying to get round. If women don't learn . . .' She paused briefly to intimidate a Lamborghini out of her path. '. . . if they don't learn at university how to sort men out, how will they cope in the big bad world?'

'Anyway, the Orange Prize isn't for lesbians.'

'You're so pedantic. I'll approve of a prize just for women when there's a prize just for men. Or not, as the case may be.'

'Then there's the Booker, which the Warburton's chasing after.'

'What's the difference?'

'The Warburton was there decades before. Set up in the will of some publisher of penny dreadfuls who wanted to encourage proper literature. It was drifting along with no one paying much attention to it when Knapper came on the scene and decided to compete with the Booker. The process was already in train, but he upped the prize money from twenty to a hundred K last year . . .'

'What!' The baroness stared at him. 'A hundred K! Are you telling me that Hermione Babcock won a hundred thousand pounds last year for her grisly novel?'

'Yes.'

'Jesus!' She looked back at the road ahead.

'But nonetheless, the Warburton got very little coverage since it's taken years for the hacks to take the Booker and the Whitbread on board and two prizes are about as much as they can cope with. Anyway, increasing the loot to a quarter of a million and having controversial judges was supposed to make it hit the headlines this year.'

'Hermione snuffing it will help. Do you think Knapper murdered her to put the Warburton on the map?'

'I think you're running ahead of yourself, Jack, but he was certainly guided by Hermione as to how to get judges that would attract public attention.' The baroness began to flash her lights at the car ahead and Amiss incautiously looked at the speedometer. He closed his eyes firmly.

The conversation did not resume until the targeted car had made way. 'Another notch on my belt. Now what do I need to know about Den Smith that I don't know already?'

Amiss opened his eyes again, but kept them firmly on the sky. 'What do you know?'

'His outstanding characteristic is being an anti-American jerk who thinks all perpetrators are victims and victims are perpetrators—especially if the perpetrators are black, Irish, or, these days at least, Muslim. What's his claim to be a judge, anyway? He's just a dilettante.'

'I wouldn't want to feed your prejudices, Jack, but I think the truth is that only the right are perceived to be dilettantes. If you're like Den and of the left you are seen to be creatively using all the various instruments at your disposal to express your righteous anger.'

'Haven't noticed him using any instrument except a bludgeon.'

'Your own weapon of choice, I might point out. Anyway, I meant vehicles rather than instruments. As well as his magazine . . .'

'*Rage*, isn't it?'

'You amaze me. What do you think of it?'

'You don't think I'd read it, do you? I've enough

36

to annoy me without courting a stroke.'

'Well, *Rage* has given him the lit. cred. and the contacts to get his one-act play performed, his novella published, occasional fulminations or even short verses into right-on newspapers and, of course, there's that late-night arts programme where he's often a visiting ranter.'

'That's where I had the fight with him last week. He was ranting about the Bush-Blair axis of evil. Gave paranoia a good name, as I pointed out.'

'What were you doing on an arts programme? You despise nearly all contemporary art.'

'I think the producer had a sense of humour. Anyway, I enjoyed myself, which is more than Den did, I think. Didn't have time to get feedback as I had to rush off.' She produced another vigorous yawn. 'I've been spared most of his outpourings. All awful, no doubt?'

'The play was hilarious. It was staged before a *Hamlet* I went to last year. All about how the Royal Family plotted to overthrow the New Labour government until they realised it was as fascist as they were—or something along those lines. There was a scene when Prince Charles arrived on stage in stormtrooper's gear to find Blair practising the goose step that will stay with me for ever. There was no dialogue, the whole thing lasted only ten minutes and was ridiculed by anyone sensible but, of course, was lauded to the skies by Den's literary mates, of whom, natch, Hermione was one.'

'Old screw?'

'Old screw from the mid-seventies, apparently, not long after his divorce from Deedee Drover.'

'Of course. I'd forgotten about him being married to Deedee Drover. What was it they used to call her?'

'Before my time.'

'Sexpot. The something sexpot.'

'Sultry sexpot?'

'No, no. A place name.'

'Solihull? Stevenage? Surbiton?'

'No. She was a Yank.' She clicked her fingers. 'Though not a Yankee. That was part of the trouble. I have it. Sex bomb, not sexpot. The Savannah sex bomb. All boobs and bottom. Opposite of Hermione when you come to think of it.'

'Why did he marry her?'

'Don't be silly, Robert.'

'I mean why did she marry him?'

'It was a sort of Arthur Miller/Marilyn Monroe thing. She wanted to show there was more to her than people thought.'

'And was there?'

'Obviously not, or she wouldn't have been dumb enough to marry Den Smith. Or Denzil Smith as he was in those days. And Denzil Drover-Smith as he quickly became.'

'Why don't I know about this? Isn't it the stuff of literary gossip?'

'Deedee died early and is as forgotten as her films and Den's been angry for so long no one ever wonders how he got that way. Besides, I knew him better than some.'

'You mean you knew him carnally?'

'Never you mind.'

'Stop being coy. I need to know.'

'No, you don't.'

'I want to know. It might get me through dull committee meetings.'

38

'I don't intend them to be dull. But, yes, we did have a short fling post-Deedee. Very short. Didn't even last one night. Fellow's a complete pillock.'

'Tell me about the Deedee business.'

'He was a young literary publisher whom she took to at a party. Handsome, I have to admit.'

'Still is, I think, for those that like the craggy, cross type.'

'Bit reminiscent of James Dean, but sadly didn't have a timely car-crash.'

'Mean and moody?'

'But not magnificent. Petulant little tyke with no bottom.' She paused. 'Metaphorically, I mean. If I remember correctly, one couldn't justifiably complain about his actual bottom.'

'So Deedee fell for him.'

'Whirlwind romance, with her flaunting him to show she'd got a brain while he flaunted her to prove he'd got a cock. Then off to Hollywood and big fancy wedding and romantic merging of names.'

'What did Den do in Hollywood?'

'Failed as a scriptwriter writing angsty stuff about Sunset Boulevard and was ditched by Deedee for a ski-instructor or some such ten years his junior.'

'So he came back home?'

'Not until after a noisy divorce. I can't remember the details, but he seems to have wanted a settlement that would have kept him in the style he'd got used to and she was a traditional kind of gel who thought alimony was for wives. Anyway he came back flush but not as flush as he'd have liked, roaringly anti-American and raving a lot about women wanting to emasculate him. A cross between Osama Bin Laden and D.H. Lawrence.'

'Why did he go to bed with you if he was worrying about being emasculated?'

She smirked. 'A question I hope he's been asking himself ever since. That night we had a rather spectacular falling-out over Vietnam which, of course, he was rabidly against.'

'And which, no doubt, you were rabidly for.'

'How did you guess?'

'So you parted brass rags?'

'Him. Not me. I wiped the floor with him in an argument and he couldn't take it. One of those fragile bullies was young Denzil.'

'But in retrospect wasn't he right and you wrong?'

'Robert, even if I'm wrong I'm wrong for the right reasons and even if Denzil's right he's right for the wrong reasons. Got that?'

'Got it.'

'Besides, the only thing wrong with the Vietnam war was that the Yanks didn't know how to win it. And even so they saved Singapore and plenty of other places from going communist.'

'Much though I'd love to argue with you about Vietnam, Jack, I think we'd better get back to the committee. We haven't got very far.'

His phone vibrated. 'Yes, Georgie . . . Well done . . . Really? How rude . . . And Geraint . . . I suppose that's logical . . . Yes, I'll be in touch as soon as we land, which should be soon.'

He grinned as he put the phone back in his pocket. 'Congratulations, Jack. Geraint Griffiths put up only a brief fight and Den said you were a fascist ball-breaker but accepted that Knapper's word was law.'

'It's rather touching that early memories are

coming back,' she responded cheerily. 'I look forward to a proper renewal of our old acquaintanceship. Last week was too brief to count.'

The car turned into the driveway of St Martha's. 'It's looking really good, Jack.'

'Certainly it's looking good. We collared another big bequest from an impressionable Indonesian a few months back and some of it's been deflected towards a good landscape gardener. He isn't Capability Brown, but he's the best there is around. He's done something inspired with the damp corners. Don't fail to inspect the new fernery.'

Narrowly missing three young women with whom she exchanged cheery waves, the baroness turned sharply left, drove around to the back of the college and parked the car snugly between two trees.

'Your private parking place, I presume?'

'Certainly my private parking place. What's the point of being Mistress if you don't get a private parking place? Get out.'

'Give me one minute, Jack,' he asked as she locked the doors. 'I must ring Geraint or he'll think I'm avoiding him.'

'You can ring him from my office.'

'You inhibit me when I'm being hypocritical.'

'Have it your own way. Breakfast's due in my office in five minutes. Mary Lou's joining us.'

'I'll be there as soon as I can get away.' He squared his shoulders assertively and rang Griffiths.

CHAPTER FOUR

A barrage of wolf-whistling greeted Amiss when twenty minutes later he opened the door to the baroness's office. Mary Lou Denslow, Bursar of St Martha's, left the table by the window and hurried over to him. 'Every nice girl loves a sailor,' observed a coarse voice as they embraced. Squinting into the sunlight, Amiss saw the source appeared to be Jack Troutbeck; further squinting ascertained that on her head was standing a grey parrot.

'Meet Horace,' said Mary Lou. 'He's Long Jack Troutbeck's latest acquisition.'

'Sit down and eat,' said the baroness. 'Introductions can wait.' She marched over to a large cage near the window and unceremoniously dumped the parrot on top of it.

There was loud ringing as Mary Lou was solicitously placing a napkin on Amiss's knee and the baroness was uncovering a chafing dish. 'I rejected the idea of scrambled eggs,' said the baroness over the shrill peals, 'since they need to be eaten immediately and I'm a long way from the kitchen, so . . .'

'Shouldn't you be answering the phone?'

'That's no phone. That's my parrot. I've diverted calls and cancelled meetings until we've decided on strategy. Switch your own phone off and eat.'

The ringing sound stopped abruptly. 'Rubbish,' squawked the parrot. 'It is a far, far better thing that I do . . . rubbish.'

'Than I have ever done,' cried the baroness and

42

Mary Lou in unison. 'It is a far, far better thing that I do, than I have ever done.'

Horace ignored them and reverted to whistling, while Mary Lou poured coffee and Amiss helped himself to kedgeree. 'Why a parrot?' he enquired, when he had swallowed the first few forkfuls.

The baroness jabbed her finger at his plate. 'What do you think of the kedgeree?'

'Wonderful.'

'You're so uncritical. I'm not entirely happy. There's something about the texture of the . . .'

'Praise the haddock, Robert,' intervened Mary Lou.

'Praise the Lord,' roared the parrot. 'PC rubbish.'

'Praise the Lord and pass the ammunition,' howled Mary Lou and the baroness. 'Praise the Lord and pass the ammunition.'

The parrot fell silent.

'Excellent haddock, if I may say so,' said Amiss.

The baroness frowned.

'She's put out,' said Mary Lou. 'Rang the kitchen to complain that the haddock wasn't finnan and found out it was. As if they'd dare have any other kind. But she's put out and discomfited. Can't bear being wrong.'

'My facts may sometimes be wrong,' said the baroness stiffly, 'but my opinions are always right.'

'You talk a better class of garbage than anyone I've ever met, Jack,' said Mary Lou fondly. The baroness grinned ecstatically.

'Aaaa'm only a bird,' contributed Horace. 'Not bloody likely.'

'Aaaa'm only a bird in a gilded cage,' yelled the two women. 'Aaaa'm only a bird in a gilded cage.'

Amiss sighed. 'It's one thing to try to talk over Horace's musings, ladies, but I can't help thinking that having to shout over your pedagogy will not help me in my increasingly vain attempt to give a coherent briefing on the Warburton.'

'Sorry, Robert. It's just that he's prone to forget where he is half-way through or get muddled and we have to correct it immediately. Jack, I think you should put him to bed.'

The baroness pushed her plate away and got up. 'Horrie, Horrie, it's time for a nap,' she crooned, picking up a stick and holding it out. The bird put its head on one side. 'Bugger Bognor,' he gabbled. 'I never heard such rubbish. Aaaa'm only a bird. Stuff and nonsense. PC claptrap. Good Horrie.'

'That's right,' said the baroness. 'Good Horrie. Nice Horrie. Come here, Horrie.' He hopped down, she stroked his head for a few seconds, thrust stick and parrot into the cage, waited until he was settled on his perch and then enveloped his home in a black velvet cloth. 'He's good at picking up things to say but rather slow about grasping the importance of shutting up on request,' she explained. 'Still, he's young. He'll learn. Now what did Griffiths say?'

'Hold on a minute. Fill me in on Horace.'

'Eat up, eat up. *Treasure Island* was on television a few months ago and I fancied myself with a parrot on my shoulder.'

'As opposed to your head?'

'He can do shoulder. It's just he prefers head. We're negotiating.'

Mary Lou poured Amiss some more coffee. 'She ordered Horace from Harrods the morning after seeing the movie, impervious to my warning that a

44

parrot is not just for life but for several generations.'

'I've already dealt with that,' said the baroness carelessly. 'I've added a codicil to my will leaving him to the college as a sacred trust. If they don't take him, they don't get anything else.'

Amiss finally remembered the name he had been struggling to recall. 'If *Treasure Island* was the inspiration, why isn't he called Flint?'

'Because I'm not a pirate with a peg leg, Robert. I name my own parrots. Horace does, however, occasionally give a nod to Robert Louis Stevenson by shouting "pieces of eight".'

'So why didn't you tell me about him before now?' asked Amiss, slightly offended.

'Wanted to imprint myself on him first so he'd make a good impression.'

'Did he arrive talking?'

'"Who's a pretty boy?" was about the extent of his vocabulary. But we're working on it and he learns fast. Between what we teach him and what he picks up he's doing well.'

'Sometimes too darn well,' said Mary Lou. 'And a word of warning, Robert. Don't get fresh with him. He bites everyone.' She held out her left hand. 'Look.'

Amiss grimaced. 'Nasty.'

'Doesn't bite me,' said the baroness, beaming.

'Everyone except Jack. Parrots, it turns out, are monogamous, and Jack's his mate.'

'He's mine rather than me being his,' said the baroness. 'Have to maintain a sense of hierarchy. When the chips are down, he's only a parrot and I'm me.'

Amiss put his coffee cup down with a bang. 'Was

it Horace that you wanted Plutarch to meet?'

'Yes.'

'Jack, are you out of your mind? She'd eat him.'

'Rubbish. One nip from Horace and Plutarch would learn her lesson. It might make her treat other birds with a bit more respect as well. Anyway, it was just a whim of the moment. Now eat up, eat up and let's get on with matters Warburtonian. What was Geraint Griffiths's reaction to me?'

Amiss looked enquiringly at Mary Lou. 'She's given me the headlines and all the dramatis personae she could remember,' she assured him. 'I'll tell you if I'm lost.'

'Geraint was fine—by his standards. He's not stupid, so he must have known he wasn't really a runner, but he was pressing his case as a bargaining counter to make sure neither Den nor Rosa had a chance. By the time I'd told him a few stories about Jack's views on political correctness he began to think he'd suggested her himself. "The crucial point is that the forces of conservatism should be mustered in defence of the values of Western fuckin' civilisation", he told me. "Whatever they say about Jack Troutbeck, I know we can rely on her to defend the citadel against the fuckin' barbarians."'

'Decent of him. He'd better be sure I don't mistake him for one. Now where are we on the fuzz front? Any news of young Inspector Pooley?'

'I haven't heard anything since we spoke last night.'

'Shall I?' asked Mary Lou. She took a phone from her bag and pressed a couple of keys. 'Ellis? Me, darling. I'm here with Jack and Robert and they're thirsting for news about the late Lady

Babcock. Right. Right. My, that's interesting . . . Hold on.' She turned to Amiss and the baroness. 'They're sure it's poison and think it might have been ricin.'

'Dear old Hermione,' grunted the baroness. 'Fashionable to the last. Nothing old-fashioned like arsenic. Ask him if he's on the case yet.'

'Jack wants to know if you're on the case, Ellis . . . Brilliant . . . I will . . . Me too. Bye.'

She beamed. 'He's trying, and it's possible. He'll keep us posted. More coffee?'

Amiss held out his cup. 'Yes, please. Now, Jack, it's time we got a grip.'

'That's my line. You've signally failed to give me a coherent briefing.'

'That's completely your fault. We got distracted onto your reminiscences of you and Den in the sack.'

Mary Lou sat bolt upright. 'You're not serious. Not Jack and Den Smith. You couldn't have, Jack. He's awful. I know you've got about a lot, but I thought even you were fussier than that.'

'Don't be so intolerant. It was a long time ago, I was young, I succumbed only once and he came off worst.'

'Still, you did succumb.'

Amiss grinned maliciously. 'Don't be unkind to her, Mary Lou. All the girls do at one time or another. Including, I understand, Hermione, Rosa and Wysteria Wilcox. It'll be quite an old girls' reunion.'

'I know I'm a simple-minded American,' said Mary Lou, suppressing a grin at the outraged expression on the baroness's face, 'but leaving sex out of it, would someone explain to me why anyone

47

listens to that creature? On that programme he was on with Jack, he said America was the most evil empire in the history of the universe and all its citizens were legitimate targets for the oppressed. I know we're a young and naïve country and we over-consume, but we're kinda well-meaning and I can't understand why anyone could hate us that much.'

'Inverted snobbery,' snorted the baroness. 'You Yanks are rich and successful and fundamentally decent: of course they hate you. And you elected George Bush, who is not literary London's American politician of choice, which means you deserve annihilation purely on aesthetic grounds.'

'His stuff on America's only part of it. From what I've heard he seems to hate England even more,' said Mary Lou.

'How often do I have to tell you that our so-called intellectuals are self-loathing, Mary Lou, and that the best way to their hearts is to knock everything British. Correction. English. You remember all that Bloomsbury wankery about betraying my country rather than my friend? This crowd of neo-Bloomsberries just take it further and see betraying their country and its allies as an end in itself. They wrap up their treachery in highbrow piffle and egalitarian rhetoric.'

'Are they as bad as she says, Robert?'

'Well, I don't know if I'd label it "treachery" . . .'

'What would you call it then?' demanded the baroness.

'Virtual treachery. In practice, I doubt if they'd actually sell the country out to al-Qaida.'

'Only because neo-Bloomsbury women don't want to be stuffed into burkas,' snarled the baroness. 'They'd sell us out to Brussels soon enough.'

'Can't argue with that. I've been at a couple of dinners where Den raved away drunkenly over the *petit fours* about the awfulness of England, its blood-sucking monarchy, its corrupt and effete establishment, its ignorant plebs and its bloodstained history, and Hermione, Rosa and Wysteria and a couple of the others squealed about the only hope being to subsume ourselves in the European ideal.'

The baroness snorted venomously. 'Of course the likes of Hermione Babcock are never happier than when engaging in a spot of intellectual S & M with rough trade like Den. With the added frisson, no doubt, in the case of those three harridans, that Den would flail them for having titles and living high on the hog.'

'I grasp it in theory,' said Mary Lou. 'I'm just always staggered in practice. I read an issue of *Rage* last week and it was unbelievable. Feeble poems and a couple of angry short stories along with some third-rate polemic about the evils of everything British from the Empire to Oxbridge elitism. Hermione Babcock had a piece explaining why she refused to call herself either English or British and demanding the government instruct everyone to call themselves European.'

Amiss sighed. 'Ladies, we need to get a move on. It's after nine and I have to tell Jack what she needs to know about the other judges. Jack, will you please sit down, shut up and listen?'

'If I must,' she said, plonking herself down in her favourite armchair.

'First, Professor Felix Ferriter. He's a ghastly little literary critic.'

49

'Bit of a tautology, that, isn't it?'

'I'm a literary critic, Jack,' said Mary Lou mildly.

'Nonsense. You're a person who appreciates and writes intelligently about literature. That's different.'

'He's obsessed with Queer Studies, of which he is a visiting professor at Yale.'

Amiss suddenly had the baroness's full attention. 'You're pulling my leg.'

'I wish I were, but the truth is that Queer Studies is all the rage in fashionable Eng. Lit. circles.' He raised his hand as she began to expostulate. 'Not now, Jack. There isn't time. Mary Lou will explain it to you later, no doubt. Just for now, take my word for it that Ferriter is a luminary in the world of Queer Studies and that this colours his attitude to the Warburton.'

The baroness opened her mouth and then shut it again.

'And he's such a little shit that Georgie, who goes in for nicknames, calls him Ferriquat.'

'After the weedkiller?'

'Exactly.'

'Who's Georgie?' asked Mary Lou.

'Georgie Perkins,' said the baroness.

'Jack, for God's sake, it's Georgie Prothero, who, Mary Lou, looks after the Warburton. Jack, will you stop messing about. And at this rate we'll be at this all day.'

'Why not?' said the baroness. 'I'm enjoying myself.'

'You haven't got time to enjoy yourself. Might I remind you that today is Friday and your long-list is due in on Tuesday.'

'And that you still have some duties as Mistress,'

50

added Mary Lou. 'I can't stand in for you on everything.'

'Right,' said Amiss sternly. 'Now next there's Rosa Karp, whom, I regret to say, Georgie Prothero, Prothero, Prothero refers to as Rosa Krap.'

'Well, he's got that right anyway,' observed the baroness.

'What do you know of Rosa?'

'Patron saint of equality gibberish. Turns up all over the place mouthing platitudes about our failure sufficiently to love our gay, lesbian, disabled, ethnic fellow-persons. If she had her way all the able-bodied, white, male Anglo-Saxons would be run out of the country.' She looked at him enquiringly. 'Fair assessment?'

'She's good-looking and articulate,' said Mary Lou. 'I've seen her on television.'

'That, my dear Mary Lou, is why she's come so far despite having no discernible brain and understanding nothing about the human condition,' said the baroness. 'What's the name of that idiotic book of hers, Robert?'

'*We Can Be Equal if We Try*. That's what got her the peerage and the Ministry for Equality.'

'She didn't last long in that job, as I remember,' said Mary Lou. 'What went wrong?'

'She was put in charge of developing equality strategies for business, and according to Georgie Prothero, Prothero, Prothero, she developed elaborate strategies to deal with discrimination that didn't just take in women, gays, lesbians, ethnic minorities, the young, the old and the disabled but also cross-dressing, sex changes and a whole host of other categories like . . .' He clicked his fingers.

51

'Like . . .'

'Bad breath?' offered the baroness helpfully.

'Criminal convictions and I can't remember what else. Anyway her idea was that every business, institution or organisation in the country would be required by law to draw up anti-discrimination plans with quotas agreed by an equality inspectorate, with heavy penalties for non-compliance. After the prime minister read her paper he chucked her out in the next re-shuffle and put equality in the hands of someone who wasn't actually barking.'

'What's she like on the committee?'

'Still a demented social engineer. Hermione outlawed books that she thought beneath her; Rosa wanted us to have what she calls "equality-proofing".'

'I.e. ?'

'She was insistent that we commit ourselves to a short-list that would be gender-balanced and ethnically diverse.'

'Regardless of the quality of the books?'

'Of course.'

'And, what was more, she wanted any offensive books ruled out of consideration.'

'Offensive to whom?'

'Offensive to her, in her capacity as watchdog.'

The baroness looked dreamy. 'Takes me back to when Mary Lou came here first.'

'And I was an innocent ethnic pawn in your epic struggle against the thought-police.' [*Matricide at St Martha's*]

'We won that one. We'll win this one.' There was a loud knocking. 'Come in,' roared the baroness, and the door opened to reveal the agitated college secretary. 'What is it, Petunia?'

'It's no good, Mistress,' said Miss Stamp, her little head quivering under her embroidered pink Alice band. 'I can't hold them off any longer. The phone's been ringing constantly for the last hour and Mr Prothero, who seems awfully nice but ever so upset, says he'll never speak to Mr Amiss again if he doesn't ring him now and put you on. He says the press are behaving like ravening monsters and you must throw them a bone.'

Amiss looked at the baroness.

'Oh, all right. If I must, I must. Put him on and I'll sort him out.'

CHAPTER FIVE

'What a fusspot! But I've set him straight, don't you think?'

The baroness handed Amiss's phone back to him. He looked at her with grudging admiration. 'You certainly know about chutzpah, Jack. Anyone would have thought you were completely on top of things.'

'I am. Didn't you dragoon me into this because you knew I would be?'

'I forget that you can be tactful when you want to be. Your paean to the Warburton was as eloquent as it was insincere.'

She gave a bark of laughter. 'It was certainly as insincere as it was eloquent. Get me Knapper.' She shoved over a piece of paper. 'Or Knapperoonie, as your little chum quaintly calls him. Here's the number of his direct line.'

'Before you talk to him, you need to know about Dervla and Hugo.'

'Why?'

'In case Knapper expects you to have heard of all the committee.'

'I'm not sitting a bloody exam.'

'All right, all right. But just in case, Dervla's a singer-stroke-actress who's our voice of yoof, and Hugo—or Sir Hugo, as he's keen to be referred to—is a literary editor who's red-hot on the European perspective.'

'There's no hope you're making them up?'

' 'Fraid not.'

She gestured impatiently. 'Knapper!' He

shrugged and dialled.

'Hello. Mr Knapper? Robert Amiss from the Knapper-Warburton committee . . . Yes indeed, it's quite a shock . . . Yes, it's really excellent, isn't it? Georgie did brilliantly to find someone of the calibre of Lady Troutbeck at such short notice . . . Because of her devotion to scholarship, I should think . . . You'd better ask her yourself. She's just here. I'll pass you over. Goodbye.' He pressed the mute button. 'Wanted to know why you took it on and wonders if you'll be frightened if it turns out Hermione was murdered. Remember he liked her.' He pressed the button again and handed her the phone.

'Jack Troutbeck here, Mr Knapper . . . Not at all . . . Yes, obviously a resourceful chap . . . No, no. Glad to help, though I'll be expecting a substantial five-figure donation to St Martha's . . . That'll do. Now you realise that with this kind of time-scale I need a free hand? . . . Good . . . They're too old to get fidgety about murder surely? . . . Oh, I don't know. Young people are tougher than you'd think. I'll steady her nerves if necessary . . . Yes, I find the trouble with murder is it gets the press all excited . . . Fine. Must fly. Goodbye.'

'Satisfactory,' she grunted, as she strode across the room, removed the black cover from the cage, released Horace and plonked him on her shoulder. 'Who's been a good Horrie then? Good Horrie. To be or not to be, that is the question.'

'Prothero, Prothero, Prothero,' contributed the parrot, in a passable imitation of an irritable Amiss.

'He has a tendency to be undiscriminating,' observed the baroness.

'Like Rosa.'

55

'Huh?'

'Nothing. How much will Knapper cough up?'

'Thirty grand. That'll help the wine cellar. I want to stock up on Eastern European wine as part of my sanctions against the frogs for their pusillanimity over Iraq.' The phone on her desk rang. 'Bring them here . . . Oh, all right, I'll send Robert.

'The books have arrived. They're in the hall and too heavy for Petunia. Fetch them.'

Horace flew off her shoulder and parked himself on a high bookshelf. 'Not bloody likely! Rubbish. I'm only a bird. Every nice . . .'

'I'm only a bird in a gilded cage,' bellowed the baroness. 'I'm only a bird in a gilded cage.'

Horace swooped onto her head.

'Owwwwwwwww!!!!!!! Be careful, for Christ's sake, Horace. That hurt.' Immovable and unperturbed, the parrot began an imitation of popping a champagne cork.

Amiss surveyed the scene. 'If you don't mind, Jack, I'll work in a corner of Mary Lou's office. I've got calls to make, I have to think and I find you and Horace strangely distracting.'

She looked surprised. 'Really? I'd have thought you'd have got used to us by now. But as you wish. See you here for a pre-lunch snifter at twelve-thirty.'

With total concentration, she applied herself to her in-tray.

*　　　*　　　*

'So what's the news?' the baroness demanded, a few hours later.

56

'Uniformly excellent,' said Amiss, as he savoured his gin and tonic. 'For a start, Horace is talking quietly, which is a nice change.'

'He's more subdued when he's in his cage. Cramps his style a bit.'

'Let's leave it cramped for the moment, if you don't mind. Now, on the books front, I've reduced the two hundred to fifty and the ten I've just given you will keep you going this afternoon. You'll have your long-list before I leave this evening.'

'Why are you leaving?'

'Novel. Plutarch. Remember? And I'm meeting Ellis tonight. He's been assigned to the case on the grounds that it would be helpful to have a copper who knows something about books, so we're meeting for a late dinner to exchange notes.'

'Most satisfactory. What else?'

'Georgie reports that while rumours are circulating about Hermione's death not being straightforward, the press haven't yet been tipped the wink about murder, so we should have a brief respite.'

'Haven't the cops said anything?'

'They're waiting until the medics are ready to go public on the post-mortem, which will be tonight. Tomorrow should be lively.'

'And the committee?'

'They won't know about Hermione until it's official. Some of them have grumbled about you refusing to hold an emergency meeting.'

'What's wrong with them? I'll never understand why people want pointless meetings. Do they seriously think I have time to leg it up to London in order to sit round a table bemoaning the loss of Hermione Babcock?'

'I think they thought it important that you all get to know each other.'

'I already know more about most of them than I could ever possibly want to,' she said, shuddering slightly. 'Sufficient unto the day is the evil thereof.'

'Most of them, on the other hand, are consumed with curiosity to know more about you.'

'They've got nothing better to do, that's the top and bottom of it.'

'Georgie did, however, get it through to them that you needed time to read the books.'

'Didn't stop Griffiths and Rosa trying to get through to me. I presume Griffiths wanted to be sure I didn't pass up his favourites and Rosa wanted to tell me what was beyond the pale.'

'So you didn't speak to them?'

'Certainly not. I instructed Petunia to tell them to get lost.'

'I've had Wysteria, Dervla, Felix and Hugo on the phone. I'd agreed to Georgie telling everyone you and I used to be colleagues on *The Wrangler* [*Publish and be Murdered*] on the grounds that it would become public anyway, so they wanted the low-down.'

'And?'

'Wysteria's apprehensive. Doesn't seem to have happy memories of you.'

'Afraid I'll call her Trixie, probably. Which I will if she's stroppy. What did you tell her?'

'That you're a thorough professional.'

'Meaningless drivel.'

'Not to Wysteria, who seemed comforted.'

'And the literary editor? What do you call him?'

'Sir Hugo Hurlingham. You must have heard of him.'

'Frightful old wanker, I seem to remember.'

'Portentous is the word, I think. Well, he said in hushed tones that although this was not to go any further, he had heard on excellent authority something very disturbing about you.'

'Oh, good. What?'

'You are reputed to be a Eurosceptic.'

'Rubbish, I'm a Europhobe. I thought everyone knew that.'

'Well, I'm sorry to tell you this, but old Hugo hasn't quite placed you yet. Anyway, I reassured him that—whatever your views—you were an experienced university politician who would not let any prejudices you might have cloud your judgement.'

'Sometimes I think you should have stayed in the civil service, Robert. You could have made Cabinet Secretary. And Dervla whatshername?'

'Just Dervla. She doesn't sport a surname. She's just generally terrified, poor kid. She's only on the committee because youth was thought to be a good idea, she'd made it as a singer, had joined a popular soap opera, and had told interviewers she loved reading. When she came on the committee she was full of confidence, not to speak of Irish bullshit, and she jabbered about the importance of wards.'

'Wards? As in hospitals or dependants?'

'Wards as in words. Wards, wards, wards. She loved wards, she told us. And indeed by the standards of the young, she really did. But she's been patronised by Hermione and Hugo, sneered at by Wysteria, bullied by Geraint, lectured by Rosa, insulted by Den and confused by Felix and she's intellectually very bedraggled and intimidated these days, afraid of everyone except me, and not knowing from day to day what she thinks of the books.'

'What did you tell her?'

'That she wasn't to tell anyone else but that you were really a pussycat.'

'You're not supposed to tell people that. It's a secret. Besides, I'm only a pussycat when I want to be.'

'You'll want to be with Dervla. She's only a kid.'

'Hmm. What was her response?'

'Something along the lines of "Like omigahd that's so totally weird. Den said she was like . . . duuuuhh."'

The baroness winced and took a large swig of her martini. 'I get enough of this at St Martha's as it is. It's like Aids. They're all infected. I'm terrified the parrot will hear any of them talk.'

'It would be vexing, wouldn't it? They'll presumably grow out of it and the lingo will change anyway, but parrots don't adjust to fashion. Imagine him telling the St Martha's Mistress in 2050 that "Like, this is like *so* totally head-wrecking."'

She jumped up. 'Lunch time. I fear my head is about to be totally wrecked, so my stomach needs all the nourishment it can get.'

*　　　*　　　*

'I left her,' Amiss told Ellis Pooley several hours later, 'surrounded by novels and crying "Rubbish", with Mary Lou kindly but firmly refusing to allow her to jettison a book until she'd read at least a chapter.'

'She's wonderful, isn't she?'

'Your betrothed, I presume you mean? Or were you talking about Jack?'

The waiter arrived and poured Amiss's wine and Pooley's water. Pooley took a sip, shook his head and looked across at Amiss. 'I get nervous sometimes that it won't work.'

'So does she. She's not convinced that your father is ready for black grandchildren.'

'Bugger my father. Anyway he's mad about her. And it's not as if I were the heir.'

'Quite,' said Amiss. 'It's amazing the compensations there are for being a younger son. But if it's not that, what is it? Different cultures?'

'Not really. Minnesota and rural England can coexist without too much trouble. It's more the practicalities. She's in Cambridge in a job she loves and I'm in London in one I love just as much and which has antisocial hours. We're always fighting circumstances to have time together. And I keep thinking how Jim and Ann split up. Not to speak of you and Rachel.'

'Both our relationships died over rows about values rather than clashing timetables, Ellis. Though I admit they didn't help.'

Pooley looked at him worriedly. 'How are you coping, Robert? You've been at a loose end ever since Rachel left. Do you miss her a lot?'

'I'm getting over her.'

'Any other women on the horizon?'

'My mind is on higher things. Like writing a novel in your favourite genre.'

'What? You're writing a crime novel?'

'Having a go. Probably hopeless, but I am rather enjoying it. I've already murdered two

61

ex-colleagues.'

'What style is it? Cosy? Hard-boiled? And where's it set?'

'I'm certainly not going to tell an aficionado like you anything about it at this stage, Ellis. You'll get all dreamy about the greats of the past and destroy my confidence.'

Pooley looked disappointed. 'Oh, all right. I'll wait. Do you expect it to make you any money?'

'Probably not. Probably won't even get published. But between the remains of the legacy and bits of reasonably lucrative freelance writing, I've enough to keep going for now. And the Warburton pays a few bob, and in theory at least makes me useful contacts.'

'Good luck. Now, about the murder of Hermione Babcock. You've heard the news?'

'No. There wasn't anything on the six o'clock bulletin.'

'It was on the seven o'clock. Just said the police suspected she had been poisoned and probably by ricin.'

'Oh, God. I shouldn't have switched my phone off.' Amiss reached into his inside pocket.

'Just hold on a sec, Robert. Before you do anything, let's just be sure you know what you're talking about.'

'All I'm supposed to know is what the news said. Was there any indication of who you think did it?'

'None. We've no idea. It's early days, and we've only interviewed her husband, but there's no whiff of a motive.'

'I hope to God it wasn't connected with the Warburton. I know Jack takes these things lightly, but I wouldn't like to think I was putting her in danger.'

'She'd do it to you without a thought.'

'True. But that's because she thinks we're invincible. Which I don't. However, there's no point in even thinking like that. We are where we are. I'd better alert her.'

'It's OK. When I couldn't get through to you, I rang her and warned her to expect an avalanche of calls. She said the drawbridge was up and no one would breach the castle walls.'

'Oh, Christ.' Amiss jumped up. 'Give me a minute. I must talk to Georgie.'

'Who?'

'Georgie Prothero, our PR guy.'

'Oh, him. Yes. Our people have already seen him. Why do you need to ring him?'

'He'll be in a state.'

Pooley shook his head and picked up his newspaper. Amiss was back within a couple of minutes. 'Georgie's surprisingly calm. Tells me Jack rang him and instructed him to refer everyone to her, stop worrying and have a stiff brandy.'

'But I thought you said she wasn't speaking to anyone.'

'Precisely. But she'll take the blame rather than Georgie. So he's happy and she's acquired a fan.'

'Good. Now let's choose some food and then you can tell me everything about what I'll be dealing with.'

*   *   *

Coming up to ten o'clock and having snorted her way through several pages, the baroness shouted 'That's enough bilge' and hurled the book at maximum force against the oak door. Horace, who had been peacefully napping, saved himself from tumbling off her head by digging in his claws.

Mary Lou watched with interest as the baroness leaped up shouting with pain. 'That's not the way to persuade him to let go, Jack,' she commented mildly. Ignored, she shrugged and returned to her book and did not re-emerge until the parrot had been placated with crooning and stroking and a piece of fig and returned to his cage.

'I could die of psittacosis,' grumbled the baroness, as she began to pack her pipe with tobacco. 'I wonder if it's painful.'

'I looked it up after he attacked me, and my incubation period would have passed by now, so I shouldn't worry. Now what was it that caused your outbreak of violence?'

'The one about the shy, solitary monk who bonds mystically in a Sumatran rain forest with an equally shy, solitary rhinoceros. I've never read such boring drivel in my life.' She flicked a lighter, directed its enormous flame at the pipe bowl and sucked noisily.

'Robert said your old pal Wysteria Wilcox was very keen on it.'

The baroness expelled a mouthful of smoke vigorously towards the ceiling. 'Trixie always had a brain even a rhinoceros would despise.'

'Have you found anything you can bear yet?'

'How could I?' She leaned over to the pile of books to her left and picked one off the top. 'Have you sampled *Flesh-Eating*? It's about how timid, deaf Lionel Carter finds a purpose to his life when as a cleaner in the British Museum he first comes across a sarcophagus. It was popular with

64

Hermione, apparently.' It thudded to the floor.

'But you like sarcophagi, Jack. Didn't you float the idea of being buried in one in the college grounds?'

'Buried, yes. Fucked, no. And I want Roman, not Egyptian. Figures. Not hieroglyphics.'

'Did you look at the one Geraint Griffiths liked?'

'Robert tells me I have to read the whole thing, but the tirade about the limitations of the Koran had me nodding off, so I adjourned to *Proust's Madeleine*, which appears to be a volume of impenetrable existential musings on the nature of women and small cakes. I can't stand much more.'

'I thought Robert said there are some you'd like—or at least not hate.'

'Yes, but I thought I'd save them for later.' She looked at her watch. 'Put on the news.'

It was another quiet day, so the admission from the police that she appeared to have died in suspicious circumstances gave Hermione top billing.

'Family and friends can think of no reason why anyone would harm a woman so loved and respected. Asked to comment on speculation that her death might be associated with her chairing of the Knapper-Warburton Prize, the organisers refused to comment.' A photograph of the baroness waggling her finger appeared behind the newsreader. 'Lady Babcock's successor as chairperson, the controversialist, Lady Troutbeck, Mistress of St Martha's in Cambridge, was not available for interview.'

'What's a controversialist?' asked the baroness.

'Someone the BBC doesn't agree with, I guess.'

'The Irish singer and soap-star, Dervla, is a Knapper-Warburton judge. Susie Briggs spoke to her earlier this evening.'

'It's, like, weird,' confessed a worried-looking, pretty, curly-haired redhead with a bare midriff. 'It's, like, aaaaggghhh!'

'Do you think the committee will be able to function in the light of this tragedy? Especially if Lady Babcock's death turns out to be connected to the Warburton.'

Dervla looked hunted. 'I'm, like, whatever,' she proffered.

'Thank you, Dervla.' Susie Briggs faced the camera. 'Like Dervla, the rest of the committee are determined on business as usual.' A photograph of a vast head topped with wild white hair took over the screen. 'Geraint Griffiths, the well-known commentator, rang our newsroom to denounce what he described as a clear conspiracy to stifle free speech and intimidate the judges. Asked to explain what he meant, he said that all would become clear in time.'

'Thank you, Susie. Speaking in the House today, the Chancellor emphasised that . . .'

Mary Lou pressed the 'off' button. 'Back to work, Jack.'

The baroness surveyed the pile to the right of her chair. 'I'm usually given to tears only at the opera,' she said, 'but I'm on the verge of bursting into noisy, self-pitying sobs.'

'Troutbecks get on with it, Jack. Remember?'

The baroness managed a wan smile as she picked up the top book.

CHAPTER SIX

'It's me, darling,' said an excited Pooley. 'I've got terrific news.'

'You're coming here for the weekend?'

'Wish I were.'

'The Warburton's been cancelled?'

Pooley's forehead furrowed. 'No. Why would that be good?'

Mary Lou sighed. 'It would prevent Jack from running amok. I think she's about to declare war on the entire literary establishment. And she won't be using conventional weapons. More those of mass destruction.'

'Robert mentioned he didn't think she was keen on modern fiction.'

'Robert sure got that right, honey. But what's the terrific news?'

'It's the old team on the job. Jim's been asked to step in and I'll be his right-hand man.'

'How did he wangle that? Isn't a solitary murder a bit beneath him these days?'

'The Met gets very jittery when cases are high-profile. And this is high-profile. And requires tact, which even Jim's detractors admit he has in abundance. Will you tell Jack? It might cheer her up a bit.'

'I'll tell her. Though I doubt if anything could cheer her up the way things are. When are you getting started?'

'I'm just going into Jim's office now, darling. Will ring when I can. Bye.'

'I photocopied the *Who's Who* entries of Hermione Babcock and her husband,' said Pooley to Detective Chief Superintendent Milton, as they sat in the back of a car on their way to north London to interview Sir William Rawlinson.

'Anything interesting?'

'Interesting-ish.' He held out two sheets of paper. 'Do you want to read them?'

Milton squinted at the tiny print. 'I can't. Forgot my glasses. Read them to me.'

' "Babcock of Islington, Baroness created 1997 (Life Peer) of Bloomsbury in the County of London; Hermione Joan Babcock (Lady Rawlinson); writer; born 27 November 1943, daughter of the late Revd Reginald Michael Massingham and the late . . ." '

'Could you make it a bit more selective and digestible, Ellis?'

'Sorry, sir. She married first in 1964 Ralph Babcock; they were divorced in 1975 having had a son and daughter.'

'Oh, so it wasn't her maiden name.'

'No. But by the time she was divorced presumably she was well-known enough to be stuck with Babcock.'

'It must have been rather irritating; Massingham's rather more attractive, don't you think?'

Pooley nodded. 'And so is Rawlinson. She married William Rawlinson the year of her divorce and he was knighted in 1986.'

'I don't know how these things work, Ellis. You do. She remained Mrs Babcock for professional reasons while first being Mrs and then Lady Rawlinson, but later became Lady Babcock. Is that right?'

'Ms Babcock, I expect, sir. She was the type. Anyway, she was educated at grammar school and Oxford, where she got a first-class BA in English and was awarded the Chiddick Honorary Fellowship, whatever that is.'

'Speed up, Ellis. I admire your thoroughness, but spare me too much academic detail. Especially since we're nearly in Islington.'

'A couple of translations of French novels and one of her own while with Babcock, and then she seems to have taken to committees in a big way.'

'All literary?'

'Broadly cultural—authors' organisations, judging literary prizes, dishing out grants, British Council activities, that kind of thing. Edited a couple of anthologies of French short stories, did reviewing and broadcasting and churned out the odd novel as well. The last one, *Virginia Falling*, won the Warburton last year. She collected a couple of honorary degrees over the last decade or so and was given a peerage in 1997.'

'Why do people want honorary degrees if they've already got one?'

'I suppose some of them like the attention and others like being called Doctor.'

'Even if they haven't earned it?'

'I don't know much about that, sir. I'll consult Mary Lou.'

'And Rawlinson? Hurry up. We're nearly there.'

'Short entry. Babcock his second wife, first one died, no children, went into Graylings Bank straight from school and became CEO five years ago.'

The car turned into a square and pulled up in front of a white, four-storey, double-fronted Georgian house. 'Unless you expect to be in there a long time, I'll wait here, sir,' said Detective Inspector (retired) Pike.

'Thanks, Sammy. I doubt if we'll be very long. Keep an ear to the news, will you? I'd like to know if any other members of the Warburton committee are sounding off.'

'Will do, sir.'

Milton pressed the bell. 'What do you reckon it's worth, Ellis? A couple of mill?'

'Easily, sir. It's the most desirable part of Islington.'

The door was opened by a tall, good-looking man with white hair so perfectly coiffed that its wings were utterly symmetrical. He led them through the narrow hall into a large sitting room and then held out his hand. 'I'm William Rawlinson. You, I presume, are Chief Superintendent Milton.'

'Yes, Sir William. And this is my colleague, Detective Inspector Pooley. May I offer our sincere sympathy on this tragedy.'

'Thank you.' Rawlinson waved towards one of the white sofas. 'Please sit down, gentlemen. Would you care for coffee?'

'No, thank you, sir.'

'Quite sure? I'm going to have some.'

'Oh, well, in that case, thank you.'

'And you, Inspector?'

'Yes, thanks.'

Rawlinson left calling, 'Alina.'

Milton and Pooley surveyed the room. Apart

from a large number of abstract paintings, most of which featured greys or black, it was exclusively decorated and furnished in white or chrome. Pooley jumped up and rushed around the room reading the plaques under the pictures. 'Ben Nicholsons and Victor Passmores,' he reported as he sat down again.

'Mean anything to you?'

'I've heard of Nicholson. He'll be expensive.'

Rawlinson returned, threw himself into an armchair and took a packet of small cigars out of his pocket. 'Do either of you smoke?'

'No, sir.'

'Mind if I do?'

'Good heavens, no, sir.'

Rawlinson lit his cigar and looked around for a receptacle for his match. 'Damn.' He got up and went over to the mantelpiece, picked up a piece of metal, put it on the bare chrome table in front of him and dropped his match on it. He leaned back in his chair. 'So what do you want me to tell you? I've already been through the story of Hermione's illness twice.'

'I realise that, sir. And I'm loath to ask you to go through it again, but it would be very helpful if you would.'

'Hermione rang me at work on Tuesday afternoon to say she felt sick and was worried that she might be too ill to make the dinner party we were due to go to that evening if she didn't get some urgent medical help. I told her she should cancel immediately, but she didn't want to; there was some Romanian dramatist expected who's the toast of literary London and she didn't want to miss him.'

'Did she go into any details about her symptoms?'

'Just said she felt feverish and nauseous and had difficulty breathing. She tried to get hold of our doctor but he was out and she didn't think much of his partner, so I arranged for the bank's doctor to call her. He reported that he thought she'd picked up a virus and had told her to go straight to bed and drink plenty of water and see her doctor in the morning if she wasn't better. I checked with her, and, reluctantly, she'd given up on the Romanian and agreed she'd go to bed as soon as she'd finished whatever she was doing with the long-list. At about five-thirty Alina rang to say she'd found Hermione slumped over her desk. She was very alarmed, since Hermione had fallen on the piles of Warburton novels she'd been sorting and had knocked them all over the place.' He gave a slight smile and gestured towards their surroundings. 'As you can see, untidiness was not my wife's style.'

The door opened and a tiny, pleasant-faced, middle-aged Filipino in a black dress and white apron came in carrying a chrome tray. She looked with alarm at Rawlinson's ashtray, which he removed and placed on the floor. She put down her tray. 'Shall I get you an ashtray from your study, sir?'

Rawlinson smiled. 'Thank you, Alina, but this will do for the moment.' He indicated Milton and Pooley. 'These gentlemen are from the police. They may want to have a word with you later.'

She bowed slightly. 'I will be downstairs. May I pour you coffee?'

'Thank you,' said Milton. 'White, no sugar, for me, please.'

72

'And me, please,' said Pooley.

She served the three of them deftly and withdrew. 'I'm sorry,' said Rawlinson, 'we don't keep biscuits.'

'We're fine, thank you, Sir William,' said Milton.

'So Alina revived Hermione with some cold water and helped her to bed. By the time I got home, at around six-thirty, Hermione had been vomiting and looked dreadful, but she insisted she'd be fine and wanted to be left alone to sweat it out. Hermione was a very determined woman, and one tended to do as instructed. Still, I kept checking, and when at about ten her breathing became more laboured, I called an ambulance. The hospital also thought it just a virus and treated her accordingly and it was not until her kidneys and liver began to fail early on Thursday morning that the alarm bells were sounded. I arrived to see her at about eight-thirty to find her already on a life-support machine. As you will know, she died at two p.m.'

'Thank you, sir,' said Milton. 'Now, as you know, the pathologist seems to think the ricin—which was a very large dose—was administered some time in the twelve hours before she became ill.'

'And I've already given your colleagues all the information I have about my wife's movements during that period.'

'Indeed. You've been most helpful and we are working on it. But could I ask you if you've had a chance to think further about who might have wanted to kill Lady Babcock?'

Rawlinson finished his coffee and put down his cup. 'Not a clue, Mr Milton. Hermione's life was in the literary world and the Lords and while obviously she made some enemies, I had no reason to think there was anything personal going on. You know what they're like, those literary people . . . Or maybe you don't?'

Milton shook his head.

'Well, it's like any other kind of work, I suppose, it's just that ambition and greed and achievement and so on take different forms from what you'd get in industry or banking. Or probably the police. That is to say, there's an extraordinarily random element at work. For instance, I got to the top of a merchant bank because I'm reasonably clever, I understand the money market, I'm diligent, I get on with clients and I have the ability to convince people I know what I'm talking about. I expect you've done well for equivalent reasons.

'But the literary world is completely different. You can be a brilliant and hard-working writer and never get anywhere, while others with a tenth of your talent and industry bask in adulation and wealth. It's a mixture of luck and self-promotion. Thomas Gray had it right. "Some mute inglorious Milton here may rest" and all that . . . Oh, sorry, Mr Milton. I forgot. You must get very fed up with that quotation.'

'Not really, sir. Police and criminals don't quote much poetry.'

'Gray, of course, was talking about illiterates, who don't know they could have been Milton. But what about those writers who've produced the book, believe it's good and can't get it published, or if it does get published, it's ignored and they see contemporaries streaking ahead of them for no reason except that they're young, sexy, lucky in their timing or geniuses at self-promotion or

74

networking. So that's why there's so much anger and backbiting in that world—far more in my experience than you get in normal life—and for all I know some of it was directed at Hermione because of her success.'

Milton looked at Rawlinson rather uncertainly. 'Are you suggesting, sir, that there were those who might have felt that Lady Babcock had been more successful than she deserved?'

Rawlinson smiled. 'There were. Plenty, in fact. A lot of people didn't like Hermione; there were snide comments in the press and quite a few expressions of outrage that she won the Warburton. There was an awful lot of money involved, after all. It wasn't just the prestige. Indeed, I remember several really disagreeable articles. But murder's a different matter.'

'No one comes to mind in her personal life who might actually have wanted to kill her?'

'Absolutely not. No likely murderers in the family, or as far as I know, among friends.'

'I was just going to ask you about her family, Sir William. I know her parents are dead, that she was divorced and that she has two children.'

'Ralph Babcock is still about, but Hermione hardly ever saw him. Joshua lives in Hong Kong and Alex in New York. They'll both be back here for the funeral, whenever that'll be. Then there's her sister, Flora, but they were not close.'

'That'll be Dame Flora Massingham, will it?' asked Pooley.

'Yes.'

'We'll need to talk to all of them,' said Milton.

'Speak to my secretary and she'll give you the phone numbers and anything else you want.' He looked at his watch. 'I have to leave shortly. I have an urgent meeting.'

'Her close friends, Sir William?'

'Hermione didn't go in for intimate friends in the way that women do—you know, old school and university friends, that kind of thing. She specialised in occupational friendship. Currently, she was particularly thick with Wysteria Wilcox and Rosa Karp, but as much for professional reasons as anything else. I'll think about it in the car and if any names come to mind I'll tell my secretary to give you the details.'

'There has been some speculation about rows on the Warburton committee, sir.'

'Which will intensify, no doubt, when people realise that their last meeting happened within the ricin incubation period. But I'm damned if I can believe that one of her colleagues bumped her off because she didn't agree with them about some novel or other. They'd have to be raving mad. I know they had rows and I suppose a fist fight might be imaginable at the stage when the winner is chosen, but the notion that someone would be murdered before even the long-list stage is too preposterous for even a thriller-writer.'

'There could be other motives, sir, since some of the judges knew each other quite well.'

'Let me think.' Rawlinson ticked the names off on his fingers as he spoke. 'I've mentioned Wysteria and Rosa. And Hermione knew that ghastly Den Smith well and wrote for his awful magazine sometimes. So those are three she got on well with. Who else was there?'

'Professor Felix Ferriter,' said Pooley.

'Oh, lord. Yes, she talked a bit about him, but I

76

couldn't understand what she was driving at. Literary criticism is a closed book to me. And they seemed to get on too. Who didn't she like? Oh, yes. She complained often about that peculiar Welsh journalist who shouts a lot. And about some little Irish girl with a funny name whom she thought stupid and ignorant. And someone called Amiss she thought obstructive and flippant. But she wasn't afraid of any of them.' He frowned. 'That's seven including Hermione, but I'm sure there were eight.'

'Sir Hugo Hurlingham,' proffered Pooley.

'Oh, yes, of course. But he was another of her allies. She's reviewed for him for years and they were both great enthusiasts for the Barbarossa Prize.'

'Barbarossa?' asked Milton.

'Some European prize that Hermione was hoping the Warburton winner might win.' He spread his hands helplessly. 'It was all very complicated and I'm afraid I only half-listened.'

'Tell me about Den Smith,' said Milton. 'He is, I understand, rather volatile.'

'Den's professionally angry. He was an Angry Youngish Man when I met him first, raged a lot in middle-age and is now an Angry Elderly Man— which always seems ridiculous to me. Not my sort, but he and Hermione seemed to get on fine. She agrees—agreed—with him about America, which she always found impossibly crude except for certain literary enclaves in New York.'

Milton looked curiously at Rawlinson. 'Did you like your wife's friends, Sir William?'

'No, I can't say I did.'

'Because?'

'Because they weren't my kind. But it didn't matter. She wasn't keen on mine either. We had fulfilling separate lives and were happy to escort each other to professional functions where it was necessary. I have old-fashioned notions about sticking by the person you marry. So, in practice, had Hermione.'

He looked at his watch. 'I don't want to be unhelpful, Mr Milton, but I really need to get to the office. Is there anything else you desperately need to discuss today?'

'No, I don't think so, sir. May we stay on for a while and look around and talk to Alina?'

'Certainly. I'll send her up to you.' He shook hands with both of them, smiled and left.

CHAPTER SEVEN

'Even allowing for shock, reserve and all that kind of thing, I don't think William Rawlinson is very upset about his wife's death.' Pooley sat forward and gazed at Amiss intently. 'In fact, the more Jim and I looked at that house, the more I suspected he'll enjoy being without her.'

Milton stretched and then leaned back further into his armchair. 'My guess is that he probably long ago realised he didn't like her. You tell Robert all about it, Ellis. I might just go to sleep.'

'Top-up, Jim?' asked Amiss, pointing at the whisky that Plutarch's recumbent body prevented him from reaching.

'No, thanks. I'm fine. Get on with it, Ellis. We need to go soon. Sammy will be getting restive.'

'Sammy? Sammy Pike? I thought he'd retired. Why didn't you bring him up with you?'

'He has retired, but helps me out sometimes. It would offend his sense of propriety to listen to Ellis contradicting me.'

Pooley was aching to continue. 'So you've got the picture so far?'

'Hermione was as chilly, minimalist and anally-retentive at home as she was abroad.'

'Fantastically so.'

'Knowing how tidy Ellis is compared to us,' said Milton, 'it was a pleasure to see him so horrified. Her study was pristine and characterless and the dining room was worse: imagine eating off a glass and metal table while sitting on wooden seats with mirrored backs?'

'Come again?'

'The front of the back of the dining chairs—i.e. what you lean against—was mirrored.'

'Clumsy guests would make for an interesting evening.'

'And the pictures . . .!' Pooley shook his head. 'The minimalist paintings were depressing enough, but as for the art photos of bathroom fittings!'

'Do you mean photos of baths?'

'And washbasins. And loos. And bidets.'

'What an absolutely foul idea.'

'Don't forget the boarded garden,' said Milton sleepily.

'Oh, yes. There were boards over half of the garden.'

'You mean decking?'

'No, decking is suburban. These were boards. And you couldn't walk on them even if you wanted to.'

'Ah, you mean they were art.'

'Indeed they were. We asked Alina to show us outside and there, sure enough, was a plaque: "CARL ANDRÉ. 'Everything is an environment'".'

'The pile-of-bricks chap,' added Milton. 'Remember the row years ago when the Tate bought them.'

'I was in short pants, then, Jim. But I know what you're talking about. Isn't he a bit passé?'

'So is minimalism,' said Pooley. 'But maybe Hermione was a traditionalist in her own way.'

The phone rang. Amiss reached across the cat and picked up the receiver. 'Ah, Jack. How are you getting on? . . . Yes, I sympathise . . . Yes, I thought you'd like that . . . No, of course I didn't. I only selected it to cheer you up . . . No, everything's been quiet, but Jim and Ellis are here reporting on their first day on the job . . . OK.' He held the receiver towards Milton. 'Jack wants a word, Jim.'

Milton reached over. 'Good to talk to you again . . . No idea . . . Yes . . . Yes . . . Yes . . . No idea . . . Give my love to . . .' He put down the receiver. 'I haven't talked to her for ages. I'd forgotten how abrupt she is.'

'What did she want?'

'Having learned that I'd no idea who'd done it, she told me to hurry up, sort everything out, give none of them any quarter and that she'd buy us all a wonderful dinner when it was all over.'

'Don't be too enthusiastic. She's just read a novel that's got her worked up about the gastronomic possibilities of tripe.'

'What's a novel got to do with tripe?' asked Milton.

'Tripe and the modern novel are closely related,' said Amiss, 'but one of the entries is actually called *Tripe!*. With an exclamation mark. If I remember correctly it's about an Algerian terrorist who plans appalling atrocities while working in a French *triperie*. Jack likes it because it includes dozens of recipes.'

'I hope she'll have moved to something called *Great Cuisine* with or without an exclamation mark by the time she buys this dinner,' said Milton. 'Where were we?'

Pooley leaned forward and gazed at Amiss intently. 'At the Rawlinson/Babcock house, which was very interesting. It was clear from Rawlinson's room that in all the rest of the house she had imposed her tastes on him. His room was full of leather and red plush and the smell of cigars and

81

sporting memorabilia and guns and classical music and thrillers and adventure books piled higgledy-piggledy. *Who's Who* gives his recreations as music, shooting and reading about explorers.'

'And hers?'

'She didn't give any.'

'Too grand to share this information with *hoi polloi*, no doubt. What was their bedroom like?'

'Separate bedrooms actually: hers spartan; his untidy. Same with their bathrooms. The spare bedrooms, bathrooms and so on were furnished to her taste. And Alina had a room at the top chock-a-block with family photos, religious statues and pictures of Imelda Marcos.'

'Kitchen?'

'Functional, but nothing elaborate. Alina told us that Madam wasn't interested in cooking. Sounds as if they ate out a lot and when at home lived on a diet of grilled fish and chicken.'

'Did Alina say anything interesting?'

'She's been with them for ten years,' said Pooley, 'and while she said appropriately polite things about how terrible Madam's death was, she didn't give much impression of grief, did she, Jim?'

'Well she certainly didn't manage any tears, though she crossed herself a few times. But she didn't manage too many words either, for that matter. All we got out of her was that they were nice to her, there were not many visitors to stay, that Madam often had people to coffee or tea, that they sometimes had drinks parties and sometimes dinners with outside caterers. She had met the children once or twice but had nothing of interest to say about them. She could not recall Flora Massingham.'

'So who else did you see today?'

Milton yawned. 'No one. We went straight back to the Yard where Ellis set things up for the next few days and I worked on all the other cases I'm in charge of. I'm going to be hard put to spend more than a quarter of my time on this, so in practice Ellis will be running things most of the time.'

His phone rang. 'Yes, Sammy . . . Oh, God . . . All right, we'll be straight down.' He jumped up. 'Sorry, Robert, but there's a problem on another job and I'll have to look in at the Yard after all before I go home. Do you want to stay or come, Ellis?'

'I'll come with you, Jim. I want to do a bit of browsing.'

'The internet was made for Ellis, Robert. It's an adventure playground for the inquisitive.'

Pooley looked slightly hurt. 'It's very useful. I've already found out that those pictures and that Carl André must have cost a packet.'

'Well, there's a surprise. Don't get up, Robert, it'd be a shame to disturb Plutarch. How middle-aged she's becoming. Hasn't done anything uncivilised all evening.'

'You weren't here when she jumped onto my keyboard and succeeded in wiping half a chapter,' said Amiss grimly. 'I can tell you I nearly did something uncivilised.' He shoved the cat to one side and got up. She waved a faintly threatening paw in a half-hearted way, spread herself over the cushion and went back to sleep.

'Ellis told me you were writing a book. How's it working out?'

'Mostly hell. Just occasionally heaven. Always too slow.'

'What's it about?'

'You don't really want to know, Jim,' said Amiss, as he opened the front door. 'Too close to home. You go off and hunt a real murderer and I'll go back to my imaginary one. We can have a race to see who gets his man first.'

'Fifty quid we win,' said Milton, perking up.

'It's a deal.' They shook hands solemnly. 'Consider yourself the bookie, Ellis,' said Milton. ' 'Night, Robert.'

Amiss closed the door, picked up his glass and took it over and set it beside the computer.

*   *   *

Pooley was on his way to interview Hermione's sister when Milton called. 'They've examined Babcock's corpse in minute detail and can find no sign of any puncturing of the skin, so it's virtually certain that she ingested the ricin. Now as we know from Rawlinson and Alina, she didn't go out on Monday, as she was reading a book and reviewing it for a Sunday paper, so there are no other Monday suspects. See me when you've finished with Flora Massingham and we'll talk about Tuesday.' He rang off just as Pooley's cab drew up outside an attractive cottage in West Hampstead.

*   *   *

'She was a bitch,' said Flora Massingham. 'A complete and utter bitch. Resented me from the moment I was born and was generally horrible to me all the time I was growing up.'

Pooley tried not to look taken aback. 'So this was

84

more than typical sibling rivalry, Dame Flora?'

She looked at him and snorted. 'Sibling rivalry my ass, Inspector. Hermione took one look at me in the cradle and decided she hated me. Made a couple of attempts to kill me. And, yes, I know that's normal jealousy and she was only two and later she confined herself to pinching and hair-pulling, but even though she tried to hide it from our parents, she could never bear me. When she wasn't being snooty and refusing to play with me, she was telling me I was stupid.'

'How did you feel about her?'

'How do you think? There was a pathetic period when I desperately wanted to make her like me, but by the time I was eight or nine I knew it was hopeless and stayed out of her way as much as possible.'

'And in your teens?'

'She did brilliantly academically and I was mediocre, so you'd have thought that would have mollified her, but it didn't, because I had more boyfriends. She became more benign when she got into Oxford while I seemed destined for something provincial, but it all went to pot again when I landed RADA.'

Pooley looked at Flora Massingham, whose gamine face, curvaceous body, husky voice and intelligent acting had her widely known as the thinking man's crumpet, and remembered skinny Hermione Babcock's stern features. 'So the relationship went on being competitive?'

'I wasn't competitive. We lived in different worlds and it didn't bother me if Hermione did well. In fact I was quite proud of her when she got her first, which was more than she was when I got

85

my big break just afterwards. In fact she was livid that I had made the West End before I had even graduated.'

'How did you know?'

'She told me on the phone that I was so inexperienced I was bound to fail in the part, and when she came to the first night with our parents she made a very bad job of pretending to be pleased that it had gone well.'

'So you became a success immediately?'

'I was lucky enough never to be a struggling actor. Why do you want all this?'

'Because I need to know what your sister was like in order to get some idea of the motive of her killer.'

'I don't really know what she was like, Mr Pooley. My view must be jaundiced.'

'Still, it would help if you would tell me how your relationship developed.'

'We didn't see much of each other, even though to my surprise she married a would-be actor, Ralph Babcock, instead of someone donnish.'

'Where did she meet him?'

'Oh, at Oxford. He was quite a figure in the Dramatic Society. But because he really did struggle, and she was pregnant with the twins at twenty-one, when they married, Hermione's twenties were difficult. I was sorry for her. I think she'd have been happy staying on at university, doing a Ph.D. and all that and becoming something lofty in a women's college, but instead she was teaching part-time in a college of education in London and spending most evenings alone while her husband earned a pittance as a spear-carrier. Ralph never got the breaks.'

'You weren't able to help?'

She looked squarely at him. 'I don't like nepotism anyway, Inspector, but even if I had, I would never have been so unprofessional as to try to get a job for someone who just didn't have the talent. Ralph realised it eventually and became a drama teacher instead. By that time he was involved with someone else and he and Hermione broke up shortly afterwards.'

'Did you see much of the children?'

She shook her head. 'Not when they were small. Seeing the children meant seeing Hermione. Too big a price to pay. I sent them decent presents at Christmas and on their birthday and when they were older and Hermione couldn't stop them, I'd take them on outings. It was all a shame, really. If she hadn't been the way she was, I could have helped a lot.'

'And then she married William Rawlinson.'

'Nice William. Yes. I can't imagine what he thought he was doing. But presumably he loved her. He's certainly been very loyal.'

'You don't think there were problems in the marriage?'

'Nothing that would have required a prosperous, attractive, sophisticated man to kill his wife. He could have just walked out.'

She lit another cigarette, lay back against the red and purple cushions and gazed quizzically at Pooley. 'You need dirt. I realise that. But I think the family's clean.'

Pooley thought so too. 'How did she react when you became a Dame?'

'She never mentioned it.'

'You were very young.'

'I was. I've a sneaking suspicion a particular senior minister had the hots for me and pressed my damery very strongly as a populist measure at a time when I'd had a big success on television. I thought Hermione would mind a lot, but fortunately William was knighted the following year so she became a Lady. Even if she had to confine her ladyness to her married name, if you know what I mean.'

'You can't use your husband's title without using his surname, you mean.'

'Exactly. But even being Lady Rawlinson must have salved the wound a bit. And of course she was cock-a-hoop when she became a peeress in her own right. Invited me to a big party held in that morgue she called a drawing room. I went to it too. For fifteen minutes.'

'Did you see each other often?'

'Impossible not to once she became a grand figure in the literary world, as it impinges so much on the thespian. We kept up appearances: Christmas cards, air-kissing when we met and pretending to speak to each other warmly, that kind of thing, especially once the papers started going on about our enmity.'

Pooley, whose researches had already revealed hundreds of articles speculating on the relationship between the sisters, said, 'Enmity?'

'I'm surprised you didn't know about the gossip, Inspector. I'd have thought you'd have looked us up.'

Milton had long ago taught Pooley that proving one was ahead of the game was not always the smart thing to do. He looked puzzled. 'Sorry, Dame Flora. I'm afraid the arts world is not one I know anything about.'

'Better you don't waste your time. Basically, the chatterers are split between those who think I was jealous of Hermione because of her intellect, her children and later her peerage, and those who think she was jealous of me because I was famous long before her, was richer and was thought to be more fanciable. The gossip intensified when it emerged that I lived with a woman.'

'Did your sister meet her?'

'I took Jane to the peerage party and Hermione ignored her. Nothing to do with being anti-gay, you understand. Hermione was far too right-on for that. But Jane's a doctor and is therefore of no networking value. And, besides, she was tarred with my brush.'

She unleashed on Pooley a dazzling smile that made him feel momentarily faint. Then, recollecting that she was more than a quarter-century his senior and a lesbian to boot, he recovered himself. 'Could you tell me something about Lady Babcock's children, Dame Flora?'

'They're sweethearts. Not a bit like Hermione. Neither could stand the literary world—or at least, their mother's version of the literary world. They've talked to me about the horrors of being patronised and embarrassed at her soirées because they failed to impress when asked what they were reading.'

'You get on, then?'

'They're nice, straightforward, good-hearted kids. Not such kids now, when you come to think of it—must be pushing forty. I'm fond of them and I think they're fond of me. We talk on the phone and we see each other when they're in England. They

89

both left as soon as they'd graduated. Couldn't wait to get away from their mother, who never stopped criticising them.'

'And her friends?'

'They weren't what I'd call friends, Inspector. She liked fashionable people, did Hermione. Fashionable or functional. I doubt if there'll be many tears for her.'

'Lovers?'

'Were there any?'

'There are rumours.'

'There are always rumours. And I wouldn't be in the least surprised if Hermione had useful affairs. I would, however, be very surprised if they were passionate.'

'It has been suggested that she had a relationship with Den Smith.'

Dame Flora emitted a happy chortle. 'Dirty Den himself,' she said. 'Why not? He's supposed to have had everyone else in literary London. Thuggish, priapic shit that he is, he stuck his hand up my skirt once, in the back of a taxi. I slapped his face so hard he never spoke to me again. But to Hermione at a certain stage in her life, Dirty Den might have come in quite handy.'

'No passion, though.'

'No passion.' She paused. 'I think. I presume. But then what do any of us know about other people really? Maybe Hermione had a wild side I knew nothing about.'

'Who do you think killed your sister?'

'Not the faintest idea. I suppose it was someone in whose way she was standing. Or someone she gave a nasty review to. Or even maybe something to do with the Warburton. Somehow I think it would be appropriate that the murder motive had to do with ambition. Nothing much else mattered to my sister.'

CHAPTER EIGHT

Pooley's report to Milton on Flora Massingham was interrupted by a brief visitation from the Assistant Commissioner that ended in raised voices.

'What was all that about, sir?' asked Pooley, after the door had banged shut.

'Let's just say the AC so hates press attention that he becomes at times just a little irrational when dealing with issues that attract it.'

'Demanding immediate results while refusing extra resources seems extremely irrational.'

'Indeed it does. However, we'd better use the few resources we have as efficiently as possible. I'm up to my eyes and can't go with you to see Ralph Babcock, but I very much want both of us to see Den Smith this afternoon if only to protect each other against the possibility of any complaints. See you back here about two.'

*   *   *

'I've haven't seen Hermione for ages,' said Ralph Babcock. 'I really don't see how I can help you.'

'We're just trying to build up a picture of her, Mr Babcock. I've just come from Dame Flora Massingham, who has been extremely helpful.'

'I'll bet she has,' said Babcock, chuckling. 'It must be quite a relief for Flora to be able to say what she thinks of Hermione to someone who isn't going to spill it to the press.' He paused. 'Or are you one of those leaky policemen?'

'Certainly not, sir. Leaking is rank unprofession-alism.'

'Glad to hear it. What do you want to know?'

'If you could just tell me the story of your relationship from your point of view?'

'We met at Oxford. I was a star and she was in my firmament.' He laughed again. 'You're very good at the po-face, Inspector. By rights you should look surprised that a fat old teacher living in suburbia should say such a thing. But it was true. I was handsome, confident and ambitious and Hermione, who was skinny, intense and a swot, thought I was wonderful and would go places. If she hadn't thought I'd be successful, I'm sure she wouldn't have set her cap at me.'

'And her attraction was . . . ?'

'I just explained. She thought I was wonderful.' There was another chuckle. 'Maybe you new men are immune to this, but in my day, someone telling you you were God and could do anything went a long way.'

He paused again. 'And then she got pregnant. And her father was a minister. And I wasn't a complete bastard.'

'The pregnancy was an accident?'

'How do I know?'

Pooley said nothing.

'I think she probably did it on purpose. She was smart and she probably guessed I'd never have married her otherwise. What she wasn't smart enough to know was that I wasn't going to live up to expectations. I was supposed to sweep all before me and outdo Flora, but I didn't have Little Sis's star quality. In fact in truth I didn't have any talent worth speaking of. Couldn't even make a decent living. So Hermione found herself in a crap job with a depressed and unsuccessful husband and looking after twins when she didn't really have much of a maternal instinct. I'd have been sorry for her if I hadn't been concentrating on being sorry for myself.'

'She was jealous of Flora?'

'Jealous! She was obsessed with her. And yet Flora was a nice little thing who could have been a real friend. She once offered to subsidise childcare so that Hermione could do her doctorate and Hermione told her to keep her filthy money. Simple jealousy. Yet she was never done complaining that Flora wouldn't get me parts. And I knew by then that I wasn't good enough for the commercial stage so was relieved Flora never offered to try.'

There was another silence.

'It was a grim time, sir.'

'It certainly was. But it cheered up no end when I fell in love with my agent's secretary, split up with Hermione and took up a job I was good at— spotting talent in kids and encouraging them.'

A forty-something woman stuck her head around the door and offered coffee. 'That would be lovely, darling. But first tell this nice policeman what you thought of Hermione.'

'Cold-hearted bitch. Do you take milk and sugar?'

Pooley, who had stood up when she entered, sat down again. 'Just milk, please, Mrs Babcock. And Dame Flora?'

'Sweetheart. And the twins are OK too. Very good, considering.'

She left the room.

'Tessa's a bit biased. Apart from anything else, it's really got up her nose all these years that Hermione held on to the Babcock name. And she believes Hermione just used me. But I recognise that I was a terrible disappointment to her and I wasn't much help with the kids. Not like I've been with mine and Tessa's. Men weren't in those days. I spent an awful lot of time being the life and soul of parties in the name of networking while she sat at home seething. Can't have done her character much good.' Another chuckle. 'Still, it gave her the inspiration to write that all-men-are-bastards novel that created a bit of a stir, so I suppose you could say I gave her her chance.'

'Did you keep closely in touch?'

'We did the parental bit reasonably successfully. Shared the kids' holidays and that sort of thing and didn't fight too much about money. Tessa mightn't agree, but Hermione wasn't mean. A bit mercenary, yes. Wanted access to money. But not mean.'

'Was she a good mother?'

'Conscientious. Expected too much of them, if you ask me. Very disappointed that neither of them made Oxbridge. As if it matters. But I suppose she thought it reflected on her. As my failure did.'

'You have not been a failure, Ralph,' said his wife, as she swept into the room with a tray. 'You have been a fine teacher and your children love you—even her children.' Handing a mug to each of the men, she left the room again.

Pooley cupped his mug in his hands. 'I really need to know more about Lady Babcock's relationships with men, Mr Babcock, and, frankly, I don't know how to ask you the next question.'

'You want to know what she was like in the sack, is that it?'

To his chagrin, Pooley felt himself blushing. 'Well . . .'

Babcock pulled himself lazily forward, picked up a plate and waved it in Pooley's direction. Pooley shook his head and Babcock took a chocolate biscuit. 'I should think Hermione has always done what she thought was expected of her if it suited her. Are you with me?'

'Calculated, sir?'

'Calculated, Inspector. Calculated and controlled.' He demolished the biscuit in two bites. 'To my knowledge there was no corner of Hermione's life in which she wasn't a control freak. The exception was her irrationality about Flora. If it hadn't been for Flora, Hermione wouldn't have wanted to marry me: I'm sure the idea was that I would be a far more successful actor, so Hermione could patronise and belittle her sister from her vantage point at the top of glamorous London society. Hence the pregnancy. Talk about the law of unintended consequences!'

He snorted into his mug, and then reached for another biscuit. 'She thought she was pulling off a daring plan, but I didn't deliver, Flora did brilliantly and Hermione became domestically a drudge and professionally a badly-paid, unhappy instructor of disadvantaged kids whom she despised.' He burst out laughing. 'I'm not much help, Inspector, am I? I seem to be giving you an excellent motive for Hermione to have murdered Flora then, rather than for person or persons unknown to kill Hermione now.'

'I know very little about my mother's private life, Inspector,' said Joshua Babcock. 'She was not the sort of person with whom one discussed intimate matters. I'm afraid I can't help.'

Pooley moved the phone to his other ear while he tried and failed to think of an inspired question. He decided to fall back on the simple appeal. 'Mr Babcock, I need your assistance. There is no obvious motive for your mother's murder, so the police need those who loved her to help us determine why anyone should have wanted to kill her. I need to know what kind of person she was. What kind of enemies she might have made.'

'Who have you talked to?'

'Your father and stepmother, your stepfather and your aunt.'

There was a chuckle that reminded Pooley of Joshua's father. 'Hardly a list of those who loved her. Except for William, I suppose.'

'That's where you come in.'

' 'Fraid not, Inspector. It's pretty difficult to love someone who regards you as an obstacle to achievement. Alex and I weren't best pleased when she went on about the pram in the hall being the enemy of good art. And of course there was all that Virginia Woolf wankery about a room of her own.'

'Well, she certainly got that all right.'

'She sure did. Several in fact. And they certainly weren't child-friendly. Or indeed William-friendly.'

'Still, as you got older . . . ?'

'We were disappointing. Failed to be a credit to her.'

'How do you mean, sir?'

'At great expense to William we went to excellent schools that got us out from under Mama's feet during term-time, but we performed no better than competently, academically or otherwise. We are OK to look at, but nothing to write home about.' He chuckled again. 'Took after her that way rather than Dad or Aunt Flora. We ended up—to her great embarrassment—at red-brick universities. And to her even greater embarrassment we read subjects she considered naff; engineering in my case, business studies in Alex's. Can't imagine what she told them at the Groucho. Beautiful, talented, arty children were what she required. Passable mediocrities with a yen for the practical were not.'

'Are you saying your mother didn't love you?'

'Love isn't a word I associate with my mother, Inspector. Duty is. She behaved perfectly properly towards us even if she did strongly show her displeasure when we failed to obey orders. Most of her sins were of omission, not commission.'

'And you felt about her?'

'Also dutiful. I'll do my bit at the funeral and I'll try to feel sorry she's dead. But the truth is she hasn't had any impact on my life worth talking about since I ceased to be under her control. She's never even seen her grandchildren. Or shown any interest in them. Though she always sent them cheques at Christmas.'

'Any advice on which friends I should see?'

'None. Mama seemed to me to have colleagues rather than friends and these changed according to whatever was preoccupying her at the moment. Though of course she always kept in with the magic literary circle even when her mind was on New Labour.'

'The literary circle is?'

'Influential publishers, reviewers, literary editors, literary organisations. And she never turned down an invitation to join a committee. Preferably as chair.'

'Can you suggest who should be top of my list?'

'That guy she reviewed for—what's his name, Hugo something? That madman Den Smith. Probably Wysteria Wilcox. She seems to have been having dinner with them forever and they certainly know everyone.'

'They were all with her on the Warburton committee.'

Joshua gave a shout of laughter. 'Didn't I tell you there was a magic circle?'

*   *   *

'His sister sounded just like him and echoed him almost word for word,' Pooley reported to Milton. 'They're obviously very close. "She'd have liked us to be stepping-stones to further advancement," she said. "Instead, more often than not, we seemed to be millstones."'

'Anything more about Sir William?' asked Milton.

'Just the same sympathetic noises as Joshua. And when it came to friends she also mentioned Wysteria Wilcox and Den Smith. Said she couldn't understand how anyone could put up with him. Thought he was off his head.'

'I'm looking forward to this encounter.' He took his glasses out of his inside pocket. 'Pass me Smith's *Who's Who* entry. I've come prepared.'

99

Den Smith had declined to be interviewed at home ('I will not have my privacy invaded'), at the Yard ('I will not set foot in Gestapo headquarters') or Milton's club ('I refuse to obey a dress code imposed by dinosaurs'). After much negotiation, he had grudgingly suggested an upstairs room in a Notting Hill pub. 'Slow down, Sammy,' said Pooley, as they neared the rendezvous. 'Look, Jim, that's his house on the corner.'

'That looks worth as much as Rawlinson's,' observed Milton.

'Easily.'

'It's very big for one person.'

'He uses it for his various causes. That's where "Anti-Fascism '88" was launched. I've been reading about it on the Net. Reagan had just been re-elected and Smith and Hermione called luvvies, literati and smart academics of the left to arms against the Thatcher-Reagan forces of evil.'

'What happened to it?'

'Acres of piss-taking by the right-wing press followed by the total failure of the campaigners to decide on what they wanted to achieve. Den's desire to overthrow the state in the name of democracy seems to have been too much for most of them. There was a huge row and *Rage* targeted a whole new batch of enemies.'

'Here we are, sir,' said Pike.

'Thanks, Sammy. Don't hang around. We'll get a taxi back.'

'Are you sure you don't want me to wait outside the room, sir? He sounds like a nasty piece of work.'

'His bile is worse than his bite, I think,' said Milton, grinning at his own wit.

*   *   *

Wearing a black rollneck, Smith was sitting across the table in the tiny room with a half of bitter in front of him, ostentatiously reading Kafka. ('I'm surprised he thought we'd get the reference,' said Milton afterwards.) 'Good afternoon, Mr Smith. Detective Chief Superintendent James Milton and Detective Inspector Ellis Pooley,' said Milton. 'May we sit down?'

'I can't stop you, but I warn you I'm not going to use those fascistic titles.'

'We're not interested in titles, Mr Smith. We just want your help in finding the murderer of your friend Lady Babcock.'

'I'm surprised you're not using the ricin as an excuse to lock up every Muslim in London.'

'So far there is no reason to suspect that this was a political crime. You may be associating ricin with Muslims because of recent publicity. We have no reason to do so.'

Smith glared at him. 'So what was it then? Who did it?'

'I hope you'll have some ideas on that.'

'And if I don't? What then?'

'You will, I hope,' offered Milton mildly, 'have some suggestions about where we should direct our enquiries. We're trying to build up a picture of Lady Babcock. We've talked to her family and now we're talking to her friends. You were one of her dearest friends, I think.'

The belligerence diminished slightly. 'I suppose

I was. Hermione and I go back a long way.'

'How long?'

'Since the seventies. We met on a peace march. We were both speakers.'

'You became friends?'

'Yes.'

'Just friends?'

Smith jumped to his feet with such force that he rocked the table and spilled his drink. 'Typical filth-type insinuation. How dare you! How dare you! It's no surprise you've minds like sewers, but I don't have to answer your shitty questions.'

Milton, who had been mopping the table with a tissue, spoke with no sign of annoyance. 'Please sit down, Mr Smith. I've no wish to upset you, but equally, you've no right to refuse to assist us. Either you want Lady Babcock's murderer caught or you don't. If you do, then I suggest you answer questions frankly. If you don't, why then we will have to ask you to come to a police station and help us anyway. It's your choice.'

Smith was still quivering. 'I can get a lawyer. And not one of those lawyers you can bully into submission. I can get a famous human rights lawyer who'll make you shiver in your flat-footed shoes.'

Milton looked at Smith benignly. 'If you want to go to that trouble and expense, Mr Smith, by all means go ahead. I will merely ask that you turn up at New Scotland Yard at nine tomorrow morning. And if you don't, I might have to have you arrested.'

Smith looked at him venomously and sat down. 'Fuck it. Oh, all right. Go on.'

'Did you have an affair with Lady Babcock?'

'Yes, I did. Thirty-odd years ago. So what!'

'Did it go on for long?'

'Just a few months.'

'Why did it end?'

'William Rawlinson came on the scene.'

'And she preferred him?'

'No.'

'No?'

'No.'

'But she ended your affair?'

'She wanted to marry William.'

'Rather than you.'

'I don't marry.'

'You did once.'

Smith shot him a furious look. 'Once was fucking well enough.'

'She would have liked to marry you?'

'Of course she would. But even if I would have, I couldn't afford Hermione. She needed someone well-off.'

'But you remained on good terms?'

'Yep.'

'But no longer lovers.'

'Yep.'

'Was she faithful to Sir William?'

'How the fuck would I know? We didn't have another affair, if that's what you're insinuating in your creepy way.'

'You didn't try to rekindle the passion?'

Smith looked at Milton incredulously. 'Rekindle the fucking passion? Are you off your fucking head? We're talking about Hermione Fucking Babcock, not Cleofuckingpatra. Hermione didn't do passion. She did a polite, well-behaved affair if it suited her.'

'Forgive me, Mr Smith, but I'd have thought you

were a man given to strong passions rather than convenient liaisons.'

Smith looked pleased. 'You're right up to a point, copper.' He stopped. 'Up to a point, copper. That's bloody good. You won't get the joke, of course. It's a play on . . .'

'On "Up to a point, Lord Copper". I've heard the pun before, sir.'

Sulkily, Smith continued. 'You can't have strong passions all the time. Hermione was an available fuck so there were no hard feelings when she moved over. But we kept in touch and were allies in the literary world.'

'In what way, sir?'

'Oh, I dunno. I introduced her to a few people, I suppose.'

Pooley touched Milton on the sleeve. 'May I, sir?'

'Certainly, Inspector Pooley.'

'Sir, would I be right in saying that it was because of you that Ms Babcock, as she then was, was asked to join the PEN committee?'

'It's a long time ago, but that's probably right.'

'And that began her involvement with literary committees?'

'Hermione certainly took to committees.'

'Was she particularly able in committee work?'

'She was keen. And not many people in our circles will do the work, I suppose.'

'Was she not on the Cultural Resources Council when your magazine was given a substantial grant?'

'How would I know?'

'You'd know when *Rage* received the hefty subsidy that made it viable.'

'How do you know about this?'

104

'Please answer my colleague's question,' said Milton.

'It was sometime in the early eighties.'

'Hermione Babcock was on the CRC from 1982–5, Mr Smith. She did you a big favour, didn't she?'

'Nothing that wasn't deserved. There wasn't any other magazine like *Rage*.'

'But there was quite a lot of criticism, wasn't there? Suggestions of cronyism, if I'm not mistaken?'

'Don't remember.'

'Since when you and she have been on innumerable committees—together and apart. She was on the Pilkington when you won the prize for a poem that was denounced as appalling by many, wasn't she? And you gave *Virginia Falling* an enormous puff that put it in the reckoning for the Warburton, I gather.'

Smith's face flushed. He jumped up, kicked his chair to the floor, pushed the table violently and screamed: 'You red-haired fucking cunt! You piece of fucking filth with a fucking pretend toff's accent. You moron with fucking pretensions. I'm outta here. And you can send the Home fucking Secretary after me to throw me into one of your fucking dungeons and torture me if you like. I'll never give in to your fucking police state.'

He stormed out.

'He's certainly got a way with words,' observed Milton.

'Sorry, Jim. Perhaps I provoked him too much.'

'Nothing to be sorry about, Ellis. I wouldn't have missed it for anything. It's a wonderful thing for an uneducated policeman to have the privilege of encountering the intelligentsia. Now let's go.'

On their way towards the street, the barman stopped them. 'Den seemed right upset,' he said. ' 'E were shouting.'

' 'E certainly were,' said Milton. 'Is he often like that?'

'Oh, yeah. Lots of the time,' said the barman. 'You don't want to take 'im too seriously. It's just 'is way. I reckon 'e should go on one of them anger management courses, but 'e tells me it's 'is artistic temperament.' He snorted. 'Lorra bollocks, if you ask me. I think 'e's just a bad-tempered git. But if you'd like to 'ang on, I'd say he'd be back in about 'alf-an-hour.'

'Thank you, but no. Could you give him a message?'

'Yeah. I'll give 'im a message.'

'Just tell him the filth will be back.' As he pushed open the door to the street, Milton turned and smiled at the gawping man. 'Soon,' he added.

CHAPTER NINE

Mary Lou was half-way through reading the latest government communiqué about ethnicity and higher education when the baroness rang and shouted at her incoherently about cats and lesbians. 'Don't come to me looking for sympathy, Jack. I'm just being threatened by the teach-your-grannie-how-to-recognise-an-egg department.'

The baroness emitted a loud sob. 'I must have sympathy. You've no idea how I'm suffering.'

Mary Lou looked at the uninviting pile of paper on her desk. 'OK. I'll drop by shortly. In the meantime, pull up your socks and get a grip like you're always telling everyone else to do.'

*   *   *

As he sat on her desk, Pooley tried to keep his eyes away from the buxom charms of DS Barbara Lupoff. While castigating himself for his unprofessionalism, the exculpatory thought occurred that it was hardly surprising his eye should stray considering he so rarely saw the woman with whom he was wildly in love.

'So the butler and the waiter agree with the chef that he never left the kitchen.'

'Absolutely, sir.'

'And you've no reason to doubt that, Barbara?'

'None, sir.'

'And you really think the waiter . . .' He checked her interview notes again, '. . . András Jungbert is out of the picture.'

107

'Sir, he can scarcely speak a word of English and he's only been in the job three weeks.'

Pooley nodded. 'Yes, yes. But we must always keep an open mind in case he turns out to be the deceased's illegitimate son or spurned lover or something.'

'If he was her spurned lover she'd have recognised him when he waited on her, wouldn't she, sir?'

'Sorry, Barbara. My mind was wandering. Now, I see you think Francis Birkett isn't worth considering either?'

'He's been the butler at Warburton HQ for twenty years, sir. I talked to people who've known him a long time and they say Knapper kept him on because he loved his old-fashioned courtesy and reliability. Confidential matters are often discussed over lunch or dinner in the executive dining room, and Birkett is known to be utterly discreet. Indeed, he told me he always makes sure the waiters are foreign in case they picked up any information they shouldn't have.'

'What did you make of him?'

'Respectable, sir. Dull, nice and respectable, just like he looks. You'd be glad to have him as an uncle but you wouldn't want him as a boyfriend.' She grinned. 'Not like András. Pity he's foreign.'

Pooley looked at her notes again. 'Nothing interesting from the checks?'

'No, sir. No record of any kind for any of the three. And the others at that dinner confirm Lady Babcock didn't know him until they all met him at their first lunch.'

'All right, Barbara. Thanks. Now, I've another job for you. Lady Babcock wrote "9.15 Ed" in her diary for the day she became ill. Sir William Rawlinson said he didn't know if it was short for Edward, Education or anything else beginning with Ed, so I'd like you to get to work on it. Obviously, you'll have to go through her manual and electronic address books, but any other bright ideas will be welcome. Report as soon as you find anything interesting.'

As he walked away, Pooley switched on his mobile phone and picked up four messages.

'This is Wysteria Wilcox, Inspector . . . what is your name? Dooley? Cooley? Gooley? The maid's writing is so slovenly I can't read it. I just want to tell you that I won't be able to stand it if there are more than two of you and if you behave roughly. My nerves are not good, I have a weak heart and I am grief-stricken at the tragic death of my dear friend. I thought I should warn you. And I insist you do not arrive one minute before four. I cannot have my precious writing time interrupted. Goodbye.'

Beep. 'Ellis, it's Jim. Griffiths can't do the later time, so I'll see him and you see Wysteria Wilcox and Rosa Karp. Talk to you later.'

Beep. 'Hello, Ellis. It's Robert. Yes, I'm happy to move the venue to your place, especially since Plutarch has just broken a bottle of whisky from sheer spite, as far as I can see, and the pong is pungent, to say the least.'

Beep. 'It's me, darling. I'm having an interesting time. Are you? Don't forget to ask me about the effect a tree falling in the forest had on Jack.'

*   *   *

109

'Come in,' called a high-pitched voice in response to the timid knock by the nervous young Filipino, who opened the drawing-room door for Amiss and then left him to it. Wysteria Wilcox, small, fragile and draped in layers of floaty and diaphanous shades of mauve and lilac and purple, was sitting at a mahogany Chippendale desk, writing with a silver fountain pen. She continued until, fed-up, Pooley cleared his throat and said, 'Good afternoon, Lady Wilcox.' Her hand flew to her throat as she turned to face him. 'Who are you?'

'I'm Detective Inspector Pooley. You asked me to come after four. It is now four-ten.'

'You gave me such a shock.'

'I'm sorry.'

'Sit down.' She pointed at a gilt chair near her desk, but as he was about to sit on it she squealed, 'Stop. You're so big and heavy you might break it.' Pooley, who was proud of his slim, athletic body, felt extremely aggrieved.

Wysteria stood up, fussed around for a moment, said, 'You'd better sit over here then,' steered him to an uncomfortable stuffed, upright armchair and settled herself bolt upright on another. 'Where's the other man?'

'He was detained.'

'I find that most unreasonable. I was expecting two of you and now the other man rudely refuses to keep his appointment.'

'He was urgently detained by another tragic murder, Lady Wilcox. London is a violent place.'

'So what do you want to ask me? I've warned you about my nerves. And my heart.'

'I want to ask you if you have any idea who might have killed Lady Babcock.'

She clutched at her bony chest. 'How can you put it so brutishly?'

'Lady Wilcox, the last thing I want to do is to distress you . . .'

Her large, soulful eyes filled with tears. 'But how can this be anything other than distressing? When you are as sensitive as am I, anything to do with violence, sudden death or indeed hatred, damages the soul . . .'

'Indeed, Lady Wilcox. But if I could just . . .'

'No, no. You have to understand. I am an artist, yes, and artists, of course, have to deal with the terror and the horror as well as the beauty of existence. But I am a sensitive too, which means I understand more than ordinary people and feel more acutely. And as well as all that, I am deeply spiritual.' She held her clasped hands out to Pooley in a gesture of supplication. 'You must try to understand me. As an artist, I live for my writing. As a sensitive, I live to commune with the inner core of the universe. As a spiritual person, I live for love.'

'And as a policeman, Lady Wilcox,' said Pooley heavily, 'I live for establishing the facts. In this case, the facts about who killed Hermione Babcock.'

Wysteria buried her face in her hands and began to sob. Pooley passed the time by looking around the drawing room and trying to price the antiques. He had just guessed £20,000 for an ormolu clock featuring disporting cherubs when she looked up, took a tiny handkerchief from her sleeve and dabbed her eyes. 'How you have upset me.'

'Frankly, Lady Wilcox, I'm the least upsetting policeman you're likely to get.'

Tremulously, she said, 'I can see that you have a white aura.'

'Good,' said Pooley briskly. 'Now, let's get started.'

* * *

What Geraint Griffiths described as his London squat consisted of a small maisonette in Kilburn in which he competed with books for enough space to live. As Milton followed the rumpled figure with the wild white hair upstairs, he trod gingerly between the tall stacks, squeezed along the landing with his back pressed against the banisters, teetered slightly as he placed his feet carefully one in front of the other to navigate the narrow pathway into what Griffiths called his parlour and then, as instructed, sat down in the only armchair. Griffiths grabbed the upright wooden chair which sat at right angles to the crowded table, turned it to face Milton and sat down talking volubly of the hardship of having to leave Wales for London to attend committees and give talks. 'Like it's a real pain to have to split my fuckin' books and never to have what I want where I need it if I didn't have the British Library I wouldn't be able to function though they won't lend books even to scholars you wouldn't believe . . .'

'I'm sorry to interrupt, Mr Griffiths, but I know you're busy . . .'

'It's Dr Griffiths boyo not that I'm keen on titles myself but you can't move for fuckin' titles in the literary world these days so I'm using what I've got which was conferred on me only last year in Aberystwyth in recognition mind you rather belatedly of what . . .'

Milton, who was wishing he had chosen Wysteria Wilcox rather than this verbal incontinent, broke in again. 'Dr Griffiths, can you please tell me if you've any idea why anyone might have wished to murder Lady Babcock?'

Griffiths took a deep breath and began to emit words even faster than before. 'Hermione? No I've no idea why anyone would fuckin' want to do that though she was morally obtuse which is why I had to tell her so often she had bad authority and I've no time for people like that in the fuckin' circumstances we face and she got up my nose not just because of that but because she was so fuckin' grand like and we people from the valleys don't like them grand especially when they're not really fuckin' grand . . .' He drew a hasty breath. 'You see boyo Hermione like she had no idea about struggle there was no fuckin' passion in her or anger or any sense that she was in tune with the great dramas that try men's fuckin' souls like and tear our universe apart now as I said to Hermione it's no good you giving us all this pc shit about how we've got to respect other people's fuckin' cultures when they're hanging gays up by the testicles I mean that's real bad authority and I'm not going to fuckin' put up with it when . . .'

Milton held up his hand. 'I'm sorry to interrupt, Dr Griffiths. Am I right that you were very anxious that *Pursuing the Virgins* should win the Warburton and that Lady Babcock was unsympathetic?'

'Unsympathetic's not the word she was fuckin' hostile though I told her and all of them over and over again that we're all of us caught up in the Homeric struggle of Western fuckin' civilisation

113

against religious bigots from the thirteenth century bent on destroying every fuckin' thing worth a fuck that we've ever done I told her "Hermione, this is no time to fuck about we must all stand up and be counted in the struggle of fuckin' good against fuckin' evil" and do you know what she said?'

'No, Dr Griffiths.'

'She said in that fuckin' pseudo-grand-aren't-I-superior way of hers that it had nothing to do with the Warburton which was about literature and not politics and I said "Hermione can't you understand you high-flown desiccated piece of shit that literature *is* fuckin' politics it's about the highest of us and the lowest of us everything we do in every part of our life in our heart in our head in our balls in our cunt it's our discourse our narrative it's all about authority good fuckin' authority or bad fuckin' authority" but Hermione she didn't have good authority all she could do was witter about mincy-wimpies like Virginia fuckin' Woolf when we're facing the ultimate clash between civilisation and the Islamofascist fuckin' barbarians like have these people any idea what . . .'

'You were obviously very angry with her . . .'

'I might have punched Hermione but if you think I'd have gone off and boiled up castor oil or whatever you have to do you must be fuckin' mad haven't you grasped I'm in the business of fighting killer ideologues not killing moral cretins who think an ideology exists only to provide topics of conversation in Islington.'

'So who might have wanted to murder Lady Babcock and why?'

'How would I know. Husband? Lover?'

'Did she have a lover?'

'I don't fuckin' know anything about Hermione Babcock's fuckin' private life which as far as I'm concerned was probably as arid as her . . .'

'Dr Griffiths, Lady Babcock was at a Warburton meeting during part of the period when the poison must have been administered. We must explore the possibility that one of the committee members killed her.'

'Is that right like I'd never have thought any of them had the fuckin' nerve to tell you the truth since they all seemed to be a shower of wimps and posturers who had the greatest difficulty seeing that basic fuckin' point I kept hammering about how what we were faced with was the dialectical challenge of the . . .'

'Dr Griffiths, from your observations, did Wysteria Wilcox have any reason to kill Lady Babcock?'

'Well now if you're to believe fuckin' Wysteria she wouldn't kill the meanest insect without having fuckin' Buddhist prayer sessions about it for days afterwards and I have to say she seemed to get on fine with Hermione being as wimpy as she was about hard fuckin' decisions so I can't see why she'd want to kill her still I've always thought she was really as hard as frozen shit so nothing would surprise me.'

As Griffiths drew breath, Milton put in hastily, 'Den Smith?'

'Oh now there's a bad depraved article Den Smith there is nothing fuckin' nothing I wouldn't think he mightn't do with that corrupt mind of his that couldn't even grasp it when I point out that we were all fucked if we didn't realise that the thesis was Bin Laden the antithesis was those fuckin'

115

fightin' him and from that we'd find the synthesis that . . .'

*   *   *

From his taxi on his way to the House of Lords, Pooley rang Mary Lou. 'So what's this about a tree falling on Jack? She shattered it, presumably.'

Mary Lou giggled. 'No, no. It shattered her— that is to say, drove her into a deep sulk that I've only just got her out of. It's a book. *A Tree Falling in the Forest.* She was at the end of her tether as it was, having spent an incredulous half-hour with *Baking Bread for Cats* . . .'

'Sorry? A cook book for cats?'

'No, a navel-gazing analysis of the lesbian condition allegedly written by a cat who is also lesbian as a result of a bad experience with a tom . . .'

'A lesbian cat?'

'Sorry, I was kidding about that bit. But the cat is the narrator. And it's pretty anti-tom. So then Jack got to *A Tree Falling in the Forest* which she hated from page one but because it's on four long-lists she had to read a lot of it.'

'And it's about?'

'A gay logger in the Yukon musing about the environmental damage he's causing with every breath he takes and every tree he cuts down. It's packed with statistics about acres of lost rain forest and apocalyptic moanings about global warming interpolated with angst-laden memories of life-denying sexual encounters . . .'

'Aren't there any straight novels any more?'

'She just hit a queer patch because of having to

116

read some of Ferriter's and Rosa Karp's favourites. Anyhow she went into a sulk because I made her read so much of it, then she plunged into Churchill's speeches and wouldn't open her mouth for about three hours. Refused even to speak to Horace. I felt like sending her to bed without her supper but in the end a large gin and tonic did the trick and she's back at work. What about you?'

'On my way from Wysteria to Rosa.'

'How awful is Wysteria?'

'Worse than awful. I'll tell you later. Must make a call to the office.'

'Bye, darling.'

'Bye,' said Pooley, making kissing noises, which were interrupted by the taxi driver. 'What's this about a lesbian cat, guv? I know us straights are in short supply these days, but I thought the animal kingdom was reliable enough. If you ask me, it's something in the water. Or they're making it compulsory in the schools. I had that Rosa Karp in the back of the cab once and when I told her what I thought of her equality she threatened to have me arrested . . .'

*   *   *

'I doubt it,' typed Amiss. 'Corpses rarely laugh . . .' The phone rang.

'I thought these books were supposed to be in English,' growled the baroness.

'Which one isn't?'

'*Crap.*'

'It's not *Crap*. It's *C-rap.*'

'Huh?'

'It's a rap novel.'

117

'It's gibberish. Can't even understand the first line. What is "I so fragged after railing the skeeza I can't walk my ass to my hoe" supposed to mean?'

'I hesitate to explain this to a woman of your delicacy, but it's roughly that the gentleman is so exhausted after enthusiastic sexual intercourse with a slut that he can't summon up the energy to pay a visit to the lady on whose immoral earnings he lives.'

After a brief silence the baroness said, 'How do you know this?'

'The internet offers translations.'

'Did you discover why the author is called Not1337?'

'Yes. But it's complicated. And, incidentally, 1337 is pronounced leet.'

She emitted a piteous cry.

'It's all right, Jack. It was on Rosa's and Ferriter's short-lists—naturally—but the rest of us never got beyond the first page.'

There was a sound of tearing paper.

'You're not desecrating this noble work, I trust?'

'Just recycling it. The parrot's cage needs lining.'

*　　　*　　　*

'So I got to the House of Lords at the time agreed,' Pooley told Amiss and Milton, as they sat surrounded by cartons of Chinese food, 'and Rosa Karp kept me waiting for the best part of an hour on the excuse that she was at a crucial meeting. When she finally arrived in the lobby I accosted her immediately and the woman she was with promptly said, "Rhonda Skeffington of the *Sketch*" and pressed her card into my hand. "Had an interesting interview?" I asked and Rhonda said that indeed she had, thanked Rosa profusely for giving her so much of her time and departed, waving cheerily.'

'What a cow!' said Amiss. 'Did Rosa look embarrassed?'

'Not enough. Mumbled something unconvincing about long-standing engagements and unavoidable overrunning, so I got very heavy about wasting police time and by the time I had finished she was apologising profusely.'

'Apologising to a WASP!' said Amiss. 'You must have roughed her up seriously.'

'Anyway it was good that she started the interview unsettled and feeling in the wrong which makes a change for Rosa Karp.'

'Is it my imagination,' asked Amiss, 'or are you becoming less nice as you get older, Ellis?'

'In our game,' said Milton, 'everyone gets less nice as he gets older.'

'As "she" gets older,' said Pooley. 'Rosa recovered enough to tell me that if I wasn't prepared to say "he or she" I should say "she", since it was a form of necessary positive discrimination to counteract the negative experienced by women over the millennia or something like that, to which I said that the only form of discrimination I was interested in was discrimination against criminals and that she'd already retarded the murder enquiry enough without going into irrelevancies.'

'My, my,' said Amiss. 'At this rate you'll be hanging suspects from the ceiling and applying electric shocks to their genitals.'

'That's what Den Smith thinks we do already.'

'If we'd a lot of suspects like Den Smith, we just

might,' said Milton. He helped himself to the last sparerib. 'I'm enjoying this,' he said. 'It feels a bit like one of those midnight feasts you'll have had in boarding school, Ellis.'

'It's not midnight, is it?' asked Pooley. 'Good lord, it is. I'd better get on. Well, the nub is that she's got no bright ideas either, though she thinks Griffiths is capable of anything.' He consulted his notebook. ' "Anti-feminist, reactionary, hectoring . . ." '

'Among the very words he used about her,' said Milton. 'Though he was coming at it from a different angle.'

'Wait'll they meet Jack,' said Amiss, pushing his plate away and picking up the wine bottle.

'Not for me, thanks,' said Milton. 'I must go in a minute. What did Rosa say about the others, Ellis?'

'Much the same likes and dislikes as the ghastly Wilcox, though with a subtly different angle. Seemed particularly upset that Hermione wouldn't be around to speak on some equality bill next week, thinks Den's crusading anti-imperialism makes him a great man, thinks Ferriter a true intellectual and admires Hugo Hurlingham because of the opposition to English insularity represented by his Europeanness.' He put down his notebook. 'Tell us what we need to know about Hurlingham.'

Amiss yawned. 'Our man in Europe. Our link with the Barbarossa Prize.'

'Which is what, exactly?'

'A new literary prize about to be funded by the European Commission with the aim of encouraging a European dimension in literature. Hugo's a sharp operator in these areas. He's apparently in love with the European ideal for all sorts of high-flown reasons, but I think it's because it gives him access to innumerable all-expenses-paid freebies abroad—meetings, conferences, lunches and dinners. And, of course, at home as well.'

He yawned again. 'Hugo's already on the guest list of all the European embassies in London, since among literary editors he's the great European drum-banger. He devotes half his literary pages in the *Sunday Oracle* to European literature.'

'So he's been involved in setting up the Barbarossa, has he?' asked Milton.

'More than that. It was he who persuaded Ron Knapper to change the rules to allow translations of novels from any country in the EU to be considered for the Knapper-Warburton. It's one of the reasons we've so many entries. The quid pro quo was that the winner of the Warburton, rather than the winner of the Booker or the Whitbread or any of the other major literary prizes, gets put in the pot for the Barbarossa.'

Pooley frowned. 'That doesn't make sense. Supposing the English translation of a French novel wins the Warburton, that means no English novel is going to be a contender for the Barbarossa.'

'That's right. But that shows your Anglo-centricity. As Hugo pointed out when I protested, anyone bothered by this would be betraying their narrow nationalism and parochialism. Anyway, a literary prize in each EU country is also being opened up to foreigners, so it's all supposed to even out.'

'Jack must have been thrilled when she heard

121

about it.'

'Thrilled is the word. She delivered herself of a tirade about how the British, being suicidally obsessed with *le* fair play, would be capable of giving prizes even to frogs, while the frogs are about as likely to allow an English novel to be awarded any of their prizes as they are to give up stuffing themselves with foie gras on the grounds that it's nasty for geese.'

'Can't argue with that,' said Milton.

'Under Hermione we might well have ended up with a foreign novel. Hugo, Rosa, Wysteria and Hermione all believed in leading by example. "The British have been bad Europeans" was one of the mantras. "In our small way," they would trill, "we have the chance to show ourselves to be good Europeans."'

'What do you get if you win the Barbarossa? And why Barbarossa anyway?'

'He was a twelfth-century Holy Roman Emperor who got a good press. And what you get if you win the prize named after him is one million euros and a piece of what will almost certainly be spectacularly naff sculpture representing the European literary ideal, whatever that is. You also become the Barbarossa Fellow, which means you're required to give a lecture at a major university in every EU country.'

'That's rather a lot of work, isn't it?' asked Milton.

'Not real work, since you can give the same lecture everywhere in conditions of great luxury. As Hugo explained it, you will receive an honorary doctorate in each university, will be celebrated and wined and dined and generally have rose petals strewn in your path.'

'Cushy number,' said Milton.

'You haven't heard the best bit. Your novel will be translated into all the EU languages—not just the ones that people actually speak, but all the officially recognised minority languages as well. So for instance in the UK you'll have your work translated into Cornish, Gaelic, Welsh and Irish as well as English.'

'I don't want to think about this,' said Milton. 'I don't want to get angry. I want to go home to bed. I'll give you a lift.'

Amiss looked distressed. 'Oh, please, before we go, Ellis, do finish giving us Rosa's views on her fellow committee members.'

Pooley consulted his notebook again. 'She thinks Dervla is mentally retarded, hates Griffiths and believes that Wilcox's sensitive exploration of the soul of woman is a vital part of the struggle.'

Milton stood up. 'The struggle for what?'

'For that future in which female values will be on top and there'll be no more violence.'

'Oh, good. That'll be something to look forward to. But for now we really must be off, Robert. Ellis and I have a meeting at eight a.m. and are then calling on Hurlingham—after which he's doing the Irish child and I'm doing Ferriter.'

'But what about me?' cried Amiss in frustration. 'What are they all saying about me?'

Pooley grinned. 'Rosa said you were insensitive and non-inclusive and Wysteria said that she had never been able to get over how much you'd hurt her feelings with some joke so inappropriate and tasteless that it ruined her whole day and still upsets her when she thinks about it. Den was a bit too preoccupied with other matters to get round to talking about you.'

'But Griffiths is a fan,' said Milton. 'Thinks you're the only one on the committee with . . . what does he call it? . . . good authority.' He put on his coat.

'Means I'm the only one who ever agrees with him,' said Amiss, reaching for his.

CHAPTER TEN

Amiss caught Pooley on his mobile as he was finishing dressing. 'Just a thought that niggled me in the middle of the night.'

'Yes,' said Pooley, as he combed his hair.

'Have you established yet if every member of the committee had the opportunity to slip her the ricin?'

'Probably. That is, no one can be ruled out. There was plenty of opportunity to slip something in her food or coffee or wine if you were bold enough. Sometimes people passed wine or poured coffee for others, though no one admits to having done so for Hermione. Except Francis Birkett and András Jungbert, of course, who helped everyone at lunch.'

'Have you checked them out?'

'Of course, I have, Robert,' said Pooley, strapping on his watch. 'Thoroughly. Someone who has spent so much time devouring crime novels knows one must always suspect the butler. Or indeed the waiter. And the PR man, whom I'm also ruling out. Both Jungbert and Birkett could have done it, but frankly, it's a bit difficult to see a motive, try as I do in my more fanciful moments.' He picked up his briefcase and left his flat. 'Not that I have many fanciful moments these days. When you have to wallow in the reality of real-life crime you find the most obvious suspect is usually the perpetrator. Not, mind you, that we've got an obvious suspect this time.'

'So it's up to me as a crime writer *manqué* to

wear the fanciful hat. Has anyone interviewed these guys?'

'Yes. And at home, in case they proved to be secret writers with a grievance. Jungbert's Hungarian and the people in his hostel confirm his English is hopeless; the chef, who never left the kitchen anyway, is French with only a bit of kitchen English, mostly expletives, lives during the week in lodgings and commutes to his family in Paris at weekends; and Birkett is a widower who lives in Streatham, has a stamp collection and some books on the subject and plays darts on Friday nights. He's been in his job for twenty years, so it seems a bit late in the day for him to start murdering people. Unless, of course, Hermione Babcock was horrible to him.'

'She was inoffensive. Much more polite than Jack's likely to be. OK. It was just a thought. Now off you go and enjoy yourselves with Hugo.'

*   *   *

Sir Hugo Hurlingham lived in a vast studio flat in Greenwich overlooking the Thames. One wall was of glass, and—as might be expected of a literary editor—another was shelved from floor to ceiling. Milton, who saw few bookish people in the course of his duties, was fascinated by the contrast between Hurlingham and Griffiths. Where Griffiths's books had been dusty, disordered and looked as if they had all been bought off barrows, Hurlingham's were pristine and arranged alphabetically. But what intrigued both policemen was the enormous display of photographs which dominated a third wall.

'Sit down, gentlemen. I'd offer you coffee, but I'm afraid I don't cater. I prefer to leave that to the fair sex and there isn't a representative on the premises right now.' He leered. 'Never available when you want them, are they?'

'We're fine, thank you, sir,' said Milton, trying to hide his distaste. Were Hurlingham's features gross or was it just his style? He walked over to the window. 'Magnificent view you've got here. Have you lived here long?'

'A couple of years. Used to live in Chelsea but my wife got the house after the divorce. Always do, these days, don't they? Still, as bachelor pads go, this is pretty good. The ladies seem to like it and that's what matters.' He gurgled.

Feeling that some kind of answer was required, Milton fell back on 'Quite.' He sat down beside Pooley on the purple chesterfield.

'Now what would you like to know, gentlemen?'

'Well, what we most need to know is who might have wanted to kill Lady Babcock.'

'This is truly a matter of the utmost gravity,' said Hurlingham, adopting an expression to match his words. 'I deeply regret, however, that I can be of no assistance to you. It is a mystery to me to imagine who could be so vile as to wish to murder such a fine lady. Her loss to literature is great; her loss to the mission of de-Anglicising this parochial little island incalculable.'

'You knew her a long time?'

'Half a lifetime, Mr Milton. Half a lifetime. I had the honour to publish her first two novels, before I abandoned publishing for the world of newspapers.' He stopped. 'Or rather before I was abandoned by publishing.' His voice rose. 'There

127

was a time when publishing was an occupation for gentlemen. Over the past couple of decades it has become almost exclusively an occupation for bean-counters. There is no vision any more. No flair. When I began . . .'

Recognising the beginning of a well-worn tirade, Milton cut in, 'Forgive me, sir, but we are all short of time. For now, could you stick to telling us about your relationship with Lady Babcock?'

Hurlingham glared at him. 'What do you want to know?'

'She had, I understand, a great regard for you, sir.' The glare softened. 'It would be helpful if you could tell us about your friendship.'

'I would not wish to blow my own trumpet, but I think I can truly say that she looked up to me from the very beginning. We were much of an age, but I was by then an experienced publisher, and Hermione was just finding her feet.' He stood up. 'I'll show you.' Leading them over to the massed ranks of photographs, he immediately pointed to one at the top left. 'There we are. This was taken when her first novel was launched.'

Milton and Pooley gazed silently at the row of smiling faces and without difficulty identified a slimmer Hurlingham and, on his right, a softer Hermione. 'Isn't that Lady Wilcox?' asked Pooley, pointing at the kaftan-clad figure with droopy hair on Hurlingham's left.

'Good for you for spotting Wysteria. She's changed a lot. Not like me. But then women show their age so much more, don't you think? And of course the scandal was upsetting.'

'The scandal?'

Though clearly delighted at having a chance to

tell all, Hurlingham once more assumed a grave expression. 'I would not wish to gossip, gentlemen, but the facts are on record. Wysteria was not pleased when she discovered her husband was given to playing away from home and she took up what one might term a somewhat draconian position.'

'Which was?' asked Milton.

'First, she hired a private detective who discovered poor Freddie Wilcox was rather keen on ladies of the night, then she told Freddie she would be suing him for adultery and subpoenaing several of the aforementioned floozies.' He tittered. 'I don't know exactly what Freddie had been up to, but Wysteria described it as "depraved" and he wasn't keen to have it publicised.' He tittered again. 'She certainly exacted her pound of flesh. Freddie had to sell most of the family treasures to pay her off.'

'Lady Wilcox is tougher than she looks, then?'

'Tougher?' Hurlingham gave a belly laugh. 'Wysteria Wilcox is probably tougher than you look, Chief Superintendent.'

'And tougher than Lady Babcock?'

'Hermione was no softy either, as I eventually discovered.'

'Would you describe yourself as having been her mentor in the early days?'

'I think it would not be too much to say so.'

'You were her publisher for roughly how long, sir?'

'About five years. Look, there we are at the party Hermione gave when I moved to the *Sunday Oracle*.'

And there they were again, though this time

Hermione and Wysteria were together at the edge of the group and Hurlingham had his arms around two younger women. Wysteria, Pooley noted, had by now had her ethereal makeover.

Hurlingham waved a finger at the display. 'You'll find her here and there over the years, but here's a contemporary one.' He pointed towards the lower right-hand corner. 'Here's a photo of all of us Warburton judges. Oh, no. That's last year's. Here's this year's.'

'You were a judge last year as well?' asked Milton. 'Is that unusual?'

'Indeed I was. And of course I urged that I should not be asked to take on the burden again this year, but Hermione was insistent. She said she wanted some continuity, and that in any case, in view of my connection with the Barbarossa Prize, I was irreplaceable.'

'Ah, yes. The Barbarossa Prize. I'd be grateful if you'd fill us in on that, sir.'

* * *

'So he started in,' Pooley told Amiss as he walked through St James's Park *en route* to the Ritz and Dervla, 'and he talked about how all the countries of the European Union were now institutionally and spiritually united, how they soon would form a complete economic and political entity, and how far-sighted, visionary people like him in every country were working to promote cross-cultural links and in the long-term a culturally coherent Europe. There was a lot about conflict resolution, healing and . . . hold on a minute.' Pooley balanced the phone between ear and shoulder as he fished his notebook out of his pocket and flipped through it. 'Ah, yes. Got it. "Respect for difference as the essence of humanity" . . .'

'Surely he didn't leave out winning hearts and minds? It's a constant theme.'

'Rings a bell. And I seem to remember something about building bridges.'

'And plenty of references to peace and love,' added Amiss. 'Yep, that's our Hugo. He can witter on like that for hours. Mind you, he's a nasty old coot as well as a boring pompous one. You presumably sussed that he's a dirty old man?'

Pooley emitted a grim laugh. 'Now why doesn't that surprise me? Not-safe-in-taxis sort of dirty old man I presume, from the way he talks?'

'Worse. Onto-that-casting-couch-or-your-book-goes-on-the-reject-pile sort, I've heard. Apparently, if you want a nice big fat review in the *Sunday Oracle*, it helps to be female, it helps to be young and it particularly helps to be pleased to receive the advances of Hugo Hurlingham.'

'Surely people aren't prepared to do that?'

'All those years a cop and you still get shocked, Ellis. It's touching. Look, if actresses do it, why not writers? Have you any idea what it's like trying to get a review of any size—even a review at all—in a major newspaper? Especially for fiction. There are something like a hundred thousand books published every year in the UK alone.'

'Good God. I'd no idea.'

'Mind you ninety per cent of them would never get near a literary page. But still . . .'

'Even so, how does Hurlingham get away with what sounds like near-rape?'

'Oh, he's not quite as unsubtle as I've made out.

131

Publishers and agents know about his tastes and tip him off about exciting pneumatic young novelists . . .'

'You're seriously telling me that publishers and agents expect young women to sleep with Hugo Hurlingham?'

'Stop sounding like a Sunday-school teacher, Ellis. They know he's susceptible to young women and that he'll take them to lunch and may make a pass. But they know too that he has some genuine interest in talent, that he may confine his attentions to lunch and a bit of thigh-massage and that it's up to the young woman in question to decide how far she's prepared to sacrifice herself for her art.'

'The whole literary world seems to be a sewer,' said Pooley grimly.

'It's not all bad. It's just that you've got a prime collection of powerful shits on this committee.'

'But the hypocrisy of Hurlingham,' cried Pooley, as he strode up the steps from The Mall to Waterloo Place. 'I suppose you're going to tell me he doesn't believe all this European stuff he spouts.'

'Oh, I think he possibly does believe quite a lot of it. He's certainly been boring the arse off *Oracle* readers for years with great slabs of reviews of impenetrable foreign fiction.'

'How does he get away with it?'

'Because the *Oracle* prides itself on being highbrow. Because Hurlingham's such an institution that his literary pages are in part the parish magazine of the literati. They all buy it to find out what A.S. Byatt is saying about Martin Amis or Martin Amis about Saul Bellow or Hermione about Wysteria, or what scatological poem Den has just composed. One of the things Hugo did from the beginning of his tenure, I understand, has been to make sure that his reviewers are bang in the centre of the literary establishment. He doesn't choose them for their insight into literature or their ability to grab the reader, but because they sit on the committees, hand out the grants and award the prizes and the fellowships. He chooses the people with power. And he gives them *carte blanche* to be horrible about their enemies and fawning about their allies.'

'The whole thing stinks.'

'You're telling me. I haven't told you about the scandal of the calling-in of extra books, have I?'

'There's more?'

'Yep. Now, the way the books come in is that small publishers—those who publish fewer than twenty books in a year—can submit one for the Warburton. Medium size—say fewer than fifty, can submit two. Bigger than that you can submit three. Now, this is a fraught business that causes many writers to fall out with their publishers.'

'I can imagine: "How dare you put that lightweight forward and not me!"'

'Exactly. And, of course, publishers don't always put in their best books.'

Pooley frowned. 'Why not?'

'Because they have to keep some authors sweet; because their taste is bad; because they think a particular type of book is more likely to win. So, as with some other prizes, the judges are given the discretion to call in a book they particularly admire. Last year it was Den who called in Hermione's. This year, Hugo called in one by his latest protégée, Wysteria called one in by a charming young man who danced attention on her and had given a wonderful review to her last novel, Hermione called in one by a fellow of the Oxbridge college of which she's an Honorary Fellow and Den called one in for slightly more principled reasons—it being a rant against America that began with the torture of an innocent captive in Guatanamo Bay. By way of contrast, Geraint called in an anti-Islamist book he's frantically plugging—*Pursuing the Virgins*.'

'Ferriter?'

'Let me think. Oh, yes, *Otherness as Loss*, that one about the cross-dressing bishop.'

'I thought all bishops were cross-dressers,' said Pooley.

'Only incidentally,' said Amiss. 'This one went in for dressing as a nun.'

'And you, Robert?'

'I called in a brilliant crime novel I still think was better than anything else we've considered and argued that it deserved to be considered as a straight novel because it had been classified as crime only for marketing reasons. Hermione stuck rigidly to her position on genre fiction and, though Dervla backed me, we were walked over and it was excluded.'

Pooley shook his head. 'As I said. Corrupt, corrupt, corrupt.'

'I repeat, you're seeing the worst of it with the Warburton. There are honest people out there too. And, incidentally, in case Hugo has inspired you to think longingly of the superiority of our European partners, may I say that compared to the French, British literary prizes are squeaky-clean. A clique of French publishers stitch up all the literary prizes.

British judges often choose books on merit.'

'Thanks for all that, Robert. Right, I'd better prepare myself mentally for Dervla. In some ways she's going to be worse than Hurlingham. At least he speaks English.'

'Be kind to her, Ellis. She's not a bad kid. And keep your dirty hands off her.'

Sniggering, he put down the receiver and applied himself to his computer and the knotty problem of how to conceal a twenty-stone body in a roof garden.

*   *   *

Dervla sprawled full-length along the sofa, a can of Coke in one hand and a cigarette in the other. Her cropped pink top revealed to the north much breast and to the south a flashing diamond in her navel. Pooley kept his eyes rigidly on her little face, which underneath all the make-up was woebegone. 'I'm, like, stressed out,' she said. 'And I'm talking totally.'

'Is it Lady Babcock's death that's upsetting you, Miss Dervla?'

She turned and propped herself on her elbow and gave him a watery smile. ' "Miss Dervla". That's, like, so cool, but it's a bit, y'know.'

'Shall I call you Dervla and you call me Ellis?'

She nodded with evident relief.

'So, Lady Babcock's death is upsetting you, Dervla?'

She shook her head. 'It's more I'm, like, bummed out.'

'Fed up in general, do you mean?'

She looked puzzled. 'Yeah, like I said, totally

135

bummed.'

'Because?'

'I'm y'know, happy. Not.'

He said nothing, but put on his best enquiring look.

'It's not like I just had all the usual crap,' she said in a rush of articulacy. 'And I'm, like, OK with media stuff, right. But when I saw . . . I thought Oh!My!God!'

Pooley stayed silent and then, suddenly, she pulled from under her body a tabloid newspaper and thrust it at him. A whole page was given to a photograph of a dishevelled-looking Dervla flashing a pair of diminutive knickers from under her microskirt as she was pushed into a car by a youth in ragged jeans and a T-shirt saying 'KNACKERS'. 'DERVLA'S KNICKERED AND KNACKERED BY KNASTY KNICK' was the headline over a story that suggested she was a) drunk, b) drugged, c) had betrayed her loyal boyfriend Conor (pictured overleaf looking clean-cut) for a well-known bed-hopper called Nick from a heavy metal band, d) was a snob with pretensions who claimed to read books, e) was a joke among the nobs on the posh Knapper-Warburton committee and e) was so heartless she went out partying the night she learned Lady Hermione Babcock had sensationally been murdered.

'Nasty is right,' said Pooley. 'The story, I mean. I don't know about the chap.'

Dervla began to cry. 'I look, like, *such* a total slut. And it's, like, *so* not true.' From the disjoined words and sobs that ensued, Pooley put together the story of how Dervla had been fulfilling a long-standing engagement to open a club, how

136

Nick and his band had been the supporting act, how she had had no drugs and very little to drink and was dishevelled because the driver had had to park around the corner and she'd had to run through wind and rain and how Nick had gone off in a separate car when he'd seen her into hers.

'Isn't this routine for someone in your position?'

'Yeah, you know but this was like, I'm, like, out of my brain, and, like, *such* a Samantha, and, as well, I'm, like, a total airhead everyone's laughing at and . . .' She started to sob again. 'And that's, like, true. Lady Babcock and the others, they all think I'm, like, two tracks short of an album.'

'You've been very successful very young,' said Pooley, 'which is more than the other members of the committee were. And when it comes to the Warburton you're in a world that's strange to you but is normality to them. Of course you're at a disadvantage. Doesn't mean they're clever and you're stupid.'

Dervla sat upright and looked at him with incredulity. 'You're, like, amazing.'

'Thanks. So will you try to forget about this malicious nonsense and help me?'

She managed a wan smile. 'OK. I read somewhere that if you sit on the pity pot too long you get nothing out of it but a ring on your butt.'

'Couldn't have put it better myself.'

She giggled.

'The truth is, Dervla, that it looks as if it had to be one of the committee who poisoned Hermione Babcock.'

'Ohmygahd. You cannot be serious! That's unreal.'

'I'm serious. But I suggest you shouldn't tell the

137

press about this.'

'Oh, pul-ease. Like it wasn't already so . . .' She searched for the *mot juste*. 'So totally . . . aaaaggghhh!'

'I'm going to be very unprofessional and tell you that you are not a likely suspect.'

She giggled again.

'So I'd like to hear your opinion of your fellow committee members. Start by telling me how you became involved in the Warburton.'

'Joe called. My agent. He goes, "Hey, you like reading books, Dervla. And I could get you big bucks to do a chicklit book. So raise your profile with the publishers. Be a judge. Here's your chance to show you're more than just a singer with a good ass." And I was like, maybe. So then I meet Georgie Prothero for, like, dinner and he goes, "You're just what we need to give us a fresh image blah, blah, blah," and I go, "But isn't this majorly serious? Like awesome. Can I do it?" and he goes, "Jerry Hall did the Whitbread and she's not Einstein," and I'm, like, a bit rat-arsed from the vodka and Red Bull and I go, "Why the feck not?"'

'So you agreed after that evening with Georgie Prothero?'

'Seemed cool.' She sounded defensive. 'It's not like I don't read. But then it went totally . . . duuuhhh.'

'How?'

'I meet the others and they're nearly all old and cross and I'm Ohmygahd what have I got into but it's too late. And then they say anything I like is so not serious and nearly everything we've got to read is totally ughhhhhhhhh.'

'What do you like to read?'

'Stories. Bridget Jones. Jane Austen. Maeve Binchy. Zadie Smith. And mysteries. I love mysteries. But Hermione. Not. Anything like that was out. I'm like, hello? We can't have it 'cos people like it? And they're, "What do *you* know?" So nearly everything I've got to, y'know, read, is either horrible or boring. Sends me straight to sleep when it doesn't give me nightmares.'

'So what did you think about the other members of the committee?'

'Horrible. I know it's, like, bad to speak ill of the dead, but that Hermione Babcock, she made me feel like a complete loser. Totally. When I said "I'm, like, I can't believe you won't have any book I like", she goes . . .' Dervla made a creditable attempt at a frosty English accent, ' "Dervla, I think you should leave such decisions to people who know what they're talking about." And so there's more blah, blah, blah from the others and they're all, like, Hermione's so right.' She paused. ' 'Cept for Robert Amiss. He's all right, Robert. I could fancy him. He's, like, funny. Human.' She thought for a second. 'Especially compared to them.'

'Robert Amiss was on your side?'

'Yeah. But Hermione, she's "Who do you think you are?" to him too.'

'Tell me something about the others. Geraint Griffiths, for instance?'

'He's like weird. Totally. He's got, like, one idea he's always going bla-de-bla-de-bla about. Like it's us against Muslims, and I'm like, well that's whatever, but we're supposed to be, like, judging books. Not, like, fighting a war. So then he shouts at me about how there won't be books if the Muslims, like, win and is that what I want.' She lit another cigarette gloomily.

'Did you argue with him?'

'How could I? I mean!'

'Did he bully you?'

'Yeah. A bit. But at least, like, he means it. I don't think he's, like, horrible just to be horrible.' She took a big draught of Coke, choked on the bubbles and dropped the can, which sprayed liquid all over her and the sofa and doused her cigarette. After several ohmygahds and more spluttering and wiping up, she lit up again and stretched out.

'You were talking about how Geraint Griffiths wasn't horrible just to be horrible.'

'Oh, yeah. Now Den Smith, he's horrible to be horrible. He's *so* not real, but always roaring anyway. About crap if you ask me. Intellectuals! More like cornerboys. Den going "You're a fuckin' bigot, Geraint" and Geraint going "And you're a blind fuckin' fool."'

'Rosa Karp?'

Dervla leaned over confidingly. 'Ellis, I'm not, like, educated. Left school at sixteen when I won that talent contest. But, y'know, education's not, like, everything. If you ask me, Rosa Karp hasn't a brain in her head. Just a rule book. Like nuns used to be in the olden days.'

'Tell me more.'

'I'm, like, struggling to know what's going on. Everyone using words I don't know. And arguing about ideas I don't, like, understand. But Rosa, if you really listen, she doesn't have a single opinion of her own. It's all that pc stuff that's supposed to make you think like you don't. I mean, I'm cool about race and gays and stuff, but Rosa, she's out-of-it. Unreal.'

'And that affects her choice of books, does it?'

'She shouldn't be let near books. She's the sort thinks Harry Potter shouldn't be allowed on the shelves 'cos he isn't a disabled female and Hogwarts only caters for wizards and there's, like, no inclusion programme for muggles. There wouldn't be any literature if people like Rosa Karp were in charge. And none of us would be let think.'

('It was interesting,' Pooley would say later, 'how as she began to talk about something substantial, "like" and "ohmygahd", and "so" and all the rest of it receded a bit. Maybe there's hope.')

'What did you think about Professor Ferriter?'

'Pillock. He's old, but he tries to talk to me like he was my age. Not, like, to communicate with me better. But to impress me. He, like, tries to be Professor Peter Pan.'

'Wysteria Wilcox?'

'Aaarrgggghhhh! So aaarrgggghhhh! I've a grannie like her. All *sooooo* sweet and delicate on the outside and, like, hard as nails on the inside. Looks like a strawberry cream but inside she's *so* toffee.' She snorted. 'She'd rip the shirt off your back, Wysteria Wilcox, if she wanted it. And then she'd complain the cloth was so rough it irritated her sensitive skin. Like it was your fault. Totally.'

Pooley was by now entranced. 'Do tell me what you thought of Hugo Hurlingham?'

'I thought of him in a posh restaurant last week. Y'know he's so Europe's-where-it's-all-at and England's-so-over? But I think he's on the gravy train they're always saying Brussels is. So there I was reading this menu full of stuff I don't understand and I ask someone what's "*jus*" and they say "gravy" and I think, "That's Hugo. He's on

141

the *jus* train. To Brussels." '

Pooley looked at her and laughed. 'Dervla, don't ever let anyone ever again make you think you're stupid.'

She grinned. 'I'm feeling better. You English policemen are wonderful. That's what my English grannie always told me. She was the nice one. Not the Wysteria one. Have we finished?'

'I think Robert Amiss is the only committee member left. Anything to add to what you said about him earlier?'

'Nope. He was, like, so out-of-it. Like me. No agenda, knowwhatImean? Think he likes books.' She giggled. 'Shouldn't be on a literary committee.'

'Georgie Prothero?'

'Gimmeabreak. Georgie's a hired gun. Wouldn't know a book from a T-shirt.'

'Have you any idea who would have wanted to kill Lady Babcock?'

· 'Totally not. I mean, she was, like, terrible. But some of the others were worse. Can't think why her when they could of murdered Den.'

CHAPTER ELEVEN

'So what do you reckon, Jim?'

'That I'd like a change from Chinese food.'

Amiss felt slightly miffed. 'You seemed very keen on it last night, so it seemed a safe option. The local Indian take-away is foul and the chipper is worse.' As he spoke, Plutarch, who had clambered to the top of his armchair, launched herself at the table and landed just beside a large container, which overturned, scattering rice in all directions. Ignoring Amiss's curses and loud imprecations from Milton and Pooley, she paused briefly to grab a sparerib and then leaped with her booty to the top of a nearby bookcase.

'It's my fault,' said Amiss bitterly, as he started cleaning up. 'I forgot to proffer the Danegeld before we began to eat.' He paused to look at the enormous cat, now gnawing loudly and triumphantly. 'You could have asked, Plutarch.'

'I've never known Plutarch to ask,' said Milton. 'In fact, I'm rather reassured that she's behaving badly again. I thought she was getting old before her time. Like me.'

'Oh, Jim, you're not,' said Pooley. 'You're just overworked.'

'And disillusioned. I'm too old to adapt to the new pc world of the Metropolitan Police. It's not just that you're not supposed to be racist or sexist or any of the other ists. That's fair enough. It's that regardless of the truth you're supposed to confess you were all those bad things and agree to be born again. I have this big problem. I think I was always encouraging to women and Asians and blacks and anyone I thought was worth a damn, but I'm told I can't have been because I'm white and a man.'

Amiss looked at Pooley. 'Is it that bad?'

'It's not good. You certainly have to think twice before you tear a strip off anyone but a WASP.'

'A male WASP at that,' added Milton.

'And I was very annoyed when told by a drunken colleague at a recent party that it was a smart career move of mine to take up with a black woman.'

'But that was a classic racist response, surely?' said Amiss.

'It might have been. But this particular racist was West Indian.'

Amiss groaned. 'Even Rosa Karp might be intellectually challenged by these complexities. But what I'm sure of is that you have to hang in there; without people like you, the lunatics really will take over the asylum. Now have some more food and I'll pour you more wine and you'll feel better. But first, a safety precaution.' Before Plutarch realised he was hovering, Amiss grabbed her, rushed her into the kitchen and slammed the door. As the cries of rage and the sound of a substantial body crashing against the door began, he picked up three spareribs, opened the door a couple of inches, pushed the bones through and slammed it again. Silence descended as he mopped the blood off his hand with a paper napkin. He looked at his guests and grinned. 'It's OK. Honour is satisfied. She's not actually hungry, she's got plenty to nibble on and she'll probably take a stroll when she's finished and see if she can find some harmless little creature of the night to knock off. Meanwhile, we can get back

144

to wherever we were. Oh, yes, I was giving Jim some more wine.'

'And I was about to apologise for complaining about having Chinese again,' said Milton, as he helped himself to some beef in black bean sauce. 'I'm just grumpy tonight. Pay no attention and let's get back to business.'

'OK,' said Amiss, wielding the wine bottle. 'Now I'm a bit confused and would be really grateful for a summary of what your conclusions are to date.'

'I don't know. We've been over and over the ground and it really seems truly unlikely that Babcock was killed for any reason to do with the Warburton. And yet it seems unquestionable that the ricin was administered some time between around six a.m. that morning and three that afternoon. According to Sir William Rawlinson and Alina, Hermione had her usual breakfast of muesli, yoghurt, coffee and a vitamin pill at seven-forty-five and, as he left at eight, went to her study to read the *Guardian* and possibly make phone calls. Her diary has an entry for nine-fifteen with the word Ed opposite but nothing more. She hadn't mentioned any appointment to her husband, but then he says there would be no reason to do so. According to Alina, she left at about eight-thirty, which would have given her time to meet someone for twenty minutes or so and still reach Warburton House, as she did, at nine-forty-five.'

'But no one has any idea about Ed?'

'Not yet. Could be a person. Could be a place. Could be a product. I've a good girl working on it.'

'Slapped wrist, Ellis,' observed Milton.

'Huh?' said Amiss.

Pooley groaned. 'To say girl is technically

discriminatory and could earn an official rebuke. Anyway, the only possible suspects for now are Warburton committee members and Rawlinson?'

'And Alina.'

'Really? Did Hermione leave her money or something?'

'No,' said Pooley, 'but I doubt if Alina was a fan of Madam's.'

'I don't want to be prim about this,' said Amiss, 'but if you don't like your employer, isn't the done thing to get another job?'

Milton shook his head. 'More to it than that. We had a tip-off that she might be involved with Sir William.'

'A tip-off from whom?'

'Can't tell you.'

'Oh, don't be ridiculous, of course you can.'

'Of course we can,' said Milton. 'The spectre of disciplinary action for breathing is beginning to get to me. Tell him, Ellis.'

'It was Wysteria. Just before I left, she suddenly burst into tears, talked of how she hadn't slept a wink since Hermione's death, made a terrific fuss about how she had wrestled with her conscience all day about breaking a confidence and was also terrified that if she told me what she was going to tell me, her life would be in danger. I made reassuring noises, but she put up her hand to silence me and explained that she had communed with Hermione's spirit and had been told to go ahead and report that Hermione had told her that a couple of weeks ago she'd come in earlier than expected from an evening engagement and had caught her husband coming down the stairs from Alina's quarters.'

'Did he admit anything?'

'Apparently not. Said he'd just remembered something he had to tell her, but Hermione had begun to put some twos and twos together.'

'You can't believe anything that noxious old bitch says,' said Amiss crossly. 'She'd character-assassinate her sick grannie.'

'That may be so, but we can't ignore her testimony. That's why Jim's interviewing Sir William again tomorrow morning.'

'You, not me, Ellis, I'm afraid. That call I took as we arrived here was to tell me about another meeting with the AC tomorrow. More nit-picking and recommendations from the Department of the Bleeding Obvious. I'll have to swap with you and see Ferriter instead since Rawlinson asked me to come to his City office and Soho's much better for me. Sorry.'

'Rawlinson must be better than Ferriter, Ellis. Honestly.' Amiss spooned some more chicken in lemon sauce onto his plate. 'Oh, no. I'm being insensitive. You do hate asking people whom they're sleeping with, don't you?'

Pooley straightened his shoulders. 'I'm a policeman. I have to take the rough with the rough.'

*   *   *

Milton shook off his annoyance with the AC as he sat in the bar of the Groucho drinking coffee. He had become mesmerised by Felix Ferriter's tongue stud, for the professor had a big mouth and the stud was very visible. *What a little squirt*, thought Milton. *And a cross-looking little squirt at that.*

Being sartorially conservative, Milton did not think Ferriter well-served by his dyed, gelled red hair, his designer stubble, his black eyeliner or the leather shirt open to the waist which revealed a scrawny chest with two pierced nipples. 'So what is your opinion of your colleagues on the Knapper-Warburton, Professor Ferriter?'

'Their taste is so retro,' said Ferriter querulously.

'Sorry?'

'Retro. Y'know.'

'I don't know.'

'So yesterday.'

'You mean old-fashioned?'

'Yeah. I mean Hermione was the only one who'd embraced Queer Studies, and even she was only just beginning to get a grip on post-postmodernism and avant-pop.'

Milton tried hard to conceal his irritation. 'Professor, I am a policeman, not a literary critic. Would you please be good enough to use words I can understand?'

Ferriter bridled. 'OK, OK. What d'you want?'

'I want to know if you've any idea why anyone would want to kill Lady Babcock.'

'No.'

'You didn't notice any particular tensions on the committee?'

'No.'

'Do you mean everyone got on well together?'

'D'you mean psycho-dynamically?'

'I mean, did everyone get on well together?' asked Milton levelly.

Ferriter looked mutinous for a moment, then shrugged. 'No. There were a lot of arguments.

148

Griffiths and Den Smith were always shouting.'

'How did you and your colleagues get on with Lady Babcock?'

'Hey, dude, I can't deconstruct the whole fuckin' committee for you. I hardly knew any of them and I was thinking of the books, not the hidden narratives.' Seeing Milton's glare, he hastily added, 'She was OK as chair. Well, OK for me. Maybe not for the retro crowd.'

'Did you know her well?'

'Sort of. Lectures. Conferences. Committees. Professional discourse. But we didn't hang out. Didn't do much facemailing.'

'You didn't do much what?'

'Oh, didn't meet and talk much. Anyway, I've been moving on. Queering up.'

Milton's phone rang. It was with great relief that he heard that he was urgently needed at the office to deal with a crisis in the Ealing axe-murder case.

*　　*　　*

The phone rang just as Amiss had despatched his least favourite character over the edge of a cliff and, as a result of several yowls from Plutarch, was thinking about breaking for lunch. 'Hello . . . Ah, Ellis. How did you get on with the grieving widower?'

'Very straightforward. He admitted to it immediately. He and Hermione had had an open marriage, he said—not in the sense that they told each other about their affairs, but in that neither of them asked the other awkward questions. He had, however, denied the relationship with Alina as he could see Hermione was not pleased about it. He

149

saw her point of view. It is always bad manners to stray so close to home. And, of course, Hermione was a snob who was appalled he was sleeping with a servant. Still, he was unapologetic about Alina. It was an arrangement that suited everyone perfectly well. Hermione and he had long had a celibate marriage, Alina was a widow whose emotions were focused on her children in the Philippines and they were a comfort to each other.'

'Did he pay her?'

'He volunteered that he didn't. Said firmly that she was a good and nice woman and not a prostitute. He gave her presents from time to time but that was it.'

'Doesn't mean that she didn't think there was more to it.'

'He's said not. And she confirmed it.'

'Oh, my poor Ellis. You had to ask her about sex too.'

'It wasn't so bad since he'd rung her after I left his office and told her to come clean. She said she liked William, he and Madam did not sleep together and what was the harm? Life could be lonely and male company was nice sometimes. Asked if she had ambitions to marry Sir William she looked at me as if I was mad. Pointed out she'd never dream of marrying a non-Catholic. In fact, she said she thought it likely he'd soon want to move into a service flat and she had saved enough money to retire back to the Philippines.'

'Your conclusions?'

'They're probably both telling the truth.'

'How disappointing. What are you doing this afternoon?'

'Stocktaking. But there's a change of plan this

evening.' Pooley sounded excited. 'Mary Lou's coming up. Says she's fed up with baby-sitting Moaning Jack Troutbeck. And even more fed up with reading freshers' bad essays.'

'Oh good. At least, oh, good if we're still meeting.'

'Of course, Robert. But my place rather than yours. And take-away pizza rather than Chinese. She's hungering for her American roots and wants some fast and indifferent food as an antidote to what Jack stuffs her with at St Martha's. Even demanded Pepsi rather than wine and bad chocolate cake for afters.'

'You can take the girl out of Minneapolis . . .'

'But you can't take Minneapolis out of the girl. I know. Bye.'

*　　　*　　　*

'Why aren't you wearing glasses today?' asked Amiss of Georgie Prothero.

'Because this isn't a professional meeting.'

'Don't follow you.'

'I don't need glasses. I only wear those because they make me look serious and I can hide behind them. You don't count.'

Amiss surveyed Prothero critically. 'I see what you mean. You're a bit too pretty for your own professional good, aren't you?'

'I look like arm-candy, Robert. That's *bad* in my game. Good PR people have to look duller than the people or products they're pushing.' He reached for a sandwich. 'I'm *dread*ing tomorrow's meeting.'

'Why particularly?' asked Amiss, pouring them

both more tea.

'Because *every*one's even crosser than usual. Because they've *all* been complaining to me *all* hours of the day *every* day. Because I hate *everyone* on the committee. I had to talk to that rather dishy inspector about them this morning and I realised how much I *hate*d them. He *is*, isn't he?'

'Who's what?'

'Inspector Pooley. *Dish*y.'

'Didn't notice it myself. But he's clever.'

'He certainly is. He seemed almost to know what I was thinking before I said it.'

'Were you frank with him?'

'Of *course* I was. You know me. When I spill, I spill. And when someone with a bod like that asks me to *spill*, I really *spill*. He knows how I hate every single horrid judge.'

'Except me.'

'Except you.'

'And Dervla.'

'Well, all right. I don't hate *Derv*la, but trying to get any sense out of her gives me a headache. I hate *all* the others.'

'You can't hate Jack Troutbeck yet.'

'I don't know her well enough to *hate* her, but she told me this morning to stop being such an old *wo*man.'

'What were you being an old woman about?'

'I was just being *thought*ful. Doing my *job*. Checking she knew how and when to get to Warburton House tomorrow and advising her about where she should park.'

'Ah, yes. She has a slightly unorthodox approach to parking so your instructions would have seemed irrelevant.'

'And she was *so* troublesome about food.'

'In what context?'

'She hadn't realised that we're given lunch after the meetings and she de*man*ded to know what was on the menu.'

Amiss worked hard at keeping his face straight. 'And you said?'

'I told her it was wonderful food and cited the salmon *en croute* we had last time.'

'And she, no doubt, asked if the salmon was wild?'

'You really know her, don't you. Yes, she did. So I said I didn't know and she snorted and started going on about the evils of fish farming with a digression on how few people knew how to make decent pastry.'

'You'd better get used to it, Georgie. Jack likes her grub. And she likes her grub good.'

Prothero's voice rose. 'As if I hadn't en*ough* to worry about. Look at the *long*-lists! I would defy the en*tire* Foreign Office to find a way of reaching a decision that doesn't involve *half* the judges walking out.'

'That's Jack's problem. Not yours.'

'The Big Knapperoonie will blame *me*. I'll be back to doing PR for incontinence pads.'

His phone rang. He looked at the screen and cast his eyes up to heaven. 'Oh, God, it's Hys*ter*ia. I don't feel strong enough to take the call. She was on for an *hour* this morning being poisonous about you, Dervla and the Gee Gee. And even her unfortunate *maid*, who'd shattered her nerves by giving her the wrong cup and saucer at breakfast or something like that. I put the phone down for fifteen minutes in the middle and she didn't even

153

notice I'd gone.'

'What did she say about me?'

'Same as she said about them. No soul. Black aura. That sort of thing. Oh, yes. And she said she was sure the two of you were having an affair.'

'Me having an affair with Dervla? I'm no paedophile.'

'No. With the Gee Gee.'

'With Geraint? Is she off her head? I mean more than usually so?'

'She can't see any other explanation as to why you agree with him about her favourite book.'

'*Anorexia Phlegmata!* Too damn right I do. Do you know what it's about?'

'Well I assumed it was about some babe who was starving herself and being brave about it. But Hysteria said it was deeply perceptive and fastidiously spiritual. Or did she say spiritually fastidious?'

'It's pretentious, unreadable crap about a day in the life of Julia who works in Harrods' Food Hall and feels sick in a hundred different ways depending on whether she's being confronted by a carrot or an aubergine—interspersed with encounters with customers being brutally insensitive by actually asking her to pass them some vegetables. Along the way she nurtures a hopeless passion for the Indian on the cheese counter who never speaks to her. That enables her to meditate in a pseudy fashion among the potatoes on bits of the Bhagavadgita . . .'

'Huh?'

'Sacred Hindu stuff. Anyway, I had to read the whole fucking book because Wysteria was so keen and all I wanted was for the manager to transfer

154

Julia to the meat section so she'd have to deal with the problem of selling beef.'

Prothero shivered. 'At least I haven't had to read these books.' His phone rang again. He peered at it. 'Oh, I think she's left a message.' He nibbled a cucumber sandwich. 'I feel strong enough now,' he said and dialled the answering service. As he listened he began to look more angry than depressed. 'How *can* she be so awful?' he said when the call ended. 'Who *does* she think I am?'

Amiss raised an enquiring eyebrow.

'She's in Cambridge tonight reading in a bookshop and it's going to go on later than expected and she'll be too tired to go back to London tonight because of the *gru*elling day ahead of her. Can't bear the thought of coming up by train tomorrow, though, as it's likely to be *so* full it'll bring on her claustro*pho*bia and the people will be *so* noisy and terrible it'll bring on a *mi*graine too. Can I arrange for a car, would you please? It's the least that can be done for her considering how much she's *suff*ering.' He grabbed another sandwich. 'Old bitch! Besides, if I hire a car for her and some of the others find out they'll be demanding cars *every*where.'

'You said she was in Cambridge, Georgie. Jack's in Cambridge.'

Prothero brightened. 'Of course she is. Do you think she'd be prepared to give Wysteria a lift?'

Amiss suddenly felt very happy. 'I'm sure she'll be absolutely delighted.'

CHAPTER TWELVE

'So what did you make of Georgie Prothero, Ellis?'

'Amusing but a bit temperamental. No use, really. He didn't tell me anything I didn't already know.'

'Murderer?'

'If you can think of a good reason why he should kill someone he's only ever met professionally.'

Amiss smirked. 'Well, he liked you.'

'I don't want to hear,' said Pooley.

'Tell us about Ferriter, Mary Lou,' said Milton. 'Revolting little creep. How can he possibly be a professor?'

'Felix Ferriter is an asshole,' said Mary Lou. 'An alpha asshole and an alpha plus apparatchik.' As she spoke, Amiss observed that Pooley had not lost the habit of looking slightly shocked when his beloved let fly. 'For someone with a second- if not third-rate brain, he's been a staggering success. And all because he's a dedicated follower of academic fashion.' She reached out for a slice of Pizza Continental. 'Poor Jack. She'd sure have a seizure if she could see us now.'

'You haven't confessed your guilty gastronomic secrets to her?'

'No. If she knew I sometimes nip out for a McDonald's she'd not be able to sleep nights.'

'Why didn't she come up with you?'

'Because the poor old thing still has a couple of books she just has to read and she's already overwrought. When I left she had just jumped up and down—literally—on *Uluroo*.'

'*Uluroo?*' asked Pooley.

'It's a godawful Australian aboriginal novel,' said Mary Lou.

'To be precise,' added Amiss, 'it's a look at Australia through the mind of a sentimental and intellectually-challenged kangaroo, which is presumably why Jack chose to leap on it rather than tear it apart.'

'How bad is it that she was just about to embark on *Closer to the Candle Flame?*'

'Bad. Very bad,' said Amiss. 'It's French and about a girl whose phobia about moths leads her periodically to run naked through the streets when she fears her clothes are full of eggs. But being an existentialist, she spends the time in between musing on the moral implications of choosing such behaviour. It's one of Hugo Hurlingham's recommended reads: he can never get enough of existentialists.'

Mary Lou took a happy draught of Pepsi. 'But I guess it's all going to get worse. She also had to sample one you said Ferriter was keen on.'

'Which is?' asked Milton.

'*This Hole my Centre.* Sure, I can see you don't believe me, Ellis, but as God is my witness, that's what it's called. It apparently explores the notion of the anus as the cradle and the anus as the grave through the eyes of an Albanian rent boy in Rome.'

'Not just the eyes unfortunately,' said Amiss, as he refilled his glass with the Bordeaux which Mary Lou had spurned.

'You see, as you know, Ferriter's a recent and enthusiastic convert to what he calls QueerStud.'

'I find the whole business completely confusing,' said Milton. 'I thought queer was a banned word years ago.'

'Unless you're gay,' explained Mary Lou. 'It's like I can call another black nigger, but if you do it you'll be in court. Anyway, Ferriter—who is, I should add, quite notorious in our profession—started his career as a straightforward Marxist critic because that's what his professor was.'

'This is completely beyond me,' said Milton. 'What do Marxists think about literature? I thought they concentrated on history and politics.'

'No, no. Marxists take a view on most things and literature's there to provide evidence of the wicked inequalities of society. Ammunition in the great struggle against the imperialistic and capitalistic oppression of the masses et cetera, et cetera, et cetera.'

'It's easy, really,' said Amiss. 'Marxist literary critics are like all Marxist commentators: they're in the business of finding facts to bear out the conclusions they want to reach.'

'Sounds like Geraint Griffiths,' said Milton.

'Geraint is an ex-Marxist who didn't so much move on as do a U-turn,' pointed out Amiss. 'He's an ideologue who's become an enemy of ideologies.'

'In a pretty ideological way,' said Pooley.

'Once a fanatic, always a fanatic,' said Milton. 'Which takes us back to Ferriter.'

Mary Lou frowned. 'Ferriter's a fanatic only about his own career. He takes up these intellectual fashions at the drop of a hat and discards them just as lightly. He's a natural linguist, I guess. But instead of learning real languages, he picks up a new language of criticism in no time at all. Writes like he talks—a mixture of yoof-drivel

158

and incomprehensible and meaningless jargon that pleases whatever constituency he's making eyes at.'

Milton snorted. 'You can say that again. Meaningless is what he does best. That and being so self-centred he's got nothing useful to say about anyone.'

'That figures. Anyway Marxist lit. crit. got him a foot on the Oxbridge ladder. Then he floated into Derridean semiotics.'

'Into what?' asked Milton.

'Don't ask,' said Mary Lou. 'But it was cool at the time and got him a chair in the provinces in his early thirties. There was a brief dalliance when he thought Edward Said was where it was all at so he claimed some Irish roots and went on about the colonised unconscious, then, bingo, suddenly, to great applause, he converts to feminism—a.k.a. gynocritical discourse—denounces phallocognition and gets a visiting chair at Harvard where they're madly chasing after Yale in their espousal of crackpot ethnic and gender studies and badly need a token male. Then, kiss my butt, you take your eye off him for two seconds and he's in at the birth of Queer Studies.'

Amiss pushed his plate away. 'I should know the answer to this, but I couldn't be bothered finding out. Is it to do with combing through literature looking for overlooked gays? Shakespeare's Dark Lady of the Sonnets was a boy—that sort of thing?'

'That was the primitive stage, Robert. Ferriter and his sort are engaged in "queering" literature on a grand scale. The QueerStud view now is that queer is normal and straight's an aberration.'

'Ferriter's gay, I presume,' said Pooley.

'Certainly dresses like one,' said Milton.

'It's not quite that simple,' said Mary Lou. 'Being the thorough little guy he is, he turned himself into a practitioner. As a feminist, he'd got in touch with his feminine side but didn't actually change sex. But once a proponent of QueerStud, he turned queer along with the studies.'

'For heaven's sake, you can't just do that,' said Amiss. 'You have to have some inclination in that direction.'

'Ferriter would say that he was always bi, even if his experience was largely hetero.' Mary Lou stopped and helped herself to some more Pepsi. She looked slightly embarrassed, as befitted someone known to everyone present to have once been a lover of Jack Troutbeck. She took a sip. 'So now Felix is in touch with his inner fag: word is he's aiming to shag his way around the entire QueerStud circuit. And being a queer academic has the great bonus that by and large, unlike feminists, gay men don't expect you to sign contracts before you can put a hand on their thigh.'

'I don't follow this,' said Amiss. 'I thought all gays were body fascists these days. Why would they want to shag a weedy little bugger like Ferriter?'

'They're body fascists when it's only about bodies. But when it comes to power, they're just the same as straights and dykes. A Professor of Queer Studies is a very attractive proposition if you have intellectual pretensions and academic ambitions.'

'And he did spruce himself up a bit, didn't he?' observed Milton. 'Body-piercing, leather and all that. Not that I can imagine anyone thinking the effect attractive. But what do I know? I'm just a middle-aged heterosexual cop who thinks the

160

country's going to the dogs.'

Mary Lou stopped talking and tucked into a final slice of pizza. Pooley was looking depressed. 'I like a few illusions, including the one that universities remain seats of learning to which we should aspire to send our children.'

'We will, darling. We will. But you have to be able to distinguish the wheat from the vast amount of chaff. I feel really sorry for these kids who're getting up to their ears in debt studying crap courses at crap universities. You'd think you Brits would have learned from all the mistakes we made in the States, but you've learned jackshit. You're dumbing down like crazy, just like we did. We get bright students at St Martha's, but it's hell to inculcate them with intellectual rigour. And it's hell to try to get through to them that most fashionable criticism isn't worth wiping your butt with.'

'You're sounding dangerously elitist,' noted Amiss. 'Rosa Karp would have you despatched to the re-education camp.'

'Since I came under the influence of Jack, I've become an unabashed elitist. But it's a hard road and it's beginning to wear me out.'

'That's Eng. Lit.,' said Amiss, smugly. 'Full of pseuds. History's different.'

'Rubbish. It's almost as bad.'

'No, it's not. There are plenty of historians writing perfectly comprehensibly and they're bestsellers.'

'They're the ones that can write, Robert. Plenty that can't are lurking in academia teaching students how to ensure nobody knows what they're talking about.'

'To think,' said Milton, 'that I used to believe

161

that professors were intelligent, peers were people of distinction and writers were dedicated to their art.'

'And policemen were honest,' said Amiss.

'Maybe things don't get worse,' said Pooley. 'Maybe it's always been like that but one just didn't know.'

'All I know is academia,' said Mary Lou. 'And it's getting much worse now that political correctness has infected staff and students. No one can say what they think any more.'

Into the general gloom, the sound of Mary Lou's phone ringing was a welcome relief. The baroness's voice was audible to everyone. 'That's it,' she bellowed. 'I won't rest until I've strangled that little shirt-lifter with the entrails of the frog-lover.'

*　　　*　　　*

Prothero woke Amiss at seven-fifteen, close to hysteria. 'What *did* your old bag mean by it?'

'What are you talking about?'

'I've just had Rosa Krap on, incan*des*cent.' To Amiss's astonishment, Prothero reported that despite her stated intention of talking to no one, the baroness had told a *Guardian* reporter her approach would not be that of Hermione Babcock since they had radically different views on fiction. 'She said she didn't share *any* of Hermione's tastes, and when the reporter asked how she felt about Virginia *Woolf*, according to Krap she said something really *aw*ful about how the only significant thing about Woolf and her circle was their *sex*-lives and that they all screwed each other since no one else would have them.'

'Can't argue with that,' said Amiss, yawning. 'Didn't Dorothy Parker say the Bloomsbury set were pairs who lived in squares and loved in triangles?'

'Wake up, Robert! You can guarantee that interview will alienate nearly *all* the committee.'

'Maybe, Georgie. But Jack doesn't get trapped by reporters. She'll have done this for a reason. Jack moves in mysterious ways and the thing to do is not to worry and to leave her to it.'

'But they'll *all* be ringing me to complain.'

'Tell them you know nothing and refer them to Jack,' said Amiss firmly. 'Now let me get back to sleep for half-an-hour. I'm a bit tired.'

*   *   *

At Prothero's request, Amiss had arrived early at Warburton House, which was just as well, for Prothero was so jittery that he was annoying the normally imperturbable Birkett. 'I'm sorry, Mr Prothero, but the menu was decided on days ago. What exactly do you want me to do?'

Prothero wrung his hands. 'I don't really know. I'm just fretting. This new chair, Lady Troutbeck, she's a foodie and things are *so* tense already I don't want a big *fuss* developing about salmon not being wild and all that sort of thing.'

'We are not having salmon today, Mr Prothero,' said Birkett frostily. 'We are having roast saddle of lamb with a vegetarian option. And, yes, it is English spring lamb and no, it has not been frozen. I trust that meets the obvious questions that may come to her ladyship's mind.'

'That admirably addresses all that might concern

her, Mr Birkett,' said Amiss firmly. 'Now, Georgie, let's have a word about the press release.'

Prothero looked distractedly at Amiss. 'Oh, all right. Thank you, Birkett. I'm sure it'll all be fine.'

*   *   *

As was customary, Rosa Karp arrived first and sat down with a brief hello; she did not waste time on people she thought irrelevant. She took from her briefcase a pile of spreadsheets which she proceeded to distribute around the table, before settling down to read her own copy intently. Ferriter was next, closely followed by Den Smith. This morning Ferriter was wearing a T-shirt with a face on it that Amiss could not quite place. 'You've made me curious, Felix. I know that person on your chest but I'm damned if I can remember who he is?'

'Gore Vidal. He's the focus for my QueerStud's strand on twentieth-century martyrs.'

'Where does the martyrdom come in?' asked Amiss politely.

'He suffered for his beliefs, like all non-hetero-affectionals.'

'As he's suffering now like the rest of us who oppose the Bush-Blair axis of capitalist/imperialist evil,' added Den Smith. Rosa looked up and murmured her agreement.

'I read an interview with Gore Vidal the other day,' said Amiss in the most courteous tone he could muster, 'and I thought him a condescending, name-dropping snob who has made millions through shocking the great American public. He lives in luxury in Italy and Hollywood while being

164

widely venerated by smart society as a sage. I could cope with that amount of suffering.'

Observing Smith going dangerously red, Amiss was relieved at the distraction caused by the simultaneous arrival of Geraint Griffiths and Hugo Hurlingham, who were chitchatting civilly about traffic. Dervla followed a moment later and Amiss, who was still buoyed up by the revelation that she found him fanciable, greeted her warmly, put her sitting beside him and told her how attractive he found her long purple suede boots. They embarked on a conversation about where she liked shopping, which he found he could follow if he concentrated very hard.

At a few minutes to ten, the baroness bounded in. 'Where's the butler?' she asked Amiss.

He pointed to the far door, through which she marched. She returned with Birkett, smiling. 'Satisfactory,' she announced as she strode to the head of the table and sat down. 'Lunch sounds satisfactory.'

She was wearing an eye-catching ensemble, chosen, Amiss deduced, to confuse. On the one hand, her fedora and severe suit—King Edward check with mid-calf skirt—were reminiscent of lesbians of the 1930s, but the cascades of pink chiffon at her throat made an aggressively feminine statement, while the vast piece of costume jewellery on her left breast—a diamanté and green enamel parrot—caused even Den Smith to goggle. 'I'm Jack Troutbeck,' she announced. 'Which ones are you?'

'Robert, will you do the honours?' asked Prothero.

Amiss came to with a start. 'Sorry, Jack, this is

165

Dervla. Dervla, this is Lady Troutbeck.'

'Hi,' said Dervla nervously.

'Hello,' said the baroness, looking her up and down appreciatively. 'Nice to have someone young and decorative in the middle of such a decrepit gathering.'

'And this is Rosa Karp,' said Amiss, pretending not to see the furious expression engendered by this remark.

The baroness nodded. 'I know,' she said rather ominously. 'And I know Denzil Smith. As he knows me. We had a reunion last week many years after a dramatic parting.' She smiled seraphically.

Smith grunted and avoided everyone's eyes.

'Beside Den is Geraint Griffiths.'

'You're welcome,' said Griffiths, 'but I should tell you that . . .'

'Later,' the baroness said. 'Let's get the platitudes over with.'

'And Hugo Hurlingham and Felix Ferriter.'

'Good God, why are you wearing a picture of that old bore?' she demanded of Ferriter. 'Met him once, and of all the self-regarding, pretentious old queens . . . !'

'And Georgie Prothero,' said Amiss hastily. Prothero, who was looking dazed, managed a wan smile. 'It's very good to speak to you in person, Lady Troutbeck. But where is Lady Wilcox? Weren't you giving her a lift?'

'I did.'

'She's in the ladies, is she?'

'I don't know where she is now. I left her downstairs having first aid.'

'Did you have an accident?'

'No, but she claimed she was having a heart

166

attack because of my driving. It was like giving a lift to a neurotic hen. She kept clucking. Indeed at times she sounded as if she were laying an egg. It's all stuff and nonsense, of course, as Robert will tell you. Nothing wrong with the way I drive.'

'Is she really ill?' asked a worried Prothero.

'Of course she's not ill. She's just looking for attention. Wysteria's a creaking gate—she'll outlive the lot of us. You'll see, she'll be along in a minute. Wouldn't want decisions reached without her. I told her to hurry up or we'd start anyway.'

Birkett left the room quietly and shortly afterwards returned with Wysteria. Amiss, who was already having a severe attack of guilt, looked with alarm at the ashen-faced little figure who tottered in on the butler's solicitous arm.

Rosa rushed to her side along with Prothero and Amiss and amid a chorus of 'Are-you-all-rights?' Wysteria fell into a chair and pawed at her chest. 'Of course I'm not all right,' she quavered. 'How could I be all right? That woman is a cold-hearted lunatic. For two hours I've lived a nightmare. A nightmare during which regardless of my desperate pleas, there was no pity, no compassion, no mercy.'

'Nonsense, Wysteria. It's all in your imagination. You're just a nervous Nellie. But you look fine now. There's nothing wrong with you and it's time we got down to business.'

'I'll leave you now, Lady Troutbeck,' said Birkett. 'Mr Prothero can fetch me if you need anything.'

'When's lunch?'

'One o'clock.'

'And you won't forget what I said about the lamb being pink.'

'I don't like pink lamb,' whispered Wysteria.

'Rubbish. It should always be pink.'

'I will make sure that there is a choice, your ladyships.'

'Waste of good meat,' grumbled the baroness. 'But if you must, you must, I suppose. Where's the coffee?'

'It will arrive at eleven unless you would prefer it at another time.'

She nodded. 'Very well. I'll want a double espresso.'

'Certainly, your ladyship.'

'And make sure it's hot.'

'I will ensure that it is extremely hot, your ladyship.'

'Good. You can leave us now, what'syourname.'

'Birkett.'

'Birkett.' She suddenly produced one of her sunniest smiles. 'Thank you, Birkett. I'm very pleased with you so far.'

'Thank you, your ladyship,' said Birkett. 'It's a pleasure to be of service.'

The baroness turned her attention to her colleagues. 'Right, the meeting is now convened.'

'Just a moment, Chair,' said Rosa.

'I will not answer to Chair,' said the baroness. 'Or Chairperson, for that matter. I am Madam Chairman.'

Rosa and Ferriter looked at her, as Amiss put it later, as if she had just announced she intended to slaughter the first-born. 'You can't,' said Rosa. 'I cannot use such an inappropriate term. No one has used it for a decade.'

The baroness beamed. 'I do. And so do my colleagues at St Martha's. However, to show

168

how extremely reasonable I am, we'll have a compromise. You may call me Chairwoman.'

'But it's gender specific and . . .' began Rosa.

'Oh, knock it off, Rosa,' said Griffiths. 'She's a woman and she's in the chair and there's no point in . . .'

'Thank you, Dr Griffiths,' said the baroness, 'but you will speak through me in future. I believe in observing the formalities. Anyone else got any beefs?' No one else spoke. 'Right, we have fewer than three hours to sort these long-lists out and produce an agreed one. I've compared them, and, on the face of it, it looks as if doing this would tax Solomon. But if it has to be done, it has to be done. Now, first I want you to . . .'

Rosa broke in. 'Chair . . . woman,' she said, with an ill grace. 'First, I want to complain about your grossly offensive remarks in *The Guardian* this morning.'

'What remarks?' asked Griffiths.

'I spoke to some reptile last night,' explained the baroness genially. 'I gather Lady Karp didn't like what I said.'

'How can you possibly justify your attack on our dear Hermione, not to speak of what you said about . . . about . . .'

The baroness leaned over and grabbed the newspaper. 'I expect she's beefing about the quote, "I've always thought those Gloomsbury wankers self-regarding snobs and creeps who would have disappeared from the public consciousness if it hadn't been for their titillating sex-lives."'

Dervla giggled, Griffiths shouted, 'Well said,' Ferriter and Smith made protesting sounds and Wysteria clutched her chest again.

The baroness looked at Rosa. 'So?'

'So, I would like you to apologise.'

'I suggest you stop being silly. I can assure you that every time I read anything you say I am not only offended; I am intellectually insulted. Here is what I propose. I will say what I like. As a quid pro quo, you can say what you like.' She turned and addressed the committee. 'Any objections?'

Smith opened his mouth and then thought better of it. The baroness turned back to Rosa. 'What was the second issue you wished to raise?'

'I've made the decision-making process much easier, as I've done a full analysis of all the long-lists according to objective criteria. That way, we can eliminate a large number of books at the very beginning, so that what we end up with will be appropriately balanced. Please look at the spreadsheet in front of you.'

'Lady Karp, who asked you to do this?'

'Hermione Babcock.'

'Hermione Babcock has been dead for several days. Do you not think it would have been . . .' she paused, 'appropriate . . . to ask me if I concurred?'

Rosa flushed. 'It didn't occur to me that you wouldn't. This has been so much a part of the consensual decision-making process until now that I assumed . . .'

'It is unwise to make assumptions where I am concerned, Lady Karp. And one assumption you should certainly not make is that I am driven by the need to achieve consensus. However, I am an open-minded woman, you appear to have done a great deal of work and I am prepared to listen to you explain what it has yielded.'

Rather flustered, Rosa shuffled her papers.

'There are ten long-lists . . .'

'Come again?' The baroness looked around the table and ticked names off on her fingers: 'Me, you, Professor Ferriter, Miss Dervla, Mr Amiss, Mr Smith, Professor Griffiths, Sir Hugo Hurlingham and Lady Wilcox. I make that nine.'

'But Hermione did a list. You're surely not going to ignore it?'

'Lady Karp, as I have already had occasion to point out, Hermione Babcock is dead and I have replaced her. I shall bear her list in mind should we become deadlocked at any stage, but that will be at my discretion.'

Rosa looked close to tears. 'But my list is based on the ten.'

The baroness's patience snapped. 'Oh, for heaven's sake get on with giving us your general conclusions. We haven't got all day.'

Rosa began to gabble. 'The ten lists have come up with on average twenty-seven titles, making a total of two hundred and seventy, but many of these are common to several lists, so there are just one hundred and thirty-four novels that need to be reduced to an agreed short-list of twenty-five. To help us decide which ones to drop, I've analysed them by author and by content according to various categories, awarding scores for certain elements; my proposal is that no book scoring less than five points should be on the long-list.'

'Fewer than five points, Lady Karp. I assume grammar isn't one of your criteria.'

Amiss clenched his teeth like an embarrassed parent. Dervla, he observed, was gazing at the baroness awestruck.

Rosa ploughed on. 'First, obviously, I have a

breakdown for each writer by such categories as gender, age, ethnicity, origin, physical ableness and sexual orientation—but there are subsections within some of these, obviously. And then I grade the progressiveness of the content into which obviously gender, ethnicity and so on are replicated, but there are also considerations such as inclusiveness, anti-racism, attitudes to the European Union, social responsibility, the progressiveness of the ideas expressed and so on.'

'Let me take a shot at this, Lady Karp. Let us suppose we have two authors, one of whom is female, seventy, Asian, lesbian and suffers from Aids and the other is a middle-aged, fit, heterosexual, male, white, Anglo-Saxon, Protestant from Tunbridge Wells. How many points would each get?'

Rosa had been taking notes. 'She would get six and he would get none.'

'Where does the sixth point come from?'

'One for a disability, but an extra one because it is a disability which attracts discrimination.'

'I see. So the man's only chance of catching up is if she has written about a middle-aged, fit, heterosexual male WASP living in Tunbridge Wells and he has written about a female, Asian, lesbian, seventy-year-old suffering from Aids?'

Rosa shook her head vigorously. 'Oh, no. We don't accept that oppressors can validly write about the oppressed.'

Ferriter nodded equally vigorously and Griffiths and Smith squawked competing noises of disagreement.

'Hold on, gentlemen. Just let me get to the bottom of this. So how many points does our male author have now?'

'He still doesn't have any, since whites lack the ability to understand the plight of the colonised and those afflicted by racism any more than the abled understand the physically challenged or the straights understand people with other sexual orientations or the young understand the old.'

'Goodness me,' said the baroness. 'Poor chap. He doesn't stand much of a chance. How would it be if she's an anti-Semite and he's a Jew?'

'It depends on if he's a Zionist or not. If he is, he's automatically disqualified. And she would lose no points for being anti-Zionist.'

'What about if she's like me, a reactionary and a Europhobe and our Tunbridge Wells scribbler is a Europhile and what you call a progressive?'

'In that unlikely event,' said Rosa rather stiffly, 'he would get a point. Maybe two, however . . .'

Griffiths was waving his arms wildly.

The baroness gazed at him benignly. 'It's all right, Dr Griffiths. Don't get worked up over this. I'm in charge and all will be well. Now, Lady Karp, can you enlighten us as to what all this has to do with literature?'

'It has to do with the relevance of literature to life. To social responsibility.'

'It's a matter of civilising cultural conversation,' added Ferriter. 'I'm with Rosa.'

'And so am I,' said Den Smith. 'Mostly.'

'No surprises there,' said the baroness gaily. 'I, however, regard everything Lady Karp has said as balls. I've gone through this charade because I'm accommodating, but here's an end to it.' She picked up the spreadsheets in front of her and tore them up. 'Now, let me make it clear how the judging is to be conducted henceforward. I have decided on the criteria and there's only one: literary excellence. If you don't accept that, Mr Prothero here can issue a statement that I'm resigning.' Observing the pleased look on several faces, she added, 'I should add that I've talked to Ron Knapper about this and he said if I resign he's scrapping the prize.' She smiled broadly. 'Everyone happy to go ahead on my terms? Yes? Good. Georgie, tell the excellent Birkett to hurry the coffee along.'

Her eyes flickered up and down the table, looking in the eyes of each committee member. 'Right, now we get started on the sensible part of this. Which means everyone volunteering in the first round to sacrifice their least favourite five. And I want no histrionics. Try to behave like grown-ups.'

CHAPTER THIRTEEN

'It was grim and hilarious by turns,' said Amiss over dinner to Pooley. 'For reasons best known to herself, Jack had set out to alienate most of the judges, which added further rancour to the inevitable arguments. Naturally, the books half the judges wanted to get rid of were the ones the other half liked most and vice versa. Not, you understand, that there is anything as simple going on as two blocs. Rosa and Ferriter are usually agreed . . .' He paused. 'Oh, yes, there was an enjoyable moment when we were considering the gay logger and Jack referred to Rosa's and Ferriter's choices as being of a particular bent, Ferriter said that proved she was homophobic and Jack said, "That, Professor Ferriter, is a fallacy, spelt 'p h a l l a c y'."'

He helped himself to more peas. 'Then there was a very jolly clash about the regional novels Rosa was so keen on, and Geraint went into an entertaining tirade about the Celtic contingent along the lines that the Scots novel was "pukelit", consisting as it did of "fucking Glaswegians saying 'fuck' between injecting themselves with heroin and throwing up", the Irish one was yet another droning exercise in misery tourism and if he had to read another piece of criminally fraudulent Welsh nostalgia about singing socialists bonding in the pits he'd puke himself.'

'Pity you couldn't have recorded the meeting and produced the edited highlights.'

'Like *Big Brother*? Now, that would be a gripping

175

show. Rosa would be first out, I think, on the grounds of being sanctimonious and boring.'

'So how many has she on her side?' Pooley took another sip of sparkling water, as Amiss took one of wine.

'Den often agrees with her, though he defends men and his right to write from the point of view of the oppressed. Wysteria isn't interested in anything except herself but it suits her usually to agree with Rosa, which Hugo sometimes does, especially if Europe comes into it anywhere. Griffiths is so focused on pushing his candidate that he only gets worked up against books he considers have bad authority, but he tends to side with Jack and me because he hates most of the others, as does Dervla, who has become positively clingy and who is happy now with Jack who was unfailingly courteous and respectful to her. As opposed to anyone else.'

Pooley looked at Amiss gravely. 'You're not being tempted, are you, Robert? Dervla's very vulnerable.'

Amiss bridled. 'Do you think she'd be better off with the sweepings of the latest boyband?'

'No, it's just that . . .'

'Oh, knock it off, Ellis. She's a nice kid but I couldn't get involved with someone who hasn't yet got the hang of how to hold a conversation. Though I have to say that between Jack urging me into bed with everyone and you warning me off someone I'm not even attracted by, I'm thinking of declaring my sex-life—or lack of it—off-limits to my friends.'

Pooley looked grave again. 'Mary Lou wanted to know if you were still pining for Rachel.'

176

'Did she now?' Amiss ate another forkful of potato and took another gulp of wine.

'Well?'

'Well, in truth, yes and no.'

'Go on.'

'I miss the old Rachel, not the Rachel who so lost her marbles as to fall into the arms of Eric Sinclair, who, as New Labour twerps go, is a megatwerp.'

'I've never really asked you how bad all that was, Robert.'

'Of course not, Ellis. We're Englishmen.'

'And I really shouldn't be asking you now, since we need to talk Warburton, but Mary Lou will tick me off if I don't seize the opportunity.'

'It won't surprise you that it was much worse than I pretended, will it? I kept hoping she would recover from the madness and rush back to me cured of the prig-virus, but of course she didn't.'

'Why of course?'

'You haven't forgotten the press coverage?'

'What I saw was pretty grim.'

'With someone like Rachel, the effect of being held up to public odium as a marriage-breaking power-crazed bimbo ensured there was no going back. And then, of course, when he lost his job owing to getting on the wrong side of the Chancellor and being made a sacrificial victim . . .'

Pooley nodded. 'I can guess. She felt bound to stick by him.'

'Exactly.'

'She's never been in touch with Jim. I think he was a bit hurt. They go back a long way.'

'She didn't want to be the cause of any split loyalties so she said she'd leave to me those people

177

who were primarily my friends. I did the same with hers. I should have told you that, but it was hard enough keeping the lip stiff without actually talking to anyone about her.'

'We'll never be New Men, will we, Robert?'

'I think we're sort of Third-Way Men, caught somewhere between Captain Oates and Felix Ferriter.'

'Felix Ferriter!'

'Well, OK, not Felix Ferriter, but touchy-feely-searching-for-their-feminine-side types.'

Pooley grinned. 'Fortunately, Mary Lou seems to prefer Oates to Ferriter.'

'So did Rachel once.'

'Have you heard from her since you split up?'

'Occasionally. We tried to stay friends but I wasn't sufficiently over it to be able to meet her, let alone to be so Hampstead I could meet her with that awful little git, so the occasional stiff phone call about practicalities was the only contact. Latterly, though, we've exchanged the odd e-mail. Even the odd frivolous e-mail, so, who knows, maybe she's recovering her sense of humour. Now, back to the committee meeting.'

Pooley took the hint. 'Was it very fractious?'

'The threat of Knapper pulling out so frightened the wits out of all of them—though Dervla and I would have been glad—that grudgingly and grumblingly they compromised. We came out at one with an agreed long-list. Jack wanted to stick out for cutting it down to twenty-five, but the prospect of being late for lunch put her off that. I was quite peevish with her, as the one she was gunning for as the last sacrificial victim was one I think very well of, but she can't stick it because it's about a neurotic Frenchman and Hurlingham liked its profound European significance. Eventually she said, with the air of one offering an enormous olive branch, that as a gesture, since Hermione had liked it, she'd let it stay on the list.'

'So it was a good day?'

'Considering. There were plenty of verbicuffs but no fisticuffs, Georgie was mad with excitement at being able to release the list on the appointed day and even lunch went without major incident. Oh, well, that is apart from the way Wysteria carried on when Jack called for a cigar. Said it would finish her off as her lungs were so delicate.'

'Jack's response?'

'Trotted out her oft-repeated Kipling lines about a woman being only a woman, but a good cigar a smoke. Wysteria stamped off followed by Rosa. Hurlingham, rather guiltily, stayed for a cigar and the rest of them chose to finish their liqueurs.'

'How did Wysteria seem after her ordeal?'

'I think she was fine and that Jack was right to say she was putting it on. Not that she hadn't been utterly terrified by the journey. Anyone would be. And I felt momentarily—but only momentarily—guilty for having been the cause. But she's as tough as she's nasty, Wysteria. Of course, she now loathes Jack even more than do Rosa, Den, Felix and Hugo, and I can't really blame her. Geraint Griffiths, however, seems to think Jack's a bit of a laugh, but then he has reason to think her authority good. She came in hard on his side when Rosa, to some acclaim, tried to have *Pursuing the Virgins* disqualified on the grounds that it was promoting racial hatred. Jack said it mightn't be literature but it was literate and that was more than could be said for most of their choices.'

Amiss's phone rang. 'Yes, Jack . . . I'm eating with Ellis . . . Sausages and mash, since you ask, and, no, they won't be Tamworth, but they're delicious anyway. Yes . . . Yes . . . I've told Ellis you smote the whole lot of them . . . You what? You unscrupulous old bat . . . But what if he? . . . Oh, OK . . . Yes, will do. Bye.'

'She really likes praise,' said Pooley.

'Don't we all? It's just that we're too reserved to demand it. Mind you, she deserves it, I suppose. Turns out she hadn't talked to Knapper at all but decided praying him in aid was the only way to swat Rosa.'

'But what happens if . . . ?'

'She's already told him. Made him laugh, apparently. Anyway, I've to go to Cambridge tomorrow so we can plot the next stage.'

Pooley's phone rang. 'My God . . . How? . . . When? . . . Are you sure it was suicide? . . . I'll be there in ten. Bye.'

He looked at Amiss. 'Oh, dear God.'

'What's happened?'

'It's Wysteria Wilcox. She seems to have drowned herself.'

*   *   *

Amiss saw Pooley off, hailed a taxi and rang the baroness, who reacted robustly. 'Don't be absurd, Robert. Wysteria's far too much of a cow to kill herself while there are still people in the world she could make miserable. I bet it's an accident.'

'I hope you're right.'

'Of course I'm right,' she said testily. 'If you've

180

taken the notion into your fat head that she topped herself because I upset her this morning, expunge it forthwith. Might I remind you that in the middle of all the metaphorical swooning-on-the-chaise-longue-and-calling-for-the-smelling-salts, she grabbed every opportunity to push the books of people she considers her protégés and nearly made Dervla cry.'

'True. Now you mention it, she was really, really unpleasant in her underhand way and you did well to bawl her out.'

'So, as I said, it's an accident. Or, of course, she might have been bumped off. Let me know if that turns out to be the case. It would raise some interesting questions.' She yawned noisily. 'But I'm off to bed now and won't be available before seven a.m. whatever happens. One way or another, things will be hotting up tomorrow so I need my beauty sleep. And I suggest you emulate me. There's nothing useful you can do between now and then since you can't admit to having inside knowledge about Wysteria popping her clogs.'

'You're probably right.'

'I'm always right. But don't forget that I want you here by eleven at the latest.'

*　　　　*　　　　*

As Amiss climbed into bed, he heard Wysteria's death being announced on the BBC's eleven o'clock news. So, it turned out, did Ron Knapper, who rang Georgie Prothero, who having tried and failed to reach the baroness rang Amiss in a state of mingled hysteria and frustration. Having calmed Prothero and persuaded him to go to bed, Amiss

181

fell asleep, but was then woken by a somewhat inebriated Dervla, who had seen the midnight news on television. As best Amiss could decipher the tumble of words, Geraint Griffiths had been on, talking of a pogrom of judges initiated by dark forces. 'Robert, I'm, like, so head-wrecked and alone,' she cried pitifully, so Amiss got up, dressed and took a taxi to the Ritz, where he held her hand as they sat on the sofa and shared a bottle of wine, spoke to her agent and made him promise to turn up at breakfast time and, at about three, put Dervla to bed and—at her insistence—slept beside her, which—at the dictates of his conscience but with extreme difficulty—he managed to do chastely in spite of her advances by dint of keeping a sheet between them. At six-fifteen he slipped out of bed, left a reassuring note for Dervla on the washbasin in her bathroom and headed off to tend to Plutarch, change and leave for King's Cross. Reaching home in time to hear the seven o'clock news, he learned that while the police still suspected accident or suicide, Den Smith as well as Geraint Griffiths was being quoted as suspecting foul play. Having got through to the baroness with this news, Amiss was told to stop fussing and leave everything to her.

*   *   *

At nine, with his phone switched off, Amiss settled into the Cambridge train and began to go through his vast pile of newspapers. The news coverage was sketchy, but all the broadsheets as well as the up-market tabloids had photographs of Wysteria looking soulful: here poised against a background

182

of apple blossom, there, with hands loosely clasped, gazing rapturously at nothing in particular.

Rosa Karp surfaced in the *Guardian* expressing her grief at having lost two such close, brilliant and wonderful friends in a matter of weeks, *The Times* featured a long quote from Geraint about attacks on free speech which was as dark as it was impenetrable and, in the *Mirror*, Den Smith pointed out the likely significance of both women having been opponents of the Iraq war. All three were asked should the Warburton go ahead: Rosa equivocated, fearing the possibility of offending the bereaved, while wanting to do what the dead would have wished, Den said he would never follow the securocrat agenda—a comment he refused to explain—and Griffiths said the future of Western democracy depended on the Warburton challenging the forces of fascism. Opening the *Sun*, Amiss was appalled to see it had eschewed Wysteria for Dervla, who was shown arriving at a recent Britpop event wearing thigh-high boots and a few scraps of sequinned denim. The headline— 'IS DERVLA NEXT?'—caused him to ring her, but there was no answer.

Readers of the news stories were pointed towards inside pages to read assessments of the Warburton long-list cobbled together the previous afternoon by Arts editors whose judgements crossed a spectrum from praise for its eclecticism to denunciations of its self-indulgence and absence of social conscience. *The Guardian* was so outraged over the shortage of regional and ethnic fiction that Amiss suspected Rosa must have been on the telephone straight after the meeting, the *Daily Telegraph* produced a general lament about the impoverished state of modern fiction and the *Daily Mail* had a 'why-oh-why?' comment piece about the craze for novels about drugs, sex and degradation.

Amiss fell asleep shortly afterwards and dreamed about Dervla's midriff.

*   *   *

'Here's 'is statement, sir,' said Detective Sergeant Kennison.

'Whose statement?' asked Pooley.

'The fella as found Wilcox's corpse tied up to his 'ouseboat. Funny bloke. Saw 'im late last night and tried to make 'im give a statement proper, but 'e said as 'ow I was leaving out the magic, and he made a big fuss, and to be honest, I couldn't spell 'alf the words, so it seemed easier in the end to let 'im write it 'isself. Like you said, last week, it's no 'arm to let 'em 'ang themselves.'

Pooley, who had recommended that course of action after a bruising encounter with Kennison's prose, took the couple of sheets of typescript and settled down to read. 'My name is Nigel Withenshaw and presently I roost in a little houseboat moored across from the Chiswick Eyot. I'd had a simply exhausting day, so very soon after I reached home, coming up to nine, as my friend Harry was cooking our little supper, I poured us each a glass of wine and took mine onto the deck to calm me and help me savour the enchanted evening.

'It was an occasion of sensual delight, for from below were coming some exquisite Schubertian strains, the air was balmy, the gentle zephyr soothed my soul and the moonlight danced on the

184

water between my boat and the glorious willows on the eyot. I revelled in the textures, the mixture of light and shade and the driftwood, whose myriad shapes intrigue my inner artist. But, soft, was that shape driftwood? Or was it perchance . . .? For a moment, I thought I'd had perhaps a little too much of what dear Keats called "the true, the blushful Hippocrene", for what I could see lying in the water resembled Ophelia—John Everett Millais's *Ophelia* that is—but with her arm caught in my anchoring rope. Fearfully, I called Harry, who confirmed that my eyes did not deceive. Together, we managed to pull our sad Ophelia on board. To my horror, I recognised her: it was my Ethereal Lady, my Free Spirit, whom I've seen before walking past the boat of an evening—on warm evenings wearing the apparel of a veritable faerie. I hailed her once, but she gave me a long, sad smile and shook her head, so I honoured her desire for seclusion. We looked for signs of life, but her frail body was cold and quiet. The Lady's soul had flown away across the horizon. We rang 999, and the rest you know.'

'See wot I mean, sir?'

Pooley looked solemn. 'I do indeed, Kennison. You were quite right to let him write his own statement. It's much more authentic that way.'

Kennison looked relieved. 'Anything else, sir?'

'Still no sign of the prelim report?'

'No, sir. Shouldn't be long.'

'Any idea where the body got into the river?'

'They're still working on it, sir. It would 'elp if we knew 'er route, but 'er maid couldn't 'elp.'

'I'll follow that up, Kennison. That's all for now.'

As Kennison turned towards the door, Pooley

asked, 'Did Mr Withenshaw happen to mention what he did for a living.'

'Well, 'e didn't mention it, but I asked 'im. 'E's a sewage engineer.'

'Thanks, Kennison. That explains a lot.'

Looking totally baffled, Kennison departed.

*   *   *

'Lady Karp? . . . It's Detective Inspector Ellis Pooley. We met at the House of Lords the other day . . . Yes, yes, it is terrible news. I quite understand how upset you must be . . . That's what I want to ask you. Lady Wilcox's housekeeper tells me that she often used to walk by the Thames, but didn't know where and I wondered if you could help . . . Yes, yes . . . Oh, really? She said that? And where do you think? . . . That's most helpful. Thank you so much . . . Yes, I'm sure I'll be able to get hold of it. Early summer, you said? . . . Thank you very much. Goodbye.'

The *Sunday Oracle*'s 'My Magic Place' was one of those features beloved by newspapers in which they fill up a page or two free in exchange for giving minor celebrities publicity. In that Rosa, Wysteria and Hermione were among those contributing, Hugo Hurlingham's hand was detectable. Rushed though he was, Pooley could not resist a quick skim which revealed that Rosa had difficulty in deciding whether she preferred to be in the centre of West Indian culture in Brixton, Asian in Southall or Turkish in Finsbury Park and that Hermione frequently enjoyed a melancholy but inspirational stroll around Gordon Square in Bloomsbury conjuring up the spirits of those great

186

intellects she felt so close to and trying to recreate the astonishing conversations in the drawing room of Number 46, where Virginia and Vanessa and Lytton and Duncan thought the unthinkable about philosophy, art and religion.

'Bingo,' shouted Pooley when he saw the caption to the photograph of Wysteria sitting among a great deal of trailing greenery. 'Lady Wysteria Wilcox at peace on the Chiswick Eyot—her favourite place of refuge.'

'It's my own little island,' wrote Wysteria. 'Not that I own it, but I feel that spiritually it is there as my refuge, somewhere I can commune with nature and the unseen forces that guide us. I live near the Thames, and when the horridness of the world bears heavily on me, if it is low tide I sometimes put on my little wellie boots, take my troubled spirit to the river and splish-splash I trip across to Chiswick Eyot. There I daydream among the willows and listen to the ancient rhythms of the river and sometimes even drift off in the arms of Morpheus . . .'

*   *   *

Amiss awoke just as the train was pulling into Cambridge station: jamming the relevant sections of the newspapers into his holdall, he jumped out. As he was leaving the station, he thought he saw Den Smith in the distance and lagged behind in case he was right. It was dry and warm, so he decided to walk to St Martha's in the hope of clearing his fuzzy head and took the opportunity to make a few calls. Prothero seemed permanently engaged and Dervla was still unobtainable, but after a few abortive attempts he reached Pooley. 'Where are we at? How bad is it?'

'I don't know, Robert. I've just seen the preliminary pathology report and that tells us what we already know: she drowned. There's no sign of heart failure or a stroke, but it is, as I say, a preliminary report. We're pretty certain she was on the Chiswick Eyot—that little island half-way along the course of the Oxford and Cambridge Boat Race route.'

'I vaguely remember it.'

'Accident's very unlikely; she'd have had to be caught unawares by the tide and been stupid enough to try to swim across the river. Suicide's possible but unlikely. Her housekeeper said she seemed no different from usual, and Rosa Karp had rung her late afternoon when she said she was shaken but recovering and was going to take a beloved calming walk to reconnect her with her muse.'

'Anyway, it's not on, Ellis. You can bet there's absolutely no chance that Wysteria would have killed herself without leaving a nasty note accusing someone vulnerable of being responsible. Someone like her unfortunate maid.'

'Of course the balance of her mind might have been disturbed as a result of her morning with Jack?'

Amiss snorted. 'Looks like murder, then?'

'I think so. After dusk someone could have walked out after her and, if she was off-guard, it would have been easy to tip her over the bank. Only a strong swimmer would have stood a chance. Sorry, Robert. I've got to go.'

'Hang on. What's the line going to be?'

188

'As of now, no reason to suggest foul play. As you know, it's a point of principle with our AC to stick his head in the sand until someone kicks him in the butt.'

'You're beginning to talk like Mary Lou.'

'I'm beginning to think like Mary Lou. Jim and the AC had a big argument; the AC told him he was seeing trouble where none existed and that Wysteria's death was a coincidental accident. He had already decided that Hermione's death had nothing to do with the Warburton but that she was poisoned at nine-fifteen on the morning of her death by someone called Ed. Unfortunately for him it was just this morning that we finally located the last Edward in Hermione's voluminous address books, Edward Cumming, who'd been in the States and hadn't heard about her death.'

'Of course,' exclaimed Amiss. 'E.C. Cumming. Damn. I didn't realise his name was Edward. He's the colleague whose ghastly book she's plugging.'

'That's the one. Turns out he met her that morning on his way to Heathrow in the Warburton car-park so she could give him a book by another protégé that she wanted him to read on the plane and review for the *Oracle*. They had a chat for a few minutes and off he went to the airport and she to the committee room.'

'So what did the AC say to that?'

'He got angrier, as he always does when he's in the wrong, and went on insisting that even if Wysteria's death wasn't an accident, it must be suicide. The best Jim could do was to get him to agree that if—but only if—any evidence emerges that Wysteria was murdered, the Met will provide some protection to the other judges.'

'It's a bit of a double-whammy having Wysteria knocked off and Ed in the clear. What's your feeling, Ellis?'

'That I wish this was all over, because I fear my friends may be at risk and I feel powerless to look after you. Watch your back, Robert. There may be a lunatic about.'

CHAPTER FOURTEEN

The baroness placed Amiss in an armchair, instructed Mary Lou to give him the cup of coffee she had already poured for him and shook her head energetically.

'Goodness me, everybody does get into such a state. Why do I always have to be the person to calm them down?'

'Drivel,' screamed the parrot from his vantage point on her shoulder. 'Bloody drivel.'

Mary Lou sighed. 'He's learned a lot more expletives during the past week or so.'

'Bollocks, bollocks, bollocks,' observed Horace obligingly. 'Balls, balls, balls. Who's a good Horrie?'

'A quiet Horrie,' said the baroness firmly as she carried him over to his cage. She came back waving a piece of paper she had taken off her desk and handed it to Amiss. 'Here's the press release I told Georgie Porgie to put out.'

'"Baroness Troutbeck, Chairwoman of the Warburton Committee, issued the following statement,"' read Amiss. '"There has been speculation in the media that Lady Wilcox, who sadly died last night, may have been murdered. In view of the undoubted murder ten days ago of Lady Babcock, this is an understandable inference, but not one I draw myself: I await the result of the inquest. The committee regrets the death of Lady Wilcox, is grateful for her contribution and extends sympathy to her family and friends."' He paused. 'Gosh, Jack, you're so tactful and hypocritical that

I'm proud of you.' He resumed reading. ' "We will be carrying on our business as usual, drawing up our communal short-list and then choosing the winner. Dr Mary Lou Denslow has kindly agreed to join our committee in Lady Wilcox's place." ' He stopped. 'Mary Lou joining the committee! What! Are you mad?'

'Denslow is willin',' said Mary Lou.

'Does Ellis know this?'

'I've just told him.'

'I bet he was thrilled.'

'Not.'

'How can you just impose Mary Lou?'

'I told the others there was safety in numbers, which was a concept they like since they seem to be getting a touch nervous. I said it wasn't easy to get hold of anyone in the circumstances, which they couldn't disagree with. I said too that I had been very worried about the racial exclusiveness and age profile of the committee, and this was an opportunity to remedy this injustice, since the literary critic I was suggesting was young and black. That silenced any potential opposition. I didn't share with them that she was American or Den might have had a seizure, and nor did I mention she was Bursar of St Martha's. They'll find all that out in the fullness of time.'

'But all those reasons are bogus, Jack. We don't need a substitute. We know all too well which books Wysteria favoured.'

'One must always seize the opportunity,' said the baroness. 'You know that, Robert. Having Mary Lou on means us sane people have another ally.'

'But you may be putting her at risk.'

'Oh, Robert,' said Mary Lou, 'don't be such a

fusspot.'

'You sound more and more like Jack every day.'

'Maybe I am more and more like Jack every day. There are worse role models.'

'I'm sure Ellis would be thrilled to hear it.'

'It would offend my finer feelings if the prize went to one of the clique's candidates because I was chicken. There's such a thing as common justice.'

'And *noblesse oblige*,' intervened the baroness.

'A concept that played pretty big in Minnesota,' said Mary Lou, grinning.

'But it's highly likely Wysteria was murdered and it's mad of you to take a risk.'

The baroness was looking very impatient. 'If one were going to fret about being murdered one would never get anything done. Anyway, we're prepared to accept police help since it won't be for long. The Cambridgeshire cops have already been on the phone talking of throwing a ring of steel around St Martha's. I told them to stop being stupid but that I wouldn't mind a rather obvious police presence.'

'You're lucky you're living in Cambridge. Jim's boss is refusing to provide any protection in London.'

'You'd better stay here then. Ring Plutarch and tell her to pack her bags and follow.'

'Absolutely not. I have to be in London. Apart from anything else I'm not leaving Dervla without someone to call on.'

'You could stay with Ellis or Jim,' suggested Mary Lou.

Amiss suddenly got cross. 'You could just as well both leave here too. You could stay with Ellis,

Mary Lou. And, Jack, you could stay with Myles.'

'Rubbish. Too busy.'

'I suppose it didn't occur to you to tell Knapper to cancel the prize?'

'Good God, no. Mind you, that's what Den, Rosa and the Ferrett wanted to do, but I dealt with them. I told them I was holding firm, as were you . . .'

'Whom you didn't bother to check with . . .'

'Of course I didn't. I know you. And that Griffiths was . . . which I already knew, and Dervla too. So those three wimps couldn't face the bad press that would come if they resigned. Pity really, we could have fixed the prize more easily.'

'Dervla. What do you mean she's holding firm? She's terrified.'

'She rang this morning. And when she found you and I were hanging in there she said she would too because she wasn't going to rat on the only people who had been nice to her. At least that's what I think she said.'

'But suppose something happens to her!'

'Oh, God, Robert, why should it?'

'We're all at risk, for Christ's sake,' he yelled. 'There's no other possibility. Someone must be trying to influence how the prize is going.'

'Can't imagine any circumstances in which they'd want to kill any of us goodies. Wysteria and Hermione were baddies. If this is what it's about, it'll be Rosa or Den next.'

'That doesn't make it all right . . .'

Mary Lou slipped over to Amiss's side and put her arm through his. 'Come for a walk, Robert. I want to show you the fernery.'

'Good idea,' said the baroness. 'I've got work to

do. Calm him down.'

Amiss looked at the baroness, who was already at her desk scrawling instructions on a piece of paper. He turned back to Mary Lou. 'What about the snipers? Shouldn't we wait until the bulletproof vests are delivered?'

'I'm prepared to take the risk if you are.' She took his hand. 'Come on, there's something I want to talk to you about.'

The baroness looked up as they left. 'When he's stopped being a prima donna, I want him back here to plot about the short-list.'

*   *   *

The new gardener had indeed done wonders with some dreary parts of the Victorian garden. Amiss gazed in admiration at a corner which had hitherto held nothing but a few dank and tenacious weeds. 'It's amazing what ferns and mirrors and imagination can do.'

'And money. Jack didn't stint.'

'But that wasn't why you dragged me out here, was it?'

'No. There are two things I want to talk about. First, I need advice about me and Ellis.'

'What sort of advice?'

'Would I be wise to get a job in London?'

Amiss stopped and faced her. 'I thought you were happy here.'

'I am, much of the job is great, I would miss Jack, and she would miss me, but I can't expect Ellis to transfer to the Cambridgeshire police . . .'

'Why not?'

'You know why not.'

'The Met's more exciting?'

'Yep. Much. And since I want to give marriage my best shot, it seems a good idea to start it off by actually living together, rather than carrying on the way we are at present.'

'What would you do? London University?'

'No. I realise more and more that while I enjoy being Bursar, I've had it with the catfight that is Eng. Lit. these days. If I have to go to a conference, I wake up depressed and there are hardly any papers I can bear to listen to. If I have to give a paper myself, it's as much as I can do not to be as rude as Jack. And students are beginning to annoy me rather than stimulate me. I think I want out.'

'To what?'

'That's what I'd like some advice about. Publishing? Journalism? Broadcasting? I know they're the sort of glamorous careers my own students are always keen on, but I'm a bit stuck for inspiration.'

Amiss sighed. 'I'm sorry for Jack. And for all of us, for whom St Martha's will lose a considerable part of its charm, but I think you're probably right. Let me think a bit about what you could do.'

'Sure. And don't tell Jack. I don't want her upset before it's necessary.'

'Your decision. And the second thing?'

'Rachel.'

'Rachel? What about Rachel?'

'We've been in touch.'

'So that's why you got Ellis to do the third-degree last night.'

'Yes, but he didn't know why as I wouldn't have wanted to make him prevaricate. Rachel rang me when she read about Hermione Babcock and wanted to know that you were OK, so I thought it would be useful to suss out the lie of the land. Then she rang this morning all worked up about Wysteria Wilcox.'

'Oh.'

'She said she'd like to ring you, but wondered how you'd feel.'

'How do you think I'd feel?'

Mary Lou stopped and faced him this time. She looked at him squarely. 'Pleased?'

'Pleased, thrilled, apprehensive, alarmed, delighted, worried, hopeful—and a lot more adjectives.'

'They'll be enough to get on with. I'll let her know. Now we'd better go in and address the little matter of the short-list.'

*　　*　　*

Rachel rang at twelve, much to Amiss's relief, as he and the baroness were coming near to blows about the merits of an Italian novel. 'Wops haven't written anything worth a damn since *The Leopard*' was the position she was sticking to, insisting that the four pages she had read of this one were sufficient to know it was dross. 'Oh, hang on, Rachel, I'll just take you outside.'

'Don't be long,' shouted the baroness. 'We've a lot to do before lunch.'

'I heard that,' said Rachel. 'Jack seems in good voice.'

'Some things don't change.'

Rachel seemed momentarily nonplussed.

'Oh, sorry, Rachel. I wasn't being snide. How are you?'

197

'I've been better. And you?'

'Ditto.'

'Are you staying in Cambridge?'

'No. I'll be going back this afternoon.'

'Is that wise?'

'I can't abandon Plutarch.'

Rachel laughed. 'And how is she?'

'Still gross in her appetites, but rather more mellow in character.'

'There was certainly plenty of room for improvement.' She paused for a moment. 'Robert, would you by any chance be free this evening? And, if so, would you like to have dinner?'

'With you? I mean, just you?'

'Oh, yes. Just me.'

'I can't think of anything I'd like better, Rachel. Where? When?'

'I'll book somewhere and let you know. Central London OK?'

'Fine.'

'Good. And it's on me.'

'Why?'

'Because that's the way I want it. Now go back to being pushed around by Jack.'

*   *   *

'Georgie Porgie's been on. Knapper's a bit bothered about Wysteria, but he's pleased about Mary Lou and thrilled about the publicity.'

'He really must believe that all publicity is good publicity,' said Amiss. 'There was plenty of rubbishing of the long-list.'

'Nothing to speak of,' said the baroness. 'Very mild, really, I thought, considering most of it's

198

crap.'

Amiss picked up a newspaper at random. '"It defies belief that a committee that includes such a champion of the marginalised as Rosa Karp could have allowed on the long-list *Pursuing the Virgins*— a novel more offensive to our peace-loving Muslim community than even Salman Rushdie's *Satanic Verses*. Even more bizarre is that she should have gone along with the choice of *Mbeike's Curse*— which implicitly blames the sexual habits of Africans rather than the drug companies for the Aids scourge in Africa."'

'Quite an achievement, when you think of it,' crowed the baroness. 'Not *Pursuing the Virgins*. Geraint's bullying did the job there. But getting *Mbeike's Curse* on took some doing.'

'Huh,' said Amiss. 'Did she tell you how that happened, Mary Lou?'

'No. You know what a rotten debriefer she is.'

'She pretended to adore *The Slut's Tale*.'

The baroness was giggling delightedly. 'You'll have to tell her. She's had more sense than to read the Gloomsberries.'

'But you know that Virginia Woolf had a big passionate number with Vita Sackville-West, Mary Lou?'

'Sure.'

'Well, one of dear old Vita's more memorable throwaway lines was apropos the irritation caused her by having to step over soapy water generated by "a dreary slut on her knees scrubbing the stairs". So this novel was an exposé of the nastiness of the Bloomsbury crew from the viewpoint of said slut.'

'What's wrong with that? Sounds eminently worthwhile.'

'In principle, yes, but sadly it was a rotten novel, which is why I was against it. So were Wysteria and Hugo, who of course hated it because it cast aspersions *inter alia* on Saint Virginia and they made much of the fact that it would be a posthumous insult to Hermione. Theoretically, Rosa should have liked it on class grounds, but she's protective of feminist patron saints so she lined up against it too. Geraint and Den loved it for ideological reasons and Jack did a great and eloquent song-and-dance about how it had moved her, and Dervla agreed and said she'd found it very sad, but after a long battle, Jack finally and reluctantly gave in to the anti-sluts in exchange for their letting *Mbeike* and a couple of others she wanted go through.'

'Normal Jack committee tactics then.'

'Don't change a winning formula,' said the baroness smugly.

Amiss picked up another newspaper. '"It beggars belief that a committee chaired by that redoubtable High Tory, Lady Troutbeck, should have placed on a long-list *Once and Future Heroes*, a preposterous fantasy about an Iraqi anti-imperialist of a philosophical disposition who leads a successful revolt against American world domination."'

'What did you get in exchange for that, Jack?'

'Den Smith to drop a couple of less preposterous favourites.'

Mary Lou nodded. 'Ah, yes. Exclude candidates who are in with a chance but allow one on the list that has rickets. Didn't they realise what you were up to?'

The baroness snorted. 'Writers are by and large

thick.'

'Or, as a kinder person would put it,' said Amiss, 'Writers are by and large politically naïve.'

'Thank heavens for that. Gives us a head start. Now, come on, come on. We have to agree on what short-list we're going to push through.'

*   *   *

They broke for lunch and switched on the radio for *The World at One*. 'There is shock and dismay in literary circles over the Knapper-Warburton Prize,' said the BBC announcer. 'Not only has the world of letters suffered two devastating blows with the murder of Hermione Babcock and the suspicious death of Wysteria Wilcox, but the committee is in turmoil over the long-list published yesterday which has elicited much criticism in this morning's press. Susie Briggs has talked to two committee members and I will be discussing what he calls an inflammatory book with Abu Mohammed, the imam of Bethnal Green mosque.'

'Inflammatory is right,' snorted the baroness. 'If that madman had his way every book in the country would go up in smoke.'

'Except the Koran and *Once and Future Heroes*,' offered Mary Lou. 'Have some salad, Jack.'

The baroness helped herself, took a forkful and shook her head. 'There's too much tarragon in the dressing, Mary Lou. Tell Nara.'

'OK.'

'And I'm not at all sure about that chicken. Not as good as usual. Tell Nara to tick off the supplier.'

Mary Lou nodded. 'Now, that's enough about food. Here's Susie Briggs.'

'Sir Hugo Hurlingham, Literary Editor of the *Sunday Oracle*, doyen of the literary establishment and last year chairman of the Warburton, spoke to me earlier . . . You must be very distressed at this second blow, Sir Hugo.'

'I am distressed beyond words, Susie. Distressed and diminished. To lose Wysteria, that rare and gentle artist, as well as dear Hermione, that great figure of literary integrity, and within a very few days, and not as a result of natural causes—what can I say? I am diminished. We are all diminished. It would not be too much to suggest that . . .'

'Oh, stop gibbering and bugger off, you old cretin,' shouted the baroness as she took a healthy glug of wine.

'Sssssshhhhhhh!' said Amiss.

'. . . for had Hermione's guiding and experienced hand still been on the tiller, we might not perhaps have had such a—quite frankly—shocking long-list.'

'Shocking? Sir Hugo,' squeaked Susie.

'I choose my words carefully, young lady. I said "shocking" and I mean "shocking". When I think of some of the great names ignored and of the thoughtful, cultured, cosmopolitan novels that have been sacrificed to make room for thinly disguised political tracts, words fail me . . .'

The baroness sniggered. 'He was very sore over losing a couple of his bosom buddies and even sorer at losing *Gesundheit*, or whatever that cheery day-in-the-life of the syphilitic German shoe-fetishist was called.' She leaned back in her chair and extracted her pipe from her pocket.

'Den Smith, another member of the Knapper-Warburton committee, also spoke to me this morning by telephone from Cambridge.'

'Cambridge?' said the baroness, vigorously prodding tobacco into her pipe. 'Why is he infesting my territory?'

'Sssssssshhhhhhh,' said Mary Lou.

'Den Smith, can you hear me? The line is rather crackly?'

'I hear you, Susie.'

'Sir Hugo Hurlingham has complained about what he called "political tracts" on the long-list and seems to be implying the list would have been different had Lady Babcock not been replaced by Lady Troutbeck.'

'Many things would have been different if Hermione hadn't died and we hadn't been saddled with a reactionary fossil,' snarled Smith, 'but that doesn't mean it's not right to have political novels. Just that it's wrong to have fascist, imperialist novels that lick George Bush's . . .'

'And there we had to leave Susie Briggs and Mr Smith,' said the presenter.

'So much for the idea of collective responsibility,' said Amiss.

'Sssssssssssssssssssssssssshhhhhhhhhhhhhhhhhhh!' said the baroness.

'We asked Lady Troutbeck to comment on those criticisms, but she said—and I quote—"I suggest that on a day when we are mourning Lady Wilcox, my colleagues might be better occupied in sober reflection than in stirring up controversy."'

'Brilliant,' said Mary Lou. 'That'll drive them bonkers.'

'They're already bonkers,' said the baroness, directing a large flame at the bowl of her pipe. 'I'm just putting my foot on the accelerator.'

'Imam Abu Mohammed is in the studio with me,' said the announcer smoothly. 'Now, Imam Abu Mohammed, I understand you are unhappy that the Knapper-Warburton committee has long-listed *Pursuing the Virgins*, a novel about what goes on in the mind of an Islamic terrorist?'

Being an Islamofascist with the excellent English that came from being British-born—indeed he was a graduate of the London School of Economics, formerly known as Kevin—Abu Mohammed was particularly popular with the BBC. 'I and all other devout worshippers of Allah are not just unhappy at this deliberate insult; we are outraged. It goes to show that there will be no protection for Muslims until Britain becomes an Islamic state.'

'But this is merely a novel about extremists—Islamists—not ordinary peace-loving Muslims. Have you read it?'

'I do not read blasphemy and filth.'

'And you wish to deny others the right to read what you disapprove of, even if you haven't read it?'

'Certainly. This is a very serious matter. I can assure you,' said Abu Mohammed, as ever choosing his words carefully, 'there will be those calling for a fatwa on this infidel author and on the committee who chose to give publicity to his infamous libel.'

'You're surely not suggesting that these people should be murdered?' asked the interviewer, his mock horror hiding his delight that the lunch-time programme was generating a story.

'I am merely reflecting what will inevitably be the view of many people whose religion has been mocked. When we have an Islamic state, perpetrators of religious libel, like those practising homosexuality, adultery, fornication and bestiality, will be stoned to death.'

'Thank you, Imam Mohammed. Today, at Prime Minister's Questions, the Leader of the Opposition . . .'

Mary Lou switched off the radio. 'It's some committee I've joined. Unless it was Muslims who did the earlier murders, it looks as if we'll have two lots of killers after us.'

The baroness emitted a cloud of smoke and smiled broadly. 'Don't pay any attention to that idiot,' she said. 'Our job is to sort out the idiots who would like to prevent me having my way. Let's get on with it.'

*   *   *

Amiss arrived at the little Italian restaurant early, and was sitting at the table reading the current *Wrangler* and drinking a Campari when Rachel touched his shoulder. He jumped up and kissed her on the right cheek. 'I don't do the kiss on both cheeks since some people started doing right, left, right,' he said. 'I'm too uncoordinated.'

She smiled wanly and sat down.

'You're looking good, Rachel.'

'Honestly, Robert?'

'Honestly, no. I was lying. You look tired and pale and too thin.'

'That's about how I feel, but I'm better than I was.' She looked up at the hovering waiter. 'I'll have a Campari too, please.'

In the awkward few moments that followed, they took refuge in exchanges about a menu which did not much interest either of them. Then, when food had been ordered and a bottle of Frascati had arrived, Rachel looked squarely at Amiss. 'I know roughly from Mary Lou what's been going on with you. Do you want to know what's been going on with me?'

'Very much.'

'Broadly, I left you for a creep.'

'What happened to the principled, high-minded Eric who was going to make the world a better place?'

'I suspect he never existed, but if he had, he didn't survive the corruption of power. And he certainly didn't survive the disappointment of losing it.'

'How long had you been together when you went off him?'

She gave a strained laugh. 'A couple of months. No, that's not true, but that's when the occasional nagging doubt surfaced. I was ready to leave and then he was fired so . . .'

'So you had to stand loyally by him?'

'Yes. How could I stop working for him and throw him out of my flat when he was down on his luck? And, in truth, I couldn't bear that anyone— including Eric—would think that I was chucking him for selfish reasons. So a mixture of compassion and vanity kept me at his side until a couple of months ago.'

'I understand the dilemma. Tell me, what was the worst thing about him?'

'He was so self-important. And never any fun. You were right when you accused me of having succumbed to a prig-virus.'

'Maybe, but I was being so irritatingly uncertain at the time that someone with a sense of purpose must have seemed very attractive.'

'That's true. We hadn't learned how to live together, Robert. And I was amazingly naïve about politicians. Now what about you?'

'We'll get to me in a minute. What are you working at now?'

'Nothing. I'm having a *crise* about what to do with myself. I don't want to go back to the Foreign Office—even if they'd have me after my bad behaviour in going off with a minister. And I definitely don't want to have anything to do with politics again. I've been looking in the appointments pages and so far haven't found anything I want. But I'm not going to rush into anything this time.'

'You sound like me.'

'Mary Lou said you were writing a book. What kind of book?'

'I don't really want to talk about it until it's finished and it'll probably never get published, but I can assure you it's not the sort of thing that would appeal to the average Knapper-Warburton judge.'

'The average judge seems to be dead.'

'Come now, it's only a minority who're dead. Anyway, it's an old-fashioned detective story, I'm doing. Retro, that's what I'm going for. There's so much mystery fiction around these days that is harrowing or disgusting that I thought fashion was sure to change. It'll be the kind of book you'll be able to give your maiden aunt without any fear of being subsequently disinherited.'

'In my present state that sounds like my sort of book. Now, what's going on with that bloody committee? I was worried when I heard about Hermione Babcock. That's what had me ring Mary

Lou. And I got really worried when I heard about Wysteria Wilcox. I thought you might be in danger and I couldn't bear not to talk to you. Even to offer you a refuge.'

Amiss smiled. 'Well now, that's the mystery solved. I murdered both of them so as to provoke you into getting in touch.'

She giggled. 'I'd forgotten how refreshing bad taste is. Let me tell you a bit about what it's like living with someone who doesn't approve of inappropriate language . . .'

CHAPTER FIFTEEN

Fighting back a rising tide of panic but trying gamely to maintain a calm exterior, Rosa Karp was spending the evening in the House of Lords chairing a meeting of 'Reclaiming our past'—a group of academics, teachers and political activists who were planning a campaign to make women's and ethnic studies a core part of the school curriculum. Although she kept trying to tell herself that—after all she had suffered at the hands of the Troutbeck monster—Wysteria had been in a sufficiently disturbed state to have let the tide creep up on the eyot, Rosa was failing to convince herself. So troubled was she that half-an-hour in, Parminda Kumar, the militant director of the outreach unit of the liaison officers' union, accused her of marginalizing her by failing to respond to her concerns about the ideological necessity of stressing the secular rather than religious nature of the Indian community. 'Post-imperial capitalist, you mean,' snarled Angela Euston, the Afro-Caribbean sociologist, and as Parminda demanded that the chair rule such offensive remarks out of order, Rosa burst into tears and ran headlong out of the room, along the corridors and out of the Lords.

*   *   *

Pleading a virus, Felix Ferriter had cancelled his well-thumbed lecture on 'Literature through the pink prism' to a London students' gay, lesbian and

209

bisexual society. He spent the evening at home compulsively watching news bulletins and wishing he could think of a face-saving excuse for going back to America. He flinched every time the clip was run of Geraint Griffiths insisting that Abu Mohammed was as good as instituting a jihad and demanding that the Home Secretary initiate his own Holy War against fascism. Having talked to him earlier, Ferriter was all too aware that Griffiths saw the Knapper-Warburton committee as the frontline troops in a glorious battle and was in maniacally high spirits about the possibility of martyrdom. Ferriter had tried to make contact with Rosa, Den Smith and Hugo Hurlingham in the hope that one of them might be weakening, but none of them could be reached. It was after ten before he disciplined himself to turn off the television and read over the first draft of his paper for the forthcoming international Queer Theory conference which flew a challenging yet ironic kite about Oscar Wilde as a symbol for the proto-post-postmodern phallus. After a few pages, he threw it aside and reached for the vodka. He pulled out his phone before going to bed and was drunk enough to fall asleep quickly. When, at midnight, the doorbell began to ring, it was a few minutes before he realised what was happening. He lay under the duvet, terrified, trying to summon up the courage to get out of bed and ring the police.

*   *   *

Dervla's agent had hired four heavies to escort her to the fashion show she was being discreetly but generously paid to attend. She wished desperately that she'd taken Amiss's advice to cry off and go to Dublin for a few days. Sitting in the front row trying to look interested and vivacious, she wondered how long she could keep up the façade. At the end of the show, she managed a glass of champagne and some air-kissing, but as she left the Savoy and faced a battery of clicking cameras and screaming reporters, she felt sick and dizzy. As the words 'Dervla, are you frightened?' floated across the ether, she crumpled to the ground.

*   *   *

Hugo Hurlingham had attended the literary agents' dining club as a guest of the chairman and had drunk enough to suspend his fears and enjoy his favourite pursuits of boasting, gossiping and character-assassinating. 'You're very brave, Hugo,' said his host. 'In your shoes I'd have quit that committee PDQ.'

'Wouldn't dream of it, old man. Job has to be done. I think I can pride myself that I've managed to steady the nerves of my colleagues.'

His host shook his head in mingled surprise and admiration. Who would have thought that the pompous old git had balls? He escorted him from the restaurant at around eleven, shovelled him into a taxi and waved him off. When he reached his apartment block, Hurlingham got out slightly nervously, much more conscious than usual of the darkness of the street. He paid the driver and, while waiting for the receipt, fished his keys out of his pocket. He had just inserted a key in the lock when the noise of the taxi driving off was drowned out by the sound of a motorbike. As he opened the door he pressed the light switch and presented to the pillion passenger a much better target than he had anticipated.

* * *

Despite his underlying nervousness, Den Smith had had a most enjoyable day. First, there had been coffee with one of his regular contributors, a young man who regarded Smith as an inspirational guru and who was suitably awestruck at his courage in defying whatever dark forces were threatening the Knapper-Warburton. The interview with Susie Briggs had given him a chance to savage the ghastly Troutbeck on the lunch-time news programme, then there had been lunch with a radical historian who wanted to consult him about the origins of American imperialism and who had given him extra ammunition with which to kick the stuffing out of the Foreign Office Minister of State during the debate that evening at the Cambridge Union.

It was three in the afternoon when he checked into the Trinity College guest room the Union had booked for him and had a nap, after which he read a bit and worked on his new poem, 'Stiff the Cunts', for which inspiration had come to him on the train. Within an hour or so he had a full draft:

There's only one way.
Stiff George W. Bush and his poodle Tony Blair,
    hired to sniff his ass.
Stiff the neo-con cunts who turn our world into a
    rodeo for their Texan whoremaster.
Stiff the racist Nazi Zionist serial killers.
Stiff the barbarians before they stiff you.

It was powerful and true, he felt, but perhaps still in need of some polishing. He tried replacing full stops with semicolons, but felt it took from the staccato effect. Then he tried capitalising the whole of the first line, but concluded reluctantly that the effect lacked subtlety. Reading it out loud to make sure the cadences were right, Smith heard a chime and realised with a start that it was six-thirty, and time to stroll up the street for a pre-dinner drink with the Union officers.

Having been asked to wear a black tie, Smith wore a red open-necked shirt, jeans and a bomber jacket. Seeing the students dressed up made him guffaw loudly, while deriding them for their slavish adherence to anachronistic styles and values kept him happy throughout most of dinner. He lost his temper, though, when the President—who had arrived late and flustered—told him that his main opponent had had to cancel and that his place would be taken by Geraint Griffiths, who was now speeding to Cambridge by car.

Not being able to admit that he feared Griffiths more than any minister, Smith took refuge in loud denunciations of the lack of courtesy involved in failing to consult him: the President's explanation that it all happened so late it was a miracle he had found a replacement was thunderously dismissed as a lie. 'I'm thinking of leaving now,' he growled but the volume of grovelling and begging that elicited persuaded him graciously to change his mind. By the time Griffiths arrived, Smith had sufficiently recovered his temper to ask him if he'd had a good journey and to agree to pose with him and the Union officers outside the building for the benefit of a freelance cameraman.

The debate would long be remembered by those present and not only because of what happened subsequently. Proposing the motion 'That this House would cage George Bush in Guantanamo Bay and throw away the key', Smith began with his now familiar account of how the mass murderers leading the fascist states of Britain and America and Israel had organised the air attacks on America in order to justify a war destined to seize the oil resources of the whole of the Middle East. Bush was not the moron he looked, explained Smith, but a brilliant, ruthless, ravening despot who had sought and found an excuse to begin enslaving the world: it was the duty of Muslims, Christians and every other moral person to defeat this evil axis by any means necessary. As he concluded his peroration, Smith hesitated about whether to recite his new poem, but decided to go for it. Griffiths's roars of laughter so enraged him that he had to be pulled back from assaulting him by the President and a few other students, but Smith recovered himself enough to shout 'Men and women, I beg to propose the motion', and sat down to thunderous applause mixed with boos and jeers.

Griffiths's onslaught on Smith was given considerable immediacy by his insistence that they were both potential victims of Smith's new best friends the Islamofascists. 'Only today,' he intoned, at only a quarter of his usual speed, 'on the BBC, that alleged bastion of freedom and democracy, the fascist cleric Abu Mohammed was allowed to threaten every member of our committee with death. Two of us have died already, but it seems we are all to be sacrificed because of the self-delusion and cowardice of those who don't realise that George Bush is our only hope of saving the world . . .' Seeing Smith on his feet waving and shouting maniacally, Griffiths gave an elaborate bow and gave way.

'They were not murdered by Muslims,' screamed Smith. 'They were murdered by MI5 at the behest of people like you in order to justify a brutal clampdown on critics of this insane, blood-soaked government.' Griffiths responded with his standard defence of democratic imperialism, worked himself into a gabbling frenzy against the tradition of British traitors and moral delinquents that included the Bloomsberries, who put their friends first, the Cambridge spies, who had put their ideologies first and these days people like Harold Pinter and Den Smith and all their cranky well-heeled Islington friends, who hated their country's allies and loved its enemies. He came to a sudden halt, formally opposed the motion and sat down to a chorus of cheers and boos.

The rest of the debate was an anticlimax, although the young stand-up comedian who was seconding the motion annoyed both guest speakers by parodying them so brilliantly that the whole audience dissolved into screams of laughter; ultimately, to Smith's fury, his side just lost the vote and a triumphant Griffiths did a victory jig before rushing off to the taxi which was to take him to London. Smith was in such a bad mood that he almost refused the invitation to come for a drink, but he wanted one badly and the President was so complimentary about his speech and about *Rage* that his face was saved and he agreed. He was mollified also by the urgency of a journalist's request for the text of his poem; pausing only to scratch 'copyright Den Smith' underneath, he handed it over and followed the President to the Union bar. After a few large whiskies he picked fights with the comedian and half-a-dozen students and, shortly before midnight, he realised that there were only two others left in the room and that the President, himself also considerably the worse for wear, was pointing to his watch and reminding him that Trinity closed at midnight.

Smith had had enough to drink to take violent umbrage at this information. Convinced that he was being insulted by being denied the hospitality that was his due, he responded to the President's offer to escort him back to Trinity by telling him to fuck himself, grabbed his jacket and stormed off. Alone and angry, he marched past the Round Church to Bridge Street and into the view of the loiterer with the mobile phone at the ready. His being on his own as he crossed the road into the semi-darkness of St John's Street was a lucky break for the man on the pillion of the motorbike waiting around the corner.

*   *   *

'It's been a wonderful evening,' said Amiss to Rachel at around midnight, as they finished yet another cup of coffee.

'The best I've had in a long time.'

He took her hand. 'I don't know what the etiquette is.'

'Nor do I.'

'Do you feel like a nightcap at my place?'

She smiled. 'Why not. I could renew my

acquaintanceship with my least favourite cat.'

They were in his flat within forty-five minutes. It took some time to satisfy Plutarch's needs and settle her down, but peace had just been achieved when the telephone began to ring. Amiss felt a surge of worry. 'Sorry, Rachel. I'd better get that. I really should have checked my mobile for messages.'

'You certainly had, Robert. At one a.m. it's likely to be serious.'

Amiss lifted the receiver. 'Hello, Ellis . . . Yes . . . Oh, sweet Jesus . . . Dead? What about the others? . . . All? . . . You're sure? . . . Yes . . . yes . . . yes . . . Yes, I do see . . . OK . . . I'll be ready . . . How long for, do you think? . . . I understand . . . They'll be able to give Rachel a lift home? . . . Thanks . . . Yep. See you shortly.'

Rachel, who had gone rigid with dread, found herself unable to speak. He sat down beside her and took her hands. 'It's all right. Well, that is, it's not all right. I'm selfishly relieved that Jack and Mary Lou and Dervla are safe, but Hugo Hurlingham and Den Smith have been killed in drive-by shootings, Hugo in London and Den in Cambridge. Not surprisingly, the cops want to take us all into protective custody and are on their way, so I guess I'd better go and pack.' He looked at her ruefully. 'I'm so sorry, Rachel. This is not a good end to a happy reunion, but I don't have any choice. And Ellis says they'll be here within fifteen minutes and I must pack for at least a few days. Not easy when you're rather drunk.'

She hugged him. 'You've certainly arranged this well as a reminder that you don't live an orthodox life. Now, what can I do to help?'

217

He hesitated.

'It's OK, Robert. I'm ahead of you. I'll look after Plutarch. Give me the spare key.'

'You're a saint. Though I'm not really happy about your coming here. It may not be safe.'

'I'll be fine. I can't imagine they're going to take you somewhere safe without telling the world there's no point in trying to get you at home. Now, come on, let's pack. Why don't you get books and papers and that sort of thing and I'll start sorting out clothes?'

He hugged her again. 'Welcome back.'

'I don't know if I'm back. I don't even know how long you're likely to be around to go back to. But so far so good.' And she disappeared into his bedroom with a purposeful air.

CHAPTER SIXTEEN

'Ridiculous,' said the baroness. 'Completely ridiculous.' She was wearing an all-enveloping creation in bottle-green velvet that she called a siren suit—one of several which comprised what Mary Lou referred to as her 'babygro' collection. She waved her pipe energetically. 'All we needed at St Martha's were a few patrolling PC Plods and we'd have been fine.' She leaned forward and helped herself to some more whisky and shook her head. 'It's very disappointing. I was looking forward to beating up puritans tonight at a debate about legalising prostitution, but I suppose I'll have to cancel.'

'I can't say I'm too bothered about legalising prostitution right now,' said Mary Lou. 'I can think of a few more urgent issues.'

'We'd have one fewer,' said Pooley acidly, 'if you hadn't taken up Jack's mad invitation to join the committee.'

Amiss felt suddenly cross. 'Look here, it's bad enough to be locked up in this suburban Gulag without the inmates falling out.'

'Did you have to put us somewhere so ugly, Ellis?' asked the baroness. 'Mock-Tudor. Really! Just look at that carpet! And as for the wallpaper . . . ! It's all deeply upsetting.'

Pooley jumped up. 'Jack, I don't think I've ever shouted at you before, but I've had enough. It's well after four o'clock in the morning, we're in the middle of a most frightful tragedy and we plods are trying to ensure the carnage doesn't get worse.

Hermione Babcock was poisoned, Wysteria Wilcox was almost certainly drowned and Den Smith and Hugo Hurlingham were shot dead. Only a complete lunatic would think there was any alternative to taking the rest of the committee into protective custody. We found two safe houses at short notice and you're doing an Oscar Wilde about the bloody wallpaper. Well, I sincerely beg your pardon for having been so remiss. Can you ever forgive me?'

The baroness pouted. 'I came when you told me to, didn't I?'

'Not quietly.' He waved at the covered cage in the corner. 'And you browbeat the protection squad into bringing a bad-tempered and raucous parrot to a place of hiding.'

Mary Lou stood up, went over to the baroness and patted her head. 'What he's trying to say, Jack, is that things are very difficult for him and it would be helpful if you would try to be supportive.'

'And uncomplaining,' added Amiss.

'And uncomplaining.'

'Even about food,' said Amiss. 'It's bound to be awful but at least we're alive to peck at it.'

The baroness yawned. 'All right, all right. I'll try not to make a fuss. Bring us up to date, Ellis.'

Pooley sat down again. 'Bad as it all has been, we've had some luck. Hugo was murdered outside his flat, but his downstairs neighbour found him so he was quickly identified and, fortunately, the local police knew to report immediately to us since they were supposed to be keeping an unofficial eye on him. Den Smith had been debating in Cambridge and one of the students followed him back to Trinity at a discreet distance because he was afraid he might be too late to get in and feared he'd run amok because he was both drunk and furious. The lad saw the shooting, ducked into a gateway and phoned 999. He's lucky to be alive; we're lucky that he was there. So that gave us time to get hold of all the . . . survivors tonight and get them into safekeeping.'

'The Cambridge cops must be a bit pissed off,' said the baroness. 'They'd taken the trouble to look after us and Den gets rubbed out on their doorstep.'

'Where's everyone else?' asked Mary Lou. 'The cop who drove us here didn't know anything.'

'Nor the one who collected us,' said Amiss.

'Who's us?' asked the baroness. 'Plutarch? Is she here?'

'Rachel. We had dinner together and she'd come home with me.'

The baroness grinned from ear to ear. 'Excellent,' she said. 'Mary Lou told me she seemed to be coming to her senses. About time too. Why didn't you bring her along here?'

'It didn't seem appropriate. I don't think one is encouraged to bring guests to safe houses, is one, Ellis? Anyway, Rachel will be looking after Plutarch.'

'My goodness, she really must have fallen for you all over again. She used to be singularly unappreciative of that excellent cat.'

'She's still unappreciative. Just more tolerant. Now, please, can Ellis tell the story from the beginning? I find myself strangely interested.'

'When I was rung with the news about Hurlingham, I got up, rang Jim, agreed on the safe-house strategy, set it in motion and warned

Mary Lou to get herself and Jack ready. Your phone was off and Dervla and Ferriter and Den Smith weren't answering, but I got through to Griffiths, who told me he was just back from a debate in Cambridge where he'd wiped the floor with Den Smith, who, unlike him, was staying overnight. That was a bit of a relief, since we thought it meant Smith was safe.

'Griffiths sounded almost pleased at the news about Hugo—not that he was glad he was dead, but that it showed his heavy warnings had been justified. Still, he was nonetheless extremely happy to hear he was going to be looked after. Jim then got through to Rosa's husband, who sounded very relieved to hear she was going to be taken away. "She's been completely hysterical, poor thing," he said. "Luisa and I have been trying to calm her for hours."'

'Who's Luisa?' asked Amiss.

'Yet another Filipino housekeeper.'

'Wonderful, these lefties,' said the baroness. 'Someone told me Den has one too. They're bleeding the Philippines dry of its workforce so they can have their houses cleaned and they still call themselves international socialists.'

Pooley ignored her. 'The husband was extremely nervous at the thought of how she'd take the news about Hugo, but he went off to tell her and get her ready to leave. I was on my way to Dervla and Jim to Ferriter when we heard from Cambridge.

'Ferriter was in an awful state, apparently. They knew he was in because the doorman said so, but he wouldn't answer either the phone or his doorbell, so in the end Jim had to get the doorman to use his master key. Jim said he kept crooning in a low, calm voice as he went through the flat, "It's all right, sir, it's just the police and we've come to look after you," but Ferriter was actually sobbing with fright and—it turned out—drink, so it took quite a while to sort him out. In the end, Jim had to help him pack.'

'And you, meanwhile, were off to see the gorgeous Dervla, you lucky old thing,' said the baroness lasciviously.

Pooley glared at her. 'Dealing with a sick, terrified child is not an erotic experience, Jack.'

'You're always so negative . . .' began the baroness, and then, remembering her promise, she waved a placatory hand. 'Carry on.'

'Turned out Dervla had fainted after some event that evening. Though she'd had four bodyguards who took her back to the Ritz, they'd just parked her on the sofa and left. Still, she's a resilient little thing and she was very rational about it.'

'So where is she now?' asked the baroness and Amiss in unison.

'In a similar hideaway with Ferriter, Rosa Karp and Griffiths.'

'The poor child,' said the baroness. 'That's cruel and unusual punishment and she doesn't deserve it. Why didn't you bring her here?'

'It's just the way it worked out logistically.'

The baroness sat up and set down her glass with a bang. 'We should all go to bed now. My view is that you have a straightforward choice. Either one of the committee is the murderer, in which case you should find everyone separate homes—except for us, since we'd have murdered each other years ago if we were ever going to do it—or none of us is, so you should find somewhere that accommodates us all.' She held up her hand. 'In any event, that child should be with us. A.s.a.p.'

'Agreed,' said Amiss.

'Agreed,' said Mary Lou.

'What's more,' said the baroness, 'my thinking is that moving in a leisurely fashion toward the publication of the short-list and the grand prize-giving evening when the winner is announced is no longer a luxury anyone can afford. We all need to get together to find a way of dealing with these . . . unusual circumstances. This, I suggest, we might do better if we were in secure premises together.'

'Got you,' said Pooley.

'Then see to it. But if it's going to take time to decide, fetch us Dervla first. Oh, yes. One more thing. What about Georgie Porgie?'

'What about him?'

'Isn't he a target? And isn't Knapper? And the butler and the chef and the waiter for all I know?'

Pooley looked worried. 'Jim and I were focusing on the committee, but now you mention it, I'll get on to him and see what he thinks.'

The baroness yawned again. 'Good. Now, if you'll forgive me for being so pathetic, it's four-forty-five and I'm going to bed.'

*   *   *

Amiss's day began at eleven, when he rolled over, peered at his watch and rang Rachel's mobile. After a few minutes, he felt reassured that last night had not been a mirage, but mindful of the unpropitious circumstances, he kept his emotions in check.

'I haven't heard any news or seen any

newspapers.'

'If I were you I'd have a shower and, preferably, have something to eat before you face what the world is saying. The story is huge and for anyone involved, it's extremely frightening. I wish I were with you.'

'Ditto. Where are you now?'

'Attending to Plutarch. She glared at me threateningly when I turned up, but the salmon seemed to placate her.'

'Was it wild?'

'It was tinned. She's a cat. Not Jack Troutbeck.'

Amiss rolled over again. 'It's so good to have you back, Rachel. Now I'll get up.'

*   *   *

'"CARNAGE ON THE COMMITTEE" is good,' observed the baroness, 'but on the whole I think I prefer "EXECUTION OF THE EGGHEADS".' She turned over a few pages. 'Well, Mary Lou, you've certainly become quite a pin-up. Dervla had better look to her laurels.'

'I'm not pleased, Jack, but at least they haven't yet found out about me and Ellis.'

'Is there any sign of said Ellis?' enquired the baroness. 'Any news of what plans he might have for us? Not that I'm complaining, you understand.'

Mary Lou shook her head and continued perusing newsprint until her phone rang and she left. Besides papers, the kitchen table also held the debris of the scrambled eggs and bacon she had prepared earlier for the three of them as well as for two hungry policemen. The baroness fished around for a while among the broadsheets for items of

225

interest and then got up and went into the living room, from which soon came sounds of loud whistling and ringing telephones. She returned with the parrot on her shoulder, but as soon as she sat down, ignoring her imprecations, he began to climb up her hair, until, crying 'Shiver me timbers', he reached his favourite spot, commenced the gentle cooing he had learned from the St Martha's pigeons and then tucked his head under his wing and fell asleep.

'I thought you were going to train him out of that,' said Amiss. 'You should pray that the tabloids don't get to hear that you wear a parrot on your head. They might infer that you're eccentric.'

She was not paying attention. 'Where's Mary Lou?'

'On the phone to Ellis, billing-and-cooing like Horace.'

'Hmmm. They don't spend enough time together. It's time they stopped pussyfooting around and got married. She's going to have to do something about that.'

'Like what?'

The baroness sighed. 'She'd better move to London.'

'How would you get on without her?'

She sighed again. 'Not the point. I've never been one to mess up Love's Young Dream and I'm not going to start now. She doesn't have to abandon St Martha's totally; she can be a Visiting Fellow. And I'll find something to distract me from my loss.'

'You're not really as selfish an old trout as you like to pretend, are you?'

'I'm more a self-centred old trout than a selfish

226

one. Now, don't tell Mary Lou what I said just yet; this is not the right time for her to be contemplating major changes. Besides I want to give more thought to what she should do in London instead of being an academic. It's time she got out of that world. I don't want her youth and beauty worn down by bureaucrats and halfwits.'

Mary Lou came bounding in. 'Ellis says Dervla will be delivered here this afternoon. Knapper has prudently gone off on a business trip to New York where he intends to stay until this is resolved, but Georgie Prothero's on his way to replace Dervla in the House of Horrors. Higher authority has decided that there's absolutely no reason to believe that this is anything more than a grudge against the Knapper-Warburton, so we'll all be reunited tomorrow in a new location.'

'Are we sure we're sure our co-judges are in the clear?' asked Amiss.

Mary Lou looked at her watch. 'Let's get the one o'clock news and talk about the judges afterwards.' They moved into the living room and she switched on the television. The portentous music played against a backdrop of the deceased quartet of judges, in front of which sat a well-made-up blonde trying to look serious. Horace woke up with a start and began wolf-whistling.

'If any of the rest of us gets knocked off, there won't be room for our photographs on the screen,' shouted the baroness over the din.

'Horace, Jack. Please!' said Mary Lou. The baroness pushed the parrot back into his cage, as the blonde was explaining that the Home Secretary had promised to make available to the Metropolitan Police 'whatever resources they need to hunt down the killer of Lady Babcock, Den Smith, Sir Hugo Hurlingham and possibly also Lady Wilcox. In the meantime, the surviving judges of the Knapper-Warburton Prize are under armed police protection at an unknown location.' Behind her the images changed to photographs of the baroness, Amiss, Mary Lou, Dervla, Griffiths, Ferriter and Rosa Karp. 'There now,' said Mary Lou. 'They managed to fit us all in just fine.'

'And now we cross to Scotland Yard where Detective Superintendent James Milton is about to read a statement to the media.'

'God, he looks terrible,' said the baroness.

'He hasn't had any sleep since the night before last,' said Mary Lou, 'and Ellis says the AC is making his life hell by blaming him for not protecting the judges even though the AC was the one who insisted Wysteria had had an accident and there was no threat.'

'We deeply sympathise with the families, friends and many admirers of these four gifted people,' announced Milton. 'We know definitely that three of the four have been brutally murdered, and although we do not wish to pre-empt the coroner, we are working on the assumption that Lady Wilcox's death was no accident either. This is a time for action rather than words. The other Knapper-Warburton judges are well and safe and we are working day and night to find the murderer.' Shouted questions flew at him. 'I'm sorry, but I will not be answering questions. We have to get on.' And Milton turned and walked back into New Scotland Yard.

'Good statement,' said the baroness. 'Economical with the bullshit.'

228

'And here is our Home Affairs correspondent, Gavin Jenkins. Gavin, this is all terrible, isn't it? Do you think the police are doing enough?'

'Well, Fiona, there's a big question mark over the police performance to date. People are asking why, after the second death, that of Lady Wilcox, were the other judges not given police protection and why the investigation was led by a Detective Chief Superintendent and not by someone of a higher rank. There will be some relief that the investigation has been taken over by Assistant Commissioner Robinson, whose professionalism is beyond reproach.'

'Thank you, Gavin. Now, the literary world is in mourning today. The Secretary of State for Culture, Sports and Media had this to say this morning.' A worried, earnest woman in black read to camera a statement considerably longer than Milton's and almost devoid of any content other than general concerned clucking about tragedies and reiterations of the government's commitment to the arts. 'But not all writers are prepared to grieve in private. Here in the studio is Billy Jones, the radical performance poet, who has just formed "Artists against Violence against Artists".' She turned to a balding man wearing a T-shirt saying 'THE CLASH'. 'Mr Jones . . .'

Jones held up a chiding hand, 'Billy, please. We're at the cuttin' edge, us, not part of the bleedin' Establishment.'

'I was a toddler when The Clash were the cutting edge . . .' remarked Amiss.

'Never heard of them,' said the baroness.

'Punk band,' said Amiss. 'Political punk.'

'Sssssssssshhhhhhhhhh!' said Mary Lou.

229

'So, Mr Jones, the purpose of your march to Downing Street is . . . ?'

'To demand that the government stop this pogrom against writers. We agree wif Den Smith, who always said it like it was. A beacon that guy, a guy what gave his life for his beliefs. Only yesterday he gave the world a last, great poem that's now electrifying the globe. "Stiff George Bush and his poodle Tony Blair,"' he intoned, ' "hired to sniff . . ."'

The presenter waved at him agitatedly. 'I'm sorry, Billy, but we cannot allow you to recite that poem on prime-time television while there are children watching.'

'Typical,' said Billy Jones. 'He's been murdered, and he's still being censored. I'll tell you one thing, Fiona, that poem's going all round the world on the Net and by the time we've finished chanting it all the way down Whitehall and in front of Downing Street and handing it out to passers-by, there'll be a lot more people out there who know why Den Smith was killed.'

'What are you suggesting, Billy?'

'I'm suggesting what everyone knows. That like Den always said, there's a lot that's sinister going on in the West. We'll be demanding of the poodle that he set up a public inquiry to see why securocrats are murdering artists.'

'What possible evidence do you have for such an assertion, Billy?'

'We're artists. We don't need evidence, we've got our intuition.'

'Thank you, Billy Jones. Now Susie Briggs will take us through the careers of these four great English people of letters—now sadly lost to the

230

nation.'

'Oh, God Almighty,' said the baroness, 'there's a paranoid lunatic born every minute. Can we not do something more useful than watch what our Irish cousins would rightly call shite?'

Amiss reached for the remote control and switched the television off. 'I was just thinking that,' he said. 'OK, guys, let's talk it through before Dervla arrives. I've scribbled a few thoughts down.' He pulled a chequebook from his inner pocket and looked at the back. 'Ah, yes. Now, only a few days ago, the prime suspects for Hermione's murder were those who could have slipped her the ricin: her husband, housekeeper, the committee, Georgie, the butler, the waiter and the mysterious Ed. Out, I think, go Sir William Rawlinson and Alina. I decline to believe either or both were prepared to hire gangs of hitmen to murder Den and Hugo so they could screw without fear of interruption. OK?'

'Fair enough,' said the baroness.

'Ditto Edward Cumming. Since Hermione was pushing his pseudy book it seems difficult to think of a motive for him to murder her. Nor indeed did he have to own up to seeing her that morning.'

'Can't rule him out,' said Mary Lou.

'I suppose not completely. He might secretly have hated his own book and have brought a flask of poisoned coffee on the off chance she'd want some. But for practical purposes, I think we forget about him for now.'

'I agree,' said the baroness. 'I'm getting bored.'

'Now,' said Amiss patiently, 'when Wysteria died, alibis were checked and some of the committee were in the clear. But that's no longer

231

relevant. Each of the drive-by shootings was done by two people, which means the murderer had at least four employees. This looks to be a managerial rather than a hands-on murderer, so for all we know, he or she could have delegated the murders of Hermione and Wysteria as well.'

'Oh, don't start that "he or she" rubbish,' said the baroness. 'He embraces she or rather her or even me if I've got anything to do with it.'

Amiss ignored her.

'So those with alibis go back to being suspects,' said Mary Lou.

'Yes,' said the baroness. 'But since we now know all the murders could have been delegated, judges are no more likely suspects than anyone else.'

'Except that individual judges might have some plausible motive.'

'Like who?'

'Let's go through them systematically,' said Mary Lou. 'Robert's right. If we're to share a house with them, it'd be good to know they're in the clear.'

'There are only five survivors from the original nine,' said Amiss. 'I didn't do it, so that leaves four, and call me a sentimentalist, but I don't see Dervla as a homicidal maniac.'

'Not least,' pointed out the baroness, 'that from what you tell me, she's so well-known she'd be instantly spotted if she went scouring the East End for competent gangsters. And anyway, none of them would have understood what she was looking for. However, I don't think we should get hung up on homicidal maniacs; our murderer might be absolutely rational.'

'Accepted. Now we're down to three.'

'Geraint is all mouth and no trousers.'

'You say that,' said Mary Lou, 'but weren't the four dead judges all against *Pursuing the Virgins*?'

'They were, but so are all the rest of us. It can't win the prize unless we're all dead, and I think someone just might smell a rat if Griffiths were the only survivor. They might even cancel the prize.'

'Still, the book has done brilliantly as a result of all the publicity,' said Mary Lou. 'Perhaps Griffiths is in cahoots with the author, or in his pay, or actually wrote it himself. Or perhaps it's the author who's doing the murdering.'

The baroness looked interested. 'A stimulating train of thought, Mary Lou. Have you considered the possibility that Griffiths may have been only pretending that he wanted *Pursuing the Virgins* to win because he's really concealing the fact that he's a Muslim extremist.'

'Thanks, Jack. Very helpful. OK, we'll put Geraint down as a possible. What do you think about Ferriter?'

'Can't think of a motive, unless it's a career move to homicidal mania,' said Mary Lou brightly. 'Next stop HomStud.'

'Rosa?'

'Maybe,' said the baroness. 'After all, the victims have been gender-balanced.'

'You two aren't taking this seriously,' said Amiss.

'How can we? Next you'll be suggesting the parrot did it.'

'Georgie?' asked Amiss stubbornly.

'For God's sake, why?' asked the baroness. 'Porgie's a child. How could he have a grievance against any of those oldies? Besides which, he's frightened of his own shadow.'

'The cops have already arrived at this

233

conclusion,' said Mary Lou, 'which is why they've decided the judges and Georgie Prothero can all shack up together.'

'Then there are Jungbert and Birkett.'

'Who?' asked the baroness.

'The waiter and the butler.'

'Ah, yes, I quite fancy the idea of Birkett the butler. He disappointed me over the lamb. Despite my instructions it was overdone: and a man who is unsound on how pink lamb should be is capable of anything.'

'That makes anyone who doesn't like bloody meat a potential mass murderer,' said Amiss. 'And it wasn't overdone. Plenty of it was pink.'

'Any ideas for a motive for Birkett?' asked Mary Lou.

'Maybe, like Griffiths, he has a secret life. Perhaps he disapproves of the honours system and is making his protest.'

'Den Smith didn't have a title,' pointed out Mary Lou.

'Birkett was trying to put us off the scent.'

Amiss drummed his fingers on the table. 'I want to get through this before Dervla arrives, Jack. Will you please stop reducing everything to farce. The cops checked Birkett out and like the waiter and the chef, he was completely clean.'

'So no one thinks any of the suspects are serious possibilities,' said Mary Lou. 'So who did it?'

'Mad Muslims?' asked Amiss.

'I don't like being fair,' said the baroness, 'but I've never heard of Muslims who go around murdering people without claiming the credit for it. Disinclined to hide their lights under bushels, I think you'll find. And for all that they have a habit

234

of being a bit random, to go out of their way to target Den Smith would seem a touch perverse.'

'Besides,' said Mary Lou, 'wouldn't they start with Geraint Griffiths?'

'Indeed, they would,' said Amiss. 'He would be highly insulted otherwise. In fact even as it is he's rather miffed he isn't the main target—while obviously being pleased he's not dead.'

'So it's someone who has something against the Knapper-Warburton Prize.'

'Or its judges.'

'Same thing, isn't it?'

'Let's assume it is,' said Mary Lou. 'Somebody— perhaps because they feel they were done down by Knapper—decides to destroy his prize.'

'Well, they've made a right hash of it then,' said the baroness. 'It must by now be well on its way to being the most famous prize in the world.'

'Perhaps Knapper decided to destroy it because he can't afford the prize money?' suggested Mary Lou.

'Hardly,' said the baroness. 'He's worth about a hundred million.'

'Someone who hates the whole literary world?' suggested Mary Lou. 'But then why would they pick on the Warburton?'

'Why not?' said Amiss. 'It did, after all, have a particularly noxious cross-representation of literati.'

'A blow against literary cliques, then?' said the baroness. 'That's not a completely stupid idea.'

'Pretty wide field,' said Amiss. 'I hadn't even finished a book, but exposure to the Warburton had me loathing the complacent closed shop represented by Hugo and Hermione and their sneering attitude to what people like to read.'

'Got it at last,' said the baroness. 'It's murder by genre novelists. The massed ranks of British crime writers clubbed together to hire hit squads.'

'From what I've heard,' said Mary Lou, 'it's more likely to be the romantic novelists. They've a reputation for being vicious.'

'If you'll forgive me, ladies, I am determined to keep to the point. And the point we've reached, I think, is that the most likely perpetrator would be a writer with a grievance.'

'And some inside knowledge of the literary world,' said the baroness.

'How much inside knowledge would you need?' asked Mary Lou. 'Your frustrated, angry author would only have to read the arts pages and the gossip columns to know about literary incest.'

'And if he or she . . . oh shut up Jack,' said Amiss, 'if said frustrated, angry author was curious about the committee and used the Net like Ellis did, said frustrated, angry author would soon know that Hugo and Hermione and Den and Wysteria were all back-scratching vigorously and profitably.'

'Excellent,' said the baroness. 'We've cracked it.'

'Except for the little matter of finding the errant author in a haystack of the disappointed.'

'Except for that,' said the baroness. 'Mary Lou, you'd better ring Ellis and tell him that's what he's got to do. And while he's about it, tell him to have another look at Birkett.' She stood up, stretched and marched across to the covered cage. 'You can come out now, Horrie. You've parrot's work to do. Get ready to cheer up young Dervla. And teach her to speak English while you're about it.'

CHAPTER SEVENTEEN

'How are you all this morning, Robert?'

'Better than yesterday, Jim. At least we've had a reasonable sleep and Dervla cooked us plenty of eggs and bacon so we're fortified for our journey.'

'How is she?'

'Dervla? Much improved. She was very shaky and tearful when she arrived, but she calmed down a lot, Mary Lou was very good with her and Jack distracted her by getting her to teach the parrot to say "faith and begorrah".'

'Did she succeed?'

'Hard to know with that parrot. It fixes you with its beady eye and keeps you guessing until a time of its own choosing.'

'Dervla told Ellis she'd had a dreadful time with Ferriter and co.'

'Yes. Apparently Ferriter and Rosa were semi-hysterical and Geraint made them worse by going on and on about Islamic conspiracies, so she hid in her room until your people arrived to get her.'

'Poor child.'

'That's what we all keep saying. I think we're getting old. How are you getting on?'

'Planning the serial murder of some of my bosses.'

'Starting with your AC?'

'Too damn right starting with my AC.'

'Presumably Ellis told you about our great brainstorming session yesterday.'

'Indeed he did, but there's not a lot we can do, what with the country being full of unsuccessful writers or would-be writers. We'd already checked with families and friends about who might have a grudge against any of the dead and I wouldn't quite know where to start with trying to find out what person or persons unknown has a grudge against the whole literary establishment. So we press on with the more mundane end of things—grubbing around among the lowlife trying to find out where the ricin came from, who did the hits, that kind of thing.'

The baroness stuck her head around the door. 'There you are, gab, gab, gab as usual. Come on, come on, transport's arrived and it's time to be off.'

'In a minute, Jack. Jim and I are just finishing.'

'Ah.' She advanced on him, making an imperious hand gesture. 'Pass him over.'

'I'm afraid she wants you, Jim. Bye.'

The baroness grabbed the phone. 'Two things.'

'Yes?'

'I've been worrying about where we'll have our celebratory dinner.'

'When we've got something to celebrate.'

'We will soon. I've decided on ffeatherstonehaugh's.'

'That'd be good. I haven't been there under the new dispensation.' [*Clubbed to Death*]

'The new chef is excellent. However, I particularly want his knuckle of veal but when I rang him this morning he told me he's having problems with the butcher. So there may be a delay.'

'I'll be patient, Jack. What's the second thing?'

'Have you given him the Third Degree?'

'Who?'

'Birkett.'

'For heaven's sake, Jack, why Birkett? Ellis said you had taken against him because of the food.'

'That wasn't wholly serious. It's just a hunch. Thought him a bit too interested in me.'

'How do you mean?'

'Kept looking at me strangely. And often.'

'All right, Jack. Just to please you, I'll have Birkett checked out again. Now can you put Robert back on?'

As the baroness marched out calling, 'Mary Lou, Mary Lou, hurry up!' Milton said to Amiss, 'Robert, Jack seems to think that Birkett was looking at her suspiciously and often. Apart from not knowing what's significant about that, is she right?'

'Everyone kept looking at her—mostly as if they couldn't believe their eyes. She was dressed in a manner one might justly call "striking" and she expressed quite a few arresting opinions over lunch. What's more, when she got to the cigar stage, she pulled her chair back and her rucked-up skirt revealed silver satin directoire knickers at which everyone, including Birkett and the waiter, gazed incredulously. Jack's not always a good reporter of how people react to her since most of the time she's under the impression that her appearance and behaviour are normal. On that occasion, even by her standards, and, indeed, the standards of Geraint Griffiths and Den Smith, they weren't.'

'Thought as much,' said Milton.

*   *   *

On the way to the new location, the baroness

239

announced she wished to stop at a wine shop and a good delicatessen; protests from the police escort were overridden. The group reached a country house in Sussex at five-thirty, about ten minutes before the Ferriter-Rosa-Griffiths contingent, now augmented by Georgie Prothero. After a brief introduction to Mary Lou, on the baroness's instructions the newcomers were shown first to their bedrooms and then to the drawing room, where they found the baroness busily filling glasses and the parrot bawling 'Prothero, Prothero, Prothero' in the corner.

'What's that fuckin' bird doing here?' demanded Griffiths.

'And why does it know *my* name?' asked Prothero nervously.

'Horace is keeping Jack company,' said Mary Lou soothingly, 'and he knows lots of names. It's just that he particularly likes the sound of Prothero.'

'It has a swagger to it,' observed the baroness.

'Don't panic,' roared the parrot. 'I'm in charge. Stap me vitals and burst me britches. Faith and begorrah.'

Dervla giggled and clapped. 'At last. That's, like, so . . . awesome.'

'Dervla put a lot of work into teaching him yesterday,' explained Amiss, 'but this is the first time he's actually uttered the words "faith and begorra".'

'Why would you want to teach him such a stereotypical Irish phrase?' asked Rosa.

Dervla looked crushed.

'For fun,' said the baroness. 'She taught it to him for fun, Rosa. It's time you got it into your earnest head that fun is good and we need all of it we can get. Especially now, which is why I've provided champagne. Help yourselves, drink to being alive and then I'll tell you what we're going to do.'

Everyone obeyed instructions, and though Ferriter and Rosa stayed glum, the others brightened up. Getting into the spirit of things, the parrot went into a sudden blast of 'God Save the Queen'.

'Good idea, Horrie,' said the baroness. 'We'll have a loyal toast as well.' She waved her glass around. 'Her Majesty,' she cried. Following suit, Amiss and Mary Lou looked appreciatively at the disbelieving faces of Ferriter and Rosa, both of whom pointedly abstained.

The baroness threw herself into the biggest armchair in the room. 'That's enough of that. Everyone sit down. Mary Lou, keep the champagne circulating. Robert, switch on the news so we can find out if any more of us are dead. Then we'll get down to business.'

'Stow the parrot,' said Mary Lou, as Horace began stapping his vitals again; the baroness grumblingly stood up again and stuffed him into his cage. She was back in her chair with her feet up on a coffee table as the BBC announced that the administrator of the Knapper-Warburton had been taken into protective custody; there followed a clip from Prothero's appearance on the night of Hermione's death. There was then a dull statement from a spokesman for several writers' organisations protesting about this assault on artistic integrity and demanding that the police find the murderers without delay so the imprisoned judges could be released. Dervla became annoyed when her mother came on crying and begging the Prime Minister to save her daughter.

'That's *sooooooo* out-of-order, Mammy.' Mammy, it emerged, had been instructed by Dervla that very morning to stay away from the press, but, being a prima donna, had been unable to resist television.

'My little girl,' she sobbed. 'My poor little Dervla. Away in a dark prison with no mammy to comfort her.'

'Your mother certainly knows how to ham it up,' observed the baroness.

'That's, like, my mammy.'

The scene abruptly changed to a motorway pile-up. 'Switch it off, Robert.'

It was a strange inversion of Reality TV, Amiss thought, as he followed instructions. Instead of the outside world watching this small group holed up in a compound, the group in the compound were watching the outside world. The baroness disturbed his train of thought.

'Right, everyone. I've talked to Knapper and told him we're going to go through with it.'

'Are we?' asked Rosa tremulously.

'Of course we are. What else can we do? Any objections?'

'I'm fuckin' with you,' said Griffiths. 'Fuckin' with you all the way.'

'I appreciate that, Geraint. But I'd appreciate it even more if you didn't say "fuckin'" every second word.'

Griffiths looked surprised. 'Do I?'

'You fucking do and it gets on my nerves.'

'What should I say instead?'

'Try "by George".'

242

'OK, I'll try, by George.'

The baroness beamed at him. 'Well done. Now that's settled. Knapper asked me to thank you all and tell you he's behind you.' She snorted. 'Three thousand miles behind you, as a matter of fact: I don't think he'll be leaving New York in a hurry. I told him that since we were enduring the heat and burden of the day, a bit of the folding stuff wouldn't go amiss to compensate people and he said that strictly without prejudice and out of the kindness of his heart he'll give everyone a bonus of twenty thousand pounds. Including Georgie.' She looked around. 'There now, that's brightened things up a bit, hasn't it?'

It had. Even Rosa managed a little smile.

'He's already given instructions to cancel the big awards dinner. There'll be a simple ceremony instead. And Knapper agrees too that we'd better hurry things up, so tonight we're choosing the short-list.'

'How can we do that?' squeaked Ferriter.

'Tricky question of etiquette here, I acknowledge. We've four dead judges and one new one who's read only a few of the books. I've given it some thought and this is what we're going to do. As a tribute to our departed colleagues, we'll put on the short-list what we believe would have been the favourite book of each of them. We'll discuss that now. And after that we'll eat the picnic I brought with me today. By tomorrow at ten I want each of the living judges—except Mary Lou—to put forward their choice of three and we'll fight it out and agree a short-list which Mary Lou will read at great speed so she can then participate in choosing the winner. Which we'll do as quickly as is

243

possible.' She looked around the circle. 'Any objections?'

It was as if there was no vitality left in any of them, Amiss would report later to Rachel. To a man they nodded obediently.

The baroness pointed at Prothero. 'You take notes.'

'Yes, Jack.'

'Yes, Madam Chairman. We're still a committee and we need to observe the conventions. Now, could I have your views on which book Lady Babcock would have chosen? Lady Karp? Professor Ferriter?'

'*Babushka Mirrored*, I think. She said it wasn't just post-modern, with its rejection of moral absolutism, but it was post-postmodern in its . . .'

The baroness cut in. 'Mr Amiss, help me place it.'

'It's the one about the novelist who's writing a book about a novelist writing a book about a novelist writing a . . .'

The baroness groaned. 'Yes, yes, it comes back to me. Seven layers of wankery. Lady Karp, do you agree with Professor Ferriter?'

'Oh, yes. Hermione was so moved by the significance of the imagery, the universality of the suffering, the cosmopolitan . . .'

'And by the fact that it was written by her colleague Edward Cumming,' added Amiss, to a glare from Rosa. 'She wasn't really prepared to give house-room to any other contender.'

'Dr Griffiths?'

'I don't know what she wanted. I didn't pay any fuck . . . by George attention, since the purpose of the whole business from where I stood, by

George . . .'

The baroness nodded. 'Fine. Unless someone objects, *Babushka Mirrored* goes on the list as Lady Babcock's choice. Whatever her reasons.'

Silence.

'Good. Mr Amiss, which book would Lady Wilcox have chosen?'

'She was dithering between two, I think: *Anorexia Phlegmata* and *Nomanis*.'

'Oh, yes,' said Rosa. 'She thought *Nomanis* was wonderful.'

The baroness scratched her head. '*Nomanis*. *Nomanis*. *Nomanis*. Oh, God, yes, I've got it: the homeless Afghan who lives in the middle of the Hogarth roundabout and describes in remorseless detail what he has in his black plastic bags and why he feels alienated. Somehow it failed to grip me.'

'Wysteria didn't think it was about gripping, Chairwoman,' said Rosa. 'She thought it was about caring.'

The baroness clapped her hand to her head theatrically, and then turned to Ferriter.

'I think that was her favourite. She saw in it a rare . . .'

'Spare us, Professor Ferriter. Mr Amiss?'

'She was certainly keen on it. You didn't get past the plastic bag, Madam Chairman, to the bit about how he was really an Afghan toff fallen on hard times who was possessed with longing for a waif-like librarian who cycled past every day and avoided looking at him. Wysteria was big on unrequited love.'

'You've completely missed the post-ironic . . .' interrupted Ferriter.

'On the other hand,' said Amiss, who was

245

beginning to enjoy himself, 'she knew the author of *Anorexia* and not, I think, the author of *Nomanis*, and that would have weighed with her heavily when it came to the choice.'

'I resent the implication that Wysteria would have been guided by anything but the highest motives,' interjected Rosa.

'Oh, please, let's cut the crap,' said the baroness. 'Dr Griffiths, have you a view?'

'As between an Afghan refugee and a neurotic shop assistant, I'll go for the fuckin' . . . sorry, by George Afghan I suppose, bearing in mind that . . .'

The baroness made an heroic attempt to be patient. 'This isn't about your opinion, Dr Griffiths. Which do you think Lady Wilcox would have chosen?'

'Oh, for by George's sake, Wysteria was completely by George unscrupulous so of course she'd have gone for the neurotic since she called it in though it wasn't worth a by George toss so she'd have had some really good reason . . .'

'Miss Dervla, what do you think?'

'I agree with Robert and Geraint,' she whispered. '*Anorexia Phlegmata* was, like, awful but . . .'

'*Anorexia Phlegmata* it is, Mr Prothero. Now we know about Mr Smith, don't we?'

'We certainly do, by George,' said Griffiths. '*Once and Future Heroes*—I'd have fought it to the death, by George, only that . . .' He paused. 'I couldn't say "bloody" instead of "by George", could I? It's getting tiring.'

'You'll get used to it, Dr Griffiths. Or you might even learn to use it less.'

He nodded resignedly. 'OK. I'd have fought it to

246

the death if Den hadn't died.'

'Add it to the list, Mr Prothero, unless there are any objections. Now, what about Sir Hugo Hurlingham?'

The subsequent discussion was quite heated, for Rosa thought he had most favoured *The Manor House of Rosemonde*, the fictionalised story of Henri Duparc, a real French composer who wrote only thirteen songs, while Amiss thought he had particularly enjoyed *La Condition Marseillaise and the Socratic Vaginal Dialogues*, a minute-by-minute account by five existentialists of how they gang-raped two nuns in a Marseilles brothel. Ferriter, however, was convinced that Hurlingham had agreed with him about the marvels of *This Hole my Centre*, especially the part where the homophobic cardinal realised that the Albanian rent boy sang like an angel at the moment of orgasm. Asked for an opinion, Dervla whispered that she thought he liked the brothel best but would have pretended to prefer the one about the composer.

Asked what he thought, Griffiths said he didn't give a by George.

'It's up to me, then,' said the baroness. 'I tend to agree with Miss Dervla and Mr Amiss that he secretly liked the gang-banged nuns. Still, since he wouldn't have admitted to that, it probably wouldn't be his wish to have the choice attributed to him. So it's between the other two. What do you think he'd have gone for, Mr Amiss? The queer-bashing bishop or the constipated frog?'

'*The Manor House of Rosemonde*, I think. He did say he thought it a very fine book. And it was by a Hungarian, so it met his EU criterion.'

The baroness raised her eyes towards the ceiling.

'Well, there's certainly nowt so queer as folk—if you'll excuse the expression, Professor Ferriter. Stick *Rosemonde* on the list, Mr Prothero, and then we'll repair to the kitchen and sort out our food and drink.'

* * *

'It was a really good picnic,' Amiss told Milton the following morning. 'A sort of hastily-constructed Babette's Feast, and Jack forced so much drink into everyone that they all relaxed a bit. Even Rosa. Mind you, Geraint Griffiths gets louder when drunk and Ferriter gets whingeier, but the rest of us got more tolerant so it didn't matter. The parrot was in good voice and people found it more agreeable to listen to him than to argue, so we all went to bed around midnight in reasonably good form.'

'Good for Jack. Now, I must rush, but first, I've news about Birkett.'

'You took her seriously?'

'No, but to shut her up I gave her a promise and I kept to it. Can I speak to her?'

'She's in the drawing room, cleaning out the parrot's cage. I'll take the phone to her.'

Amiss walked next door into the middle of an altercation, for the baroness's chore was not rendered easier by the parrot's insistence on swinging from her hair crying 'Who's a pretty boy?'

'Not you,' the baroness was shouting. 'That hurts. You're Horrible Horace—got that?— Horrible Horace.'

'Jim for you, Jack. News about Birkett.'

'Hah. Give it here and you shut up, Horrible

248

Horace. Just a sec, Jim.' She yanked the parrot off her head, howled with pain as he pulled her hair and then jammed him into his cage. 'Right. What have you found? Dismembered bodies under his patio?'

'Do you want the bad news or the bad news?'

'The bad news.'

'It's bad from your perspective: there's absolutely nothing linking Birkett to the world of literature. The only new information we've got on him is that he has a model railway in his spare room.'

'Harumph. I suppose the model railway, though culpable, is not a hanging offence.'

'That was my feeling.'

'Any family?'

'No.'

'Hah, that's suspicious.'

'You haven't got any family, Jack, have you?'

'I'm different. Besides, I don't have a model railway.'

'Anyway, he's a widower who moved to his maisonette when his wife died a few years ago. Neighbours say they've never seen any sign of children or heard any mention but obviously we'll check on that. He keeps himself to himself apart from his weekly visit to the pub and gets on fine with everyone.'

'OK, then. I'll have the other bad news.'

'This is really really bad news. Birkett's disappeared.'

'What do you mean, "disappeared"?'

'I mean disappeared. He went into work on Friday and when told that as a mark of respect that day's lunch had been cancelled, he sent the chef

249

and the waiter home and left. There's no sign of him at his home, the neighbours haven't seen him since, his morning suit isn't in his house and yesterday's post is on the mat.'

'Ooooer! That doesn't look good. Unless, of course, he's the murderer and has done a runner.'

'His passport was at home too, along with his bank card.'

'You think he's been knocked off too?'

'Looks likely.'

'But the other killings were very public.'

'Not Wilcox. She mightn't have surfaced for days.'

'Are you telling the press?'

'No option. It would be irresponsible not to.'

'It'll certainly get them worked up here.'

'You'll manage. Oh, and by the way, well done. We wouldn't know this yet if you hadn't made an issue of Birkett. Even if for the wrong reasons.'

The baroness beamed as she went back to her labours.

CHAPTER EIGHTEEN

'Hysterics won't get us anywhere, Rosa. Here, have some brandy.'

'But we could be stuck here for ever.' Rosa heaved with violent sobs. 'Don't you understand? If they're even killing waiters, no one's safe!'

'Butlers, not waiters, if we're being snobbish about it,' said the baroness. 'Now drink this and remember that, as Pollyanna would rightly point out, if Birkett has been murdered, the bright side is that none of us could have done it, so henceforward we can turn our backs on each other with impunity.'

'Er, Georgie could theoretically have done it, Jack,' said Amiss.

Prothero looked hurt.

'Oh, yes,' she said carelessly. 'I forgot about him.'

Prothero looked even more hurt.

'Well then, each of us can turn our backs on everyone except Porgie.' To the baroness's evident bewilderment, this observation caused Rosa to become even more upset. It took Mary Lou— drafted in by Amiss to administer first aid—ten minutes of patting and there-there-ing and sips of brandy to calm Rosa down. Everyone else, even Griffiths, looked on in silence.

'Right,' said the baroness. 'That's enough of that. The committee is reconvened. Pen at the ready, Mr Porgie. We have four titles on the short-list and the five old-timers now have to come up with at most another five, though fewer would be good. Dr Griffiths? Yes, I know about your endlessly pursued virgins, but what other offerings do you have for our delectation?'

*   *   *

'So what did Jack choose?' asked Rachel of Amiss.

'She didn't choose any. Rather surprisingly, she announced loftily that she had concluded that the chairman should not make suggestions of her own, but should be ready to vote at the final stage. Then she looked at the lists various people had come up with and said—rightly—that since there was no agreement on even one title we'd be there for the rest of our lives trying to reach a consensus. What about having a vote, she asked and then Griffiths announced that he thought it by George unfair that the dead judges were able to nominate a book each when the living weren't. So Jack said she saw the merit of that argument and did anyone object if therefore each judge got to nominate just one title. So that's what happened.'

'It doesn't sound like the old Jack to me, Robert. Surely there's some book she likes more than the others.'

'She's been fantastically rude about all of them, good, bad and indifferent.'

'So what's on the short-list? What is poor Mary Lou racing through as we speak?'

'She's groaning through Rosa's choice, *Childe Rolandas*, an awful book that would probably walk the Barbarossa Prize.'

'I read a review of that. Eastern European ghosts or something?'

'It's the eponymous story of a Lithuanian psychic

252

and his successful struggle to convince his fourteenth-century ancestor, Grand Duke Olgerd, that if alive today he would support the European Union. It's almost nine hundred pages long.'

'Doesn't say much for the European Union if it takes that long to make its case.'

'You said it, not me. Don't tell me you've changed your view on that along with everything else?'

'After my time with Eric, I'm an agnostic on almost everything until I can think straight again. The only thing I've a firm opinion about at present is that Plutarch has improved. That doesn't say much since she was so appalling to begin with, but it does show that there are possibilities of redemption. True, she presented me this morning with the corpse of an unfortunate mouse, but her motivation did not seem to be malign. Unless I'm deluding myself.'

'You must be feeding her well if she's behaving as civilly as that.'

'Oh, I certainly am. A bribe a day keeps the cat from your throat. What about the others?'

'Geraint, of course, chose *Pursuing the Virgins*, which Mary Lou's already read and discarded as having no literary merit. Ferriter had a real struggle between the cross-dressing bishop and the homophobic cardinal, but in the end, *This Hole my Centre*—or *Vatican Ragout*, as I prefer to call it— prevailed. Dervla went for *Sharing the Scratcher*, a tale of poverty and incest in inner-city Dublin.'

'And you?'

'I dithered mightily, as you might expect, torn between *Nothing Springs to Mind*—you know, the very funny one about Wittgenstein in the Wild

West that had escaped Hermione's cull—and *The Manor House of Rosemonde* which is really good.'

'And opted for?'

'*Nothing Springs to Mind*, which I feel a bit guilty about because it's really very slight, but Rosa and Ferriter were so condescending about it and so failed to get the joke that in a childish moment I put two metaphorical fingers up to them.'

'In the circumstances, Robert, I think you're allowed to be childish. And to choose something that makes you laugh.'

'Gosh, you really have mellowed. You'll be urging frivolity next.'

Rachel laughed. 'I'm glad Eric was useful for something.'

*　　*　　*

The newsreader was perched in front of a wall of book jackets. He looked gravely at the camera. 'Although decimated by murder . . .'

'Moron,' shouted the baroness.

'. . . in protective custody and in fear of their lives, the Knapper-Warburton judges have come up with a short-list.'

'If we'd been decimated, only nought point nine per cent of one person would be dead, you ignoramus,' she bellowed at the screen.

'Sssssssssshhhhhhhhhh!' said everyone.

'The judges wish it known that the list is unusually long since they added to it without challenge the books they think their four admired, murdered colleagues may have chosen.' The faces of the dead judges flashed up behind him.

'Might, might, might, might have chosen, not

254

may, you cretin.'

'. . . Lady Hermione Babcock, Lady Wysteria Wilcox . . .'

'Double ignoramus,' roared the baroness. 'Can't even get the fucking titles right.'

'By George titles,' said Griffiths.

'Sorry. By George titles.'

'. . . Hugo Hurlingham. The nine books chosen are . . .' After reading the list of authors and titles sonorously, the presenter swivelled right to greet a frowning woman. 'Joining us now is Maureen Becker, editor of the magazine *Reading Circle*. So what do you think of the short-list, Maureen?'

'I think they've all gone mad in protective custody,' said Maureen. 'It's a dreadful, dreadful, dreadful short-list. Six of those books are a waste of trees and . . .'

'Sorry, Maureen, we have to leave it there and go over now to Scotland Yard where a statement is being made about the missing butler, Francis Birkett.'

With the exception of the baroness, everyone tensed. Milton's solemn announcement that there was no news but everyone must hope did nothing to cheer them up. With respectively a wail, a whinge and a shout, Rosa, Ferriter and Griffiths all turned on the baroness over her performance during the news and Prothero rushed off to his bedroom to ring various friends and bemoan. Amiss jerked his head towards the door and, with Mary Lou and Dervla, slipped out.

'I'm off to my book,' said Mary Lou, sighing as she went.

'I wish, like, she'd, you know, told us,' said Dervla.

'Who? What?'

'The telly one.'

'Ah, you mean Maureen Becker? You wish she'd told us which novels she approved of?'

She nodded. 'In case, y'know.'

'In case people might guess which one you chose. Dervla, I mightn't have been particularly keen on *Sharing the Scratcher*, but I can assure you it's a million times better than the ones Rosa and Felix chose. And Geraint's isn't even what I'd call a novel. Don't worry, you've nothing to be ashamed of. Now, if you'll forgive me, I've a few phone calls to make.'

'Robert.'

'Yes?'

'Jack. She's kind of funny.'

'You can say that again.'

'I mean was she, like, trying to get them mad?'

'Maybe, but I can't think why. Unless it's revenge for how much they annoy her. She usually has good reasons for what she does but it's often hard to guess them.'

Dervla nodded and headed off towards her bedroom.

*　　　*　　　*

The committee watched several news bulletins in the early evening. Though the short-list was variously described as 'controversial', 'unexpected' and 'contentious', there were no literary figures attacking the choices directly. 'They've probably decided it's bad form to be rude about us,' observed the baroness over her champagne. 'Pity. It might have livened us up a bit. It's like a

256

mausoleum here.'

'Mausoleum is hardly the *mot juste*, Jack,' said Amiss wearily.

'Well it feels like a mausoleum. You can't imagine having a knickers-over-the-chandelier event here, can you? At least not with the present dramatis personae.' The parrot, who after a tussle had settled for her shoulder, seemed to share the prevailing gloom, contributing nothing to the conversation other than a hacking cough he had learned a week or two previously from Mary Lou.

To Amiss's relief, at that moment one of the police knocked and came in. 'I've left the food you ordered in the kitchen, your ladyship.'

'Good. Good. I'll go and inspect it. Porgie, sort out the drinks. Come on, Horrie. Let's find something to cheer us up.'

*　　　*　　　*

At nine on Monday morning, as the inhabitants of the safe house were eating boiled eggs and trying to shake off their hangovers, Milton was having yet another strained meeting with the AC. He came grumpily back to his desk to face an enormous pile of reports and was sitting there in despairing mode when his secretary put an envelope on his desk which was marked 'Second class' as well as 'Private and personal'. The letter inside was written in neat handwriting, the address was given as 'No fixed abode', it was dated 'Friday' and the postmark was Heathrow. Milton's eyes flew to the signature.

Dear Chief Superintendent Milton,

As a responsible citizen I've got nothing against the police, or indeed, against the remaining members of the Knapper-Warburton committee, except Lady Karp and Professor Ferriter, so I don't want to inconvenience you any further. The attached short tape should make things clear.

Yours sincerely,
Frank S. Birkett

PS You should know that I've sent copies of this to several newspapers, so it can't be kept quiet. And if you try to ban them from printing it, I'll get it on the Net somehow.

Milton summoned Pooley and they listened together. Birkett began by introducing himself fully, helpfully including his date of birth, his mother's maiden name and his medical card number as proof of his identity. It was clear he was reading his statement, for there were no hesitations, no pauses to find the right words. As ever, he sounded calm and polite.

'It's a simple story,' he began. 'My wife, Lizzie, and I were able to have just one child, Mary, whom we adored. She was a clever but shy and intense little thing, who lived a lot of the time in her imagination and loved to read and write.

'From the time she was a child she scribbled and scribbled. At grammar school all her teachers praised her essays and we were proud as proud. Her big ambition was to get to university to study English Literature and we were all delighted when she got to Oxford. We didn't know if she just had bad luck with her lecturers or what, but she came home at the end of the first term and said she was leaving. "Dad and Mum," she said, "it's a waste of time. It's got nothing to do with enjoying books. It's all about politics and scoring points and rubbishy theories and attacking dead people because they didn't think like us."

'We argued with her, of course. Told her it was a great chance and it might get better. Even said maybe she should try another university. But she said she hated it all so much she couldn't go on. "I don't want to end up being put off literature," she said. "It's all right. I'll get a job and I'll still be able to read and I'll write my novel. That's what I really want to do." And so she worked in a bookshop and though she didn't get paid much she liked having books around her and she wrote away in the evenings. And then, when the novel was finished, she sent it off to what she thought was the likeliest publisher who sent it back with a rejection slip so fast she knew no one had read it. So she sent it to the next most likely and so on.

'It was heartbreaking every time the post came and it was another rejection. Some of them said it was interesting or well-written but not for them. Lots of them didn't seem to have read it. Others didn't even reply. It's only since I started to learn about the publishing world that I discovered that in those days most publishers were already expecting agents to do the job of finding new authors. Mary was too green to have known that. We were all green. We were a very close little family who probably kept ourselves to ourselves too much.

'For all that Mary believed in her talent, she was a modest girl and she thought maybe the book wasn't good enough so she rewrote it and rewrote it and rewrote it and when it got turned down again and again she put it in a drawer and wrote another one. And this time she struck lucky. She had an answer from Hugo Hurlingham, who was then a publisher. He took her out to lunch, he spoke warmly about the quality and originality of her book, he promised to help her improve it and he said he would publish it enthusiastically and that she had a bright future.

'You've never seen anyone so excited and happy. Then he took her out again and asked her to go to bed with him and she said no. After that he never answered her letters or returned her phone calls. Mary had been working for so long and so hard and had had so many disappointments that this further one put her into a terrible depression. The doctor put her on some pills and, in those days, people didn't know about the side effects. She became very manic, went on about how after all she had no talent and one night she just jumped into the Thames. It took several days for her body to surface and during that time we were half-mad with worry.

'I wrote to Hurlingham and told him she had killed herself and he didn't even answer the letter. And what with grief and work and trying to help Lizzie, revenge was way down the menu at that time. I always told myself that if I got a chance I'd do for Hugo Hurlingham, but not while Lizzie was alive, and she lived on, miserably, poor thing, for another twenty years. Fortunately—because I was going to need cash—I sold our house because it was too big for just me and moved to a little rented flat nearby. And then, last year, the Warburton Prize was chaired by Hugo Hurlingham and all my old rage bubbled up again. I served him coffee and I served him lunch and I wondered about killing him.

'I had a conscience, though. He was a lot older and even though he had a big opinion of himself, he was civil enough. Maybe he had reformed, I thought. So I began reading about him and about the literary world in all sorts of newspapers and magazines, learned to use a computer and spent hours on the internet. With nothing much else to do, I got quite absorbed in it. And then by the time the prize was awarded to Hermione Babcock, who I realised by then was one of his closest friends, I realised properly how corrupt he really was. And how corrupt a lot of those people were and how little chance people like my Mary had. So I decided to do something that would do more than avenge her, but bring that squalid little world to the notice of everyone.

'I'm not a man who does things without thought, so by the time I had made up my mind what I was going to do, I heard that Babcock was going to chair the Knapper-Warburton and Hurlingham would be on the committee. Give the man another chance, I thought, just in case I'm being unfair. I've always been very proud of how fair the English are. So I went to one of those spy shops and got myself two of those bugging devices that I could clamp under the tables in the boardroom and the dining room and that transmitted to my car in the car-park outside.

'After one of those Warburton meetings, I'd sit at home evening after evening listening to every word, and—putting it together with what I'd read—I was revolted by the corruption of it all. You could see with most of them it was all about their agendas and their networks and their prejudices. Hugo Hurlingham was on the make in Europe. Hermione Babcock was pushing a few people who would give her some job she was looking for. Den Smith lived only to do down people he didn't like. Wysteria Wilcox was cruel and vain. Felix Ferriter was an academic with no love or understanding of literature—just the sort of person that had driven Mary away from university. And Rosa Karp was a time-serving, dangerous fool.

'Geraint Griffiths was pushing an agenda too, but I didn't think it was a selfish one, and anyway I agreed with him. Robert Amiss and Dervla were continually walked over, but seemed perfectly nice and harmless. As for Lady Troutbeck, who came on the scene later. Well! If I was in the business of killing people for having bad manners, then she'd be top of the list. But I'm not and anyway she seemed very sensible to me and she dealt with all the people I hated in a way I very much approved of. Anyway, I had decided that for the sake of young people like Mary I would kill the six members of the committee that the world would be better off without. I'm sorry I only managed four. For now, that is. But I'll come back to that.

'I decided from the beginning that I wasn't the kind of person that's cut out to murder people myself. The thing was to get others to do it for you. So I read crime reports, found out about a few

262

pubs where villains are easily found and tested the water by placing an order for ricin, which I duly tried out successfully in Hermione Babcock's vegetable curry. It didn't cost much, and was money very well spent.

'I really wanted the Wilcox woman drowned like the kitten the nasty old bitch pretended to be. I knew all about her favourite walk and her favourite place and all that from the internet and because she never stopped blethering about it over lunch. My criminal contact found me someone suitable and we went together to the Chiswick Eyot to suss it out. All he needed, he told me, were a few hours' notice, and I was able to give him that immediately after I heard Wilcox tell Rosa Karp at lunch that she was in such a terrible state after the car ride with mad Ida Troutbeck that she would have to go home and lie down and then go to her place of rest. My man was already hiding there when she arrived.

'That murder was a lot more expensive, but I've been a frugal man all my life and none of the direct expenses made more than a little dent in my savings. Still, I spent a lot on the drive-by shootings, and was very disappointed that only two of them came to fruition. I already knew from the internet that Den Smith would be at the Cambridge Union that night, I had rung the offices of Hurlingham, Karp and Ferriter a few days earlier to ask if they'd be available to take part in a debate and had been told they were all otherwise engaged that night, so there were teams ready to wait near all their houses after ten. And then, to my big disappointment, the look-out men, who went to suss things out a few hours earlier, reported that both Ferriter and Karp had arrived home hours before they should have, so their assassins sadly had to be stood down. Still, they got Hugo Hurlingham, who mattered most, and Den Smith, who was a great bonus.

'So what now? I planned it all very carefully over the past year. Nearly all my money is abroad and I'm going after it. I won't be back and I'll be very surprised if you'll find me under my interesting new identity in an interesting place. However, I still have my contact among the criminal classes and I still have a great loathing for Felix Ferriter and Rosa Karp. But being, like I said, a fair man, I'll give them a sporting chance. If he retires from academic life and stops making fools of those poor students and if she never again opens her idiotic mouth in public, they'll be left alone. Professor Ferriter and Lady Karp, it's quite simple. I'll have access to the internet where I'm going and I'll be checking on you. My message is quite straightforward. Shut up or die!'

Milton thought for a moment. 'Right. I'll have to take this to the AC and see if we can get the press to hold it until we've decided what to do. At the very least, Rosa Karp and Ferriter will have to be warned before this gets into the public sphere. Ellis, ring Jack, tell her it's probable all this will be over shortly and that she should say nothing but convene that damned committee and choose the winner while they still have the chance.'

Pooley nodded. 'Jack's going to be unbearably pleased with herself.'

'So is the AC if he spots that we were wrong about Birkett having no children. If we'd checked properly we'd have found out about the suicide and it might have led us in the right direction. However,

264

let's hope he's too stupid to suss it out himself.' He picked up the cassette player and strode off to the AC.

EPILOGUE

'I think we can pat ourselves on the back,' said the baroness. She was sitting at a circular table in a private room at ffeatherstonehaugh's, beaming all around her. On her right was Rachel, welcomed back into the fold with a bear hug, on her left Mary Lou, and opposite them Milton, Pooley and Amiss. 'We've plenty to celebrate apart from me being right and the chef getting good veal at last.'

'Why have you divided us by gender, Jack?' asked Amiss.

'Too long an incarceration with Rosa Karp has got to you, Robert. I have not divided us by gender, I have merely placed beside me the people I want beside me.'

'And we two are honoured because . . .?' asked Mary Lou.

'Delicacy forbids me to say anything about why Rachel is a guest of honour except that I'm pleased she's recovered from her bout of insanity and hope she will in future hold on to her wits. And to Robert.'

'Thank you, Jack. I'm so glad you're being delicate. And I'll try my best to meet your wishes on both counts.'

'In your case, Mary Lou, while I'm lamenting your loss, I'm rejoicing in your new career—not least because you owe it all to me.'

'I rather thought Mary Lou's performance on *Newsnight* had something to do with it,' observed Pooley.

'Well, of course it had, you idiot. She was, of

course, brilliant and beautiful, but if I might remind you, it was I who made Mary Lou a judge in the first place, it was I who was asked to appear and it was I who said I was too busy and bludgeoned them into taking Mary Lou instead. She'd never have been offered Hugo Hurlingham's job or the arts programme if she hadn't had that chance to wow the viewers.'

'Incontrovertible,' said Mary Lou. 'I was just the humble instrument of a higher power.'

'Drink up, drink up. Robert, attend to everyone's glasses. The starters will be along in about fifteen minutes and will be accompanied by a New Zealand Sauvignon I'm particularly keen on. But we must not waste the champagne. One must never waste champagne.'

'You owe me fifty quid, Robert,' said Milton. 'We got our man before you got yours.'

'I don't call receiving a confession through the post getting your man. Especially when you still haven't the faintest idea where he is and will almost certainly never find him.'

'I certainly hope not,' said the baroness sternly. 'I should be very annoyed if you did. Birkett might have been unsound on lamb but he was certainly sound on judges. The world's a much better place without that ghastly quartet. And besides, if you banged up Birkett, Ferriter and Karp might revert to their wicked, wicked ways.'

'I couldn't possibly comment on Birkett,' said Milton, 'but I'm prepared to waive the bet, Robert, if you've actually finished the book.'

'He hasn't just finished it,' said Rachel. 'It's good and he's got an agent. So there.'

'And you're doing what, Rachel?' asked Milton.

'Nothing until Robert and I have gone on our long, aimless and lazy wander around Europe in the naff but comfortable second-hand motorhome we've just acquired.'

'I envy you,' said Milton. 'That was something Ann and I were always going to do and never got round to doing because we were always too busy.'

'You're always too busy, Jim,' said Pooley. 'The last few weeks have just been ridiculous.'

'Things will be much better now that Robinson's been shunted sideways. He made such a balls of trying to silence the press over Birkett's letter for no sane reason that the Commissioner actually bothered to hold an investigation of how the case had been conducted and found for me against him on every contentious issue. No one, thank heaven, picked up on our failure to find out about Birkett's daughter. So I'm being promoted and he's been shuffled into a non-job.'

The jabber of congratulations which followed was drowned out by the baroness. 'Promoted to what?'

'Commander.'

'Excellent. Sounds suitably authoritative and grave.' She beamed once more. 'I must say, this is most satisfactory. Let me sum up. The case has been solved but the admirable murderer is free; Jim has been given the recognition he deserves and no longer has a craven and stupid boss; Mary Lou and Ellis are getting married, she's beginning a new lucrative career and will stay a Fellow of St Martha's and visit often enough to keep her hand in and me happy; Robert and Rachel are reunited and going off to enjoy themselves; and there's even a chance that Robert might actually have found a

269

line of work that he might stay with for five minutes.'

She leaned forward, grabbed a bottle and filled up her own glass. 'Where was I? Oh, yes. Karp and Ferriter are silenced for ever, unless Birkett does something foolish and gets caught; the literary establishment is still reeling from the appalling press it received and is perforce cleaning up its act; that preposterous piece of EU self-aggrandisement, the Barbarossa Prize, has been aborted because the twenty-five-nation committee could not even agree on what constituted literature; and Geraint Griffiths has succeeded in putting *Pursuing the Virgins* so thoroughly on the map as to force both Muslims and Christians in this country to have an honest debate about what the hell we're going to do about Islamofascists. What else?'

'A good book won the Knapper-Warburton,' pointed out Amiss.

'*The Manor House of Rosemonde* is not just a good book,' said the baroness, 'it's a fine book, perhaps even a great book. Even if it was written by a Hungarian about a frog.'

'I've been so busy I never found out how you pulled off fixing it so a good book won,' said Milton.

'You explain it, Robert,' said the baroness.

'Even by Jack's standards,' said Amiss, 'she behaved appallingly, with the aim, I realised, of ensuring that her enemies on the committee would always vote for books she seemed particularly to hate, thus ending up with a long-list full of appalling books liked at most by one or two judges. The short-list was made even more appalling by

270

her manipulating things so that there was no vote, and that crackpots—both dead and alive—got to indulge themselves by choosing ridiculous titles, except for Hugo Hurlingham, who posthumously and with help chose *Rosemonde*, which Jack continued to rubbish. Are you with me so far?'

There were murmurs of agreement.

'She then announced at the last session that the winner would be chosen by proportional representation and said something to me apparently intended to be *sotto voce* about *Rosemonde* being total crap and that she'd rather have *Once and Future Heroes*, the book that Griffiths, who actually liked Jack, hated above all— thus throwing him into a rage that caused him to give *Rosemonde* his number two. So the result of all this was that *Rosemonde* won overwhelmingly, since it turned out to be the first choice of Jack, Mary Lou and me and the second of everyone else.'

Milton took a thoughtful sip. 'I think I follow this, but I've got two questions. First, what happened when they realised that she must have been misleading them all along?'

'It took a few moments,' said Mary Lou, 'and then there was a barrage of angry questions and accusations, but fortunately just as she was telling them that all was fair in love and war, Ellis rang to say we could pack up and get ready to go home and everyone lost interest. And then of course the publication of Birkett's letter stopped Rosa and Ferriter from causing any further trouble.'

'And why, Jack, did you like the book so much if it is as European as it sounds?' asked Milton.

'It is a wonderful study of an astonishing talent who was so self-critical that he produced in his life only thirteen songs—all masterpieces of their kind—which give the titles to the chapters which in their turn, treat of the great issues of life and death and love and loss and the human condition.'

'For example?'

'"To the country where war is waged" is the first,' said Mary Lou, 'and I'm not going to make any attempt to explain to you how it caught and moved me. You'll have to read it yourself.'

'But you're such a Europhobe, Jack,' said Milton.

The baroness shook her head. 'I hate the European Union, Jim, but I love Europe. I love visiting it, I love eating its food, and looking at its art and listening to its music and sometimes even reading its books. I just want it to stay where it is— on the other side of the channel—and keep its nose out of our business.'

'So are you going to emulate Robert and Rachel and take off there soon?' asked Pooley.

'No, I'm going to China.'

'China! Why China all of a sudden?' asked Mary Lou.

The baroness looked coy. 'I'm visiting a friend I met recently.'

'Who? When? Where?'

'In Richmond Park a few weeks ago. I was passing and saw the Chinese State Circus was on. One must always go to the circus. I admired the leading acrobat and took him for a drink afterwards.'

As everyone began firing off questions simultaneously, the waiter came in with a large tray.

'You can be as inquisitive as you like, but you

won't get anything more out of me,' said the baroness, 'except that I'm celebrating too. Get pouring the white wine, Robert, for there are many courses and many bottles to be consumed before we sleep.'